More Favourite
Fairy Tales

MORE FAVOURITE
FAIRY TALES

Chosen from the Colour Fairy Books of
ANDREW LANG by KATHLEEN LINES
With illustrations by MARGERY GILL
and an Epilogue by ROGER LANCELYN GREEN

LEOPARD

This edition published in 1996 by Leopard Books,
a division of Random House UK Ltd,
20 Vauxhall Bridge Road, London SW1V 2SA

The Colour Fairy Books of Andrew Lang
were first published between
1889 and 1910.
This selection, the epilogue and the illustrations
© The Nonesuch Press Limited 1967
First published 1967

ISBN 0 7529 0212 1

Printed in Great Britain

The Tales

The Battle of the Birds

THERE WAS to be a great battle between all the creatures of the earth and the birds of the air. News of it went abroad, and the son of the King of Tethertown said that when the battle was fought he would be there to see it, and would bring back word who was to be king of the animal world for the year. But in spite of that, he was almost too late, and every fight had been fought save the last, which was between a snake and a great black raven. Both struck hard, but in the end the snake proved the stronger, and would have twisted himself round the neck of the raven till he died had not the King's son drawn his sword, and cut off the head of the snake at a single blow. And when the raven beheld that his enemy was dead, he was grateful, and said:

'For thy kindness to me this day, I will show thee a sight. So come up now on the root of my two wings.' The King's son did as he was bid, and before the raven stopped flying, they had passed over seven bens and seven glens and seven mountain moors.

'Do you see that house yonder?' said the raven at last. 'Go straight to it, for a sister of mine dwells there, and she will make you right welcome. And if she asks, "Wert thou at the battle of the birds?" answer that you were, and if she asks, "Didst thou see my likeness?" answer that you did, but be sure to meet me in the morning at this place.'

The King's son followed what the raven told him, and that night he had meat of each meat, and drink of each drink, warm water for his feet, and a soft bed to lie in.

Thus it happened the next day, and the next, but on the fourth morning, instead of meeting the raven, in his place the King's son found waiting for him the handsomest youth that ever was seen, with a bundle in his hand.

'Is there a raven hereabouts?' asked the King's son, and the youth answered:

'I am that raven, and I was delivered by thee from the spells that bound me, and in reward thou wilt get this bundle. Go back by the road thou camest, and lie as before, a night in each house, but be

9

careful not to unloose the bundle till thou art in the place wherein thou wouldst most wish to dwell.'

Then the King's son set out, and thus it happened as it had happened before, till he entered a thick wood near his father's house. He had walked a long way, and suddenly the bundle seemed to grow heavier; first he put it down under a tree, and next he thought he would look at it.

The string was easy to untie, and the King's son soon unfastened the bundle. What was it he saw there? Why, a great castle with an orchard all about it, and in the orchard fruit and flowers and birds of every kind. It was all ready for him to dwell in, but instead of being in the midst of the forest, he *did* wish he had left the bundle unloosed till he had reached the green valley close to his father's palace. Well, it was no use wishing, and with a sigh he glanced up, and beheld a huge giant coming towards him.

'Bad is the place where thou hast built thy house, King's son,' said the giant.

'True; it is not here that I wish it to be,' answered the King's son.

'What reward wilt thou give me if I put it back in the bundle?' asked the giant.

'What reward dost thou ask?' answered the King's son.

'The first son thou hast when he is seven years old,' said the giant.

'If I have a boy thou shalt get him,' answered the King's son, and as he spoke the castle and the orchard were tied up in the bundle again.

'Now take thy road, and I will take mine,' said the giant. 'And if thou forgettest thy promise, *I* will remember it.'

Light of heart the King's son went on his road, till he came to the green valley near his father's palace. Slowly he unloosed the bundle, fearing lest he should find nothing but a heap of stones or rags. But no! all was as it had been before, and as he opened the castle door there stood within the most beautiful maiden that ever was seen.

'Enter, King's son,' said she, 'all is ready, and we will be married at once,' and so they were.

The maiden proved a good wife, and the King's son, now himself a king, was so happy that he forgot all about the giant. Seven years and a day had gone by, when one morning, while standing on the ram-

parts, he beheld the giant striding towards the castle. Then he remembered his promise, and remembered, too, that he had told the
Queen nothing about it. Now he must tell her, and perhaps she might
help him in his trouble.

The Queen listened in silence to his tale, and after he had finished,
she only said:

'Leave thou the matter between me and the giant,' and as she spoke,
the giant entered the hall and stood before them.

'Bring out your son,' cried he to the King, 'as you promised me
seven years and a day since.'

The King glanced at his wife, who nodded, so he answered:

'Let his mother first put him in order,' and the Queen left the hall,
and took the cook's son and dressed him in the Prince's clothes, and
led him up to the giant, who held his hand, and together they went out
along the road. They had not walked far when the giant stopped and
stretched out a stick to the boy.

'If your father had that stick, what would he do with it?' asked he.

'If my father had that stick, he would beat the dogs and cats that
steal the King's meat,' replied the boy.

'Thou art the cook's son!' cried the giant. 'Go home to thy mother;'
and turning his back he strode straight to the castle.

'If you seek to trick me this time, the highest stone will soon be the
lowest,' said he, and the King and Queen trembled, but they could not
bear to give up their boy.

'The butler's son is the same age as ours,' whispered the Queen;
'he will not know the difference.' And she took the child and dressed
him in the Prince's clothes, and the giant led him away along the road.
Before they had gone far he stopped, and held out a stick.

'If thy father had that rod, what would he do with it?' asked the
giant.

'He would beat the dogs and cats that break the King's goblets,'
answered the boy.

'Thou art the son of the butler!' cried the giant. 'Go home to thy
mother;' and turning round he strode back angrily to the castle.

'Bring out thy son at once,' roared he, 'or the stone that is highest
will be lowest,' and this time the real Prince was brought.

But though his parents wept bitterly and fancied the child was

suffering all kinds of dreadful things, the giant treated him like his own son, though he never allowed him to see his daughters. Years passed and the boy grew into a handsome lad, and one day the giant told him that he would have to amuse himself alone for many hours, as he had a journey to make. So the boy wandered by the river, and down to the sea, and at last he went up to the top of the castle, where he had never been before. There he paused, for the sound of music broke upon his ears, and opening a door near him, he beheld a girl sitting by the window, holding a harp.

'Haste and begone, I see the giant close at hand,' she whispered, 'but when he is asleep, return hither, for I would speak with thee.' And the Prince did as he was bid, and when midnight struck he crept back to the top of the castle.

'Tomorrow,' said the girl, who was the giant's daughter, 'tomorrow thou wilt get the choice of my two sisters to marry, but thou must answer that thou wilt not take either, but only me. This will anger him greatly, for he wishes to betrothe me to the son of the King of the Green City, whom I like not at all.'

Then they parted, and on the morrow, as the girl had said, the giant called his three daughters to him, and likewise the young Prince, to whom he spoke.

'Now, O son of the King of Tethertown, the time has come for us to part. Choose one of my two elder daughters to wife, and thou shalt take her to your father's house the day after the wedding.'

'Give me the youngest instead,' replied the youth, and the giant's face darkened as he heard him.

'Three things must thou do first,' said he.

'Say on, I will do them,' replied the Prince, and the giant left the house, and bade him follow to the byre, where the cows were kept.

'For a hundred years no man has swept this byre,' said the giant, 'but if by nightfall, when I reach home, thou hast not cleaned it so that a golden apple can roll through it from end to end, thy blood shall pay for it.'

All day long the youth toiled, but he might as well have tried to empty the ocean. At length, when he was so tired he could hardly move, the giant's youngest daughter stood in the doorway.

'Lay down thy weariness,' said she, and the King's son, thinking he could only die once, sank on the floor at her bidding, and fell sound asleep. When he woke the girl had disappeared, and the byre was so clean that a golden apple could roll from end to end of it. He jumped up in surprise, and at that moment in came the giant.

'Hast thou cleaned the byre, King's son?' asked he.

'It is cleaned,' answered he.

'Well, since thou wert so active today, tomorrow thou wilt thatch this byre with a feather from every different bird, or else thy blood shall pay for it,' and he went out.

Before the sun was up, the youth took his bow and his quiver and set off to kill the birds. Off to the moor he went, but never a bird was to be seen that day. At last he got so tired with running to and fro that he gave up heart.

'There is but one death I can die,' thought he. Then at midday came the giant's daughter.

'Thou art tired, King's son?' said she.

'I am,' he answered; 'all these hours have I wandered, and there fell but these two blackbirds, both of one colour.'

'Lay down thy weariness on the grass,' said she, and he did as she bade him and fell fast asleep.

When he woke the girl had disappeared, and he got up, and returned to the byre. As he drew near, he rubbed his eyes, hard, thinking he was dreaming, for there it was, beautifully thatched, just as the giant had wished. At the door of the house he met the giant.

'Hast thou thatched the byre, King's son?'

'It is thatched.'

'Well, since thou hast been so active today, I have something else for thee! Beside the loch thou seest over yonder there grows a fir tree. On the top of the fir tree is a magpie's nest, and in the nest are five eggs. Thou wilt bring me those eggs for breakfast, and if one is cracked or broken, thy blood shall pay for it.'

Before it was light next day, the King's son jumped out of bed and ran down to the loch. The tree was not hard to find, for the rising sun shone red on the trunk, which was five hundred feet from the ground to its first branch. Time after time he walked round it, trying to find some knots, however small, where he could put his feet, but the bark was so smooth he soon saw that if he was to reach the top at all, it must be by climbing up with his knees like a sailor. But then he was a king's son and not a sailor, which made all the difference.

However, it was no use standing there staring at the fir, at least he must try to do his best, and try he did till his hands and knees were sore, for as soon as he had struggled up a few feet, he slid back again. Once he climbed a little higher than before, and hope rose in his heart, then down he came with such force that his hands and knees smarted worse than ever.

'This is no time for stopping,' said the voice of the giant's daughter, as he leant against the trunk to recover his breath.

'Alas! I am no sooner up than down,' answered he.

'Try once more,' said she, and she laid a finger against the tree and bade him put his foot on it. Then she placed another finger a little higher up, and so on till he reached the top, where the magpie had built her nest.

'Make haste now with the nest,' she cried, 'for my father's breath is burning my back,' and down he scrambled as fast as he could, but the girl's little finger had caught in a branch at the top, and she was obliged to leave it there. But she was too busy to pay heed to this, for the sun was getting high over the hills.

'Listen to me,' she said. 'This night my two sisters and I will be dressed alike, and you will not know me. But when my father says "Go to thy wife, King's son," come to the one whose right hand has no little finger.'

So he went and gave the eggs to the giant, who nodded his head.

'Make ready for thy marriage,' cried he, 'for the wedding shall take place this very night, and I will summon thy bride to greet thee.' Then his three daughters were sent for, and they all entered dressed in green silk of the same fashion, and with golden circlets round their heads. The King's son looked from one to another. *Which* was the youngest? Suddenly his eyes fell on the hand of the middle one, and there was no little finger.

'Thou hast aimed well this time too,' said the giant, as the King's son laid his hand on her shoulder, 'but perhaps we may meet some other way;' and though he pretended to laugh, the bride saw a gleam in his eye which warned her of danger.

The wedding took place that very night, and the hall was filled with giants and gentlemen, and they danced till the house shook from top to bottom. At last everyone grew tired, and the guests went away, and the King's son and his bride were left alone.

'If we stay here till dawn my father will kill thee,' she whispered, 'but thou art my husband and I will save thee, as I did before.' Then she cut an apple into nine pieces, and put two pieces at the head of the bed, and two pieces at the foot, and two pieces at the door of the kitchen, and two at the big door, and one outside the house. And when this was done, and she heard the giant snoring, she and the King's son crept out softly and stole across to the stable, where she led out the blue-grey mare and jumped on its back, and her husband mounted behind her. Not long after, the giant awoke.

'Are you asleep?' asked he.

'Not yet,' answered the apple at the head of the bed, and the giant turned over, and soon was snoring as loudly as before. By and by he called again.

'Are you asleep?'

'Not yet,' said the apple at the foot of the bed, and the giant was satisfied. After a while, he called a third time, 'Are you asleep?'

'Not yet,' replied the apple in the kitchen, but when, in a few minutes, he put the question for the fourth time and received an answer from the apple outside the house door, he guessed what had happened, and ran to the room to look for himself.

The bed was cold and empty!

'My father's breath is burning my back,' cried the girl, 'put thy hand into the ear of the mare, and whatever thou findest there, throw it behind thee.' And in the mare's ear there was a twig of sloe tree, and as the Prince threw it behind him there sprang up twenty miles of thornwood so thick that scarce a weasel could go through it. And the giant, who was striding headlong forwards, got caught in it, and it pulled his hair and beard.

'This is one of my daughter's tricks,' he said to himself, 'but if I had my big axe and my wood-knife, I would not be long making a way through this,' and off he went home and brought back the axe and the wood-knife.

It took him but a short time to cut a road through the blackthorn, and then he laid the axe and the knife under a tree.

'I will leave them there till I return,' he murmured to himself, but a hoodie crow, which was sitting on a branch above, heard him.

'If thou leavest them,' said the hoodie, 'we will steal them.'

'You will,' answered the giant, 'and I must take them home.' So he took them home, and started afresh on his journey.

'My father's breath is burning my back,' cried the girl at midday. 'Put thy finger in the mare's ear and throw behind thee whatever thou findest in it,' and the King's son found a splinter of grey stone, and threw it behind him, and in a twinkling twenty miles of solid rock lay between them and the giant.

'My daughter's tricks are the hardest things that ever met me,' said the giant, 'but if I had my lever and my crowbar, I would not be long in making my way through this rock also,' but as he had *not* got them, he had to go home and fetch them. Then it took him but a short time to hew his way through the rock.

'I will leave the tools here,' he murmured aloud when he had finished.

'If thou leavest them, we will steal them,' said a hoodie who was perched on a stone above him, and the giant answered:

'Steal them if thou wilt; there is no time to go back.'

'My father's breath is burning my back,' cried the girl; 'look in the mare's ear, King's son, or we are lost.' And he looked, and found a tiny bladder full of water, which he threw behind him, and it became a great loch. And the giant, who was striding on so fast, could not stop himself, and he walked right into the middle and was drowned.

The blue-grey mare galloped on like the wind, and the next day the King's son came in sight of his father's house.

'Get down and go in,' said the bride, 'and tell them that thou hast married me. But take heed that neither man nor beast kiss thee, for then thou wilt cease to remember me at all.'

'I will do thy bidding,' answered he, and left her at the gate. All who met him bade him welcome, and he charged his father and mother not to kiss him, but as he greeted them his old greyhound leapt on his neck, and kissed him on the mouth. And after that he did not remember the giant's daughter.

All that day she sat on a well which was near the gate, waiting, waiting, but the King's son never came. In the darkness she climbed up into an oak tree that shadowed the well, and there she lay all night, waiting, waiting.

On the morrow, at midday, the wife of a shoemaker who dwelt near the well went to draw water for her husband to drink, and she saw the reflection of the girl in the tree, and thought it was her own.

'How handsome I am, to be sure,' said she, gazing into the well, and as she stooped to behold herself better, the jug struck against the stones and broke in pieces, and she was forced to return to her husband without the water, and this angered him.

'Thou hast turned crazy,' said he in wrath. 'Go thou, my daughter, and fetch me a drink,' and the girl went and the same thing befell her as had befallen her mother.

'Where is the water?' asked the shoemaker, when she came back, and as she held nothing save the handle of the jug he went to the well himself. He too saw the reflection of the woman in the tree, but looked up to discover whence it came, and there above him sat the most beautiful woman in the world.

'Come down,' he said, 'for a while thou canst stay in my house,' and glad enough the girl was to come.

Now the son of the King of the country was about to marry, and the young men about the court thronged the shoemaker's shop to buy fine shoes to wear at the wedding.

'Thou hast a pretty daughter,' said they when they beheld the girl sitting at work.

'Pretty she is,' answered the shoemaker, 'but no daughter of mine.'

'I would give a hundred pounds to marry her,' said one.

'And I,' 'And I,' cried the others.

'That is no business of mine,' answered the shoemaker, and the young men bade him ask her if she would choose one of them for a husband, and to tell them on the morrow. Then the shoemaker asked her, and the girl said that she would marry the one who could bring his purse with him. So the shoemaker hurried to the youth who had first spoken, and he came back, and after giving the shoemaker a hundred pounds for his news, he sought the girl, who was waiting for him.

'Is it thou?' inquired she. 'I am thirsty, give me a drink from the well that is out yonder.' And he poured out the water, but he could not move from the place where he was; and there he stayed till many hours had passed by.

'Take away that foolish boy,' cried the girl to the shoemaker at last, 'I am tired of him,' and then suddenly he was able to walk, and betook himself to his home, but he did not tell the others what had happened to him.

Next day there arrived one of the other young men, and in the evening, when the shoemaker had gone out and they were alone, she said to him, 'See if the latch is on the door.' The young man hastened to do her bidding, but as soon as he touched the latch, his fingers stuck to it, and there he had to stay for many hours, till the shoemaker came back, and the girl let him go. Hanging his head, he went home, but he told no one what had befallen him.

Then was the turn of the third man, and *his* foot remained fastened to the floor, till the girl unloosed it. And thankfully he ran off, and was not seen looking behind him.

'Take the purse of gold,' said the girl to the shoemaker, 'I have no need of it, and it will better thee.' And the shoemaker took it and told the girl he must carry the shoes for the wedding up to the castle.

'I would fain get a sight of the King's son before he marries,' sighed she.

'Come with me, then,' answered he; 'the servants are all my friends and they will let you stand in the passage down which the King's son will pass, and all the company too.'

Up they went to the castle, and when the young men saw the girl standing there, they led her into the hall where the banquet was laid out and poured her out some wine. She was just raising the glass to drink when a flame went up out of it, and out of the flame sprang two pigeons, one of gold and one of silver. They flew round and round the head of the girl, when three grains of barley fell on the floor, and the silver pigeon dived down, and swallowed them.

'If thou hadst remembered how I cleaned the byre, thou wouldst have given me my share,' cooed the golden pigeon, and as he spoke three more grains fell, and the silver pigeon ate them as before.

'If thou hadst remembered how I thatched the byre, thou wouldst have given me my share,' cooed the golden pigeon again; and as he spoke three more grains fell, and for the third time they were eaten by the silver pigeon.

'If thou hadst remembered how I got the magpie's nest, thou wouldst have given me my share,' cooed the golden pigeon.

Then the King's son understood that they had come to remind him of what he had forgotten, and his lost memory came back, and he knew his wife, and kissed her. But as the preparations had been made, it seemed a pity to waste them, so they were married a second time, and sat down to the wedding feast.

The Billy Goat and the King

ONCE THERE lived a certain king who understood the language of all birds and beasts and insects. This knowledge was rather a troublesome gift, for he knew that if he were ever to reveal anything he had thus learned he would turn into a stone. How he managed to avoid doing so long before this story opens I cannot say, but he had safely grown up to manhood, and married a wife, and was as happy as monarchs generally are.

This king, I must tell you, was a Hindu; and when a Hindu eats his food he has a nice little place on the ground freshly plastered with mud, and sits in the middle of it which is quite a different way from ours.

Well, one day the King was eating his dinner in just such a nice, clean, mud-plastered spot, and his wife was sitting opposite to wait upon him and keep him company. As he ate he dropped some grains of rice upon the ground, and a little ant, who was running about seeking a living, seized upon one of the grains and bore it off towards his hole. Just outside the King's circle this ant met another ant, and the King heard the second one say:

'Oh, dear friend, do give me that grain of rice, and get another for yourself. You see my boots are so dirty that, if I were to go upon the King's eating place, I should defile it, and I can't do that, it would be so very rude.'

But the ant with the grain of rice only replied:

'If you want rice go and get it. No one will notice your dirty boots; and you don't suppose that I am going to carry rice for all our kindred?'

Then the King laughed.

The Queen looked at herself up and down, but she could not see or feel anything in her appearance to make the King laugh, so she said:

'What are you laughing at?'

'Did I laugh?' replied the King.

'Of course you did,' retorted the Queen; 'and if you think that I am ridiculous I wish you would say so, instead of behaving in that stupid way! What are you laughing at?'

'I'm not laughing at anything,' answered the King.

'Very well, but you *did* laugh, and I want to know why.'

'Well, I'm afraid I can't tell you,' said the King.

'You *must* tell me,' replied the Queen impatiently. 'If you laugh when there's nothing to laugh at you must be ill or mad. What is the matter?'

Still the King refused to say, and still the Queen declared that she must and would know. For days the quarrel went on, and the Queen gave her husband no rest, until at last the poor man was almost out of his wits, and thought that, as life had become for him hardly worth living while this went on, he might as well tell her the secret and take the consequences.

'But,' thought he, 'if I am to become a stone, I am not going to lie, if I can help it, on some dusty highway, to be kicked here and there by man and beast, flung at dogs, be used as the plaything of naughty children, and become generally restless and miserable. I will be a stone at the bottom of the cool river, and roll gently about there until I find some secure resting-place where I can stay for ever.'

So he told his wife that if she would ride with him to the middle of the river he would tell her what he had laughed at. She thought he was joking, and laughingly agreed; their horses were ordered and they set out.

On the way they came to a fine well beneath the shade of some lofty, wide-spreading trees, and the King proposed that they should get off and rest a little, drink some of the cool water, and then pass on. To this the Queen consented; so they dismounted and sat down in the shade by the well-side to rest.

It happened that an old goat and his wife were browsing in the neighbourhood, and, as the King and Queen sat there, the nanny goat came to the well's brink and, peering over, saw some lovely tender green leaves that grew out of the inside wall of the well.

'Oh!' cried she to her husband, 'come quickly and look. Here are some leaves which make my mouth water: come and get them for me!'

Then the billy sauntered up and looked over, and after that he eyed his wife a little crossly.

'You expect me to get you those leaves, do you? I suppose you don't consider how in the world I am to reach them? You don't seem to think at all; if you did you would know that if I tried to reach those leaves I should fall into the well and be drowned!'

'Oh,' cried the nanny goat, 'why should you fall in? Do try and get them!'

'I am not going to be so silly,' replied the billy goat.

But the nanny goat still wept and entreated.

'Look here,' said her husband, 'there are plenty of fools in the world, but I am not one of them. This silly king here, because he can't cure his wife of asking questions, is going to throw his life away. But I know how to cure you of your follies, and I'm going to.'

And with that he butted the nanny goat so severely that in two minutes she was submissively feeding somewhere else, and had made up her mind that the leaves in the well were not worth having.

Then the King, who had understood every word, laughed once more.

The Queen looked at him suspiciously, but the King got up and walked across to where she sat.

'Are you still determined to find out what I was laughing at the other day?' he asked.

'Quite,' answered the Queen angrily.

'Because,' said the King, tapping his leg with his riding whip, 'I've made up my mind not to tell you, and moreover, I have made up my mind to stop you mentioning the subject any more.'

'What *do* you mean?' asked the Queen nervously.

'Well,' replied the King, 'I notice that if that goat is displeased with his wife, he just butts her, and that seems to settle the question –'

'Do you mean to say you would *beat* me?' cried the Queen.

'I should be extremely sorry to have to do so,' replied the King; 'but I have to persuade you to go home quietly, and to ask no more silly questions when I say I cannot answer them. Of course, if you *will* persist, why . . .'

And the Queen went home, and so did the King, and it is said that they are both happier and wiser than ever before.

The Black Bull of Norroway

And many a hunting song they sung,
And song of game and glee;
Then tuned to plaintive strains their tongue,
'Of Scotland's luve and lee.'
To wilder measures next they turn
'The Black, Black Bull of Norroway!'
Sudden the tapers cease to burn,
The minstrels cease to play.

'The Cout of Keeldar,' by J. Leyden

IN NORROWAY, langsyne, there lived a certain lady, and she had three dochters. The auldest o' them said to her mither, 'Mither, bake me a bannock, and roast me a collop, for I'm gaun awa' to seek my fortune.' Her mither did sae; and the dochter gaed awa' to an auld witch washerwife and telled her purpose. The auld wife bade her stay that day, and gang and look out o' her back door, and see what she could see. She saw nocht the first day. The second day she did the same, and saw nocht. On the third day she looked again, and saw a coach-and-six coming alang the road. She ran in and telled the auld wife what she saw. 'Aweel,' quo' the auld wife, 'yon's for you.' Sae they took her into the coach, and galloped aff.

The second dochter next says to her mither, 'Mither, bake me a bannock, and roast me a collop, for I'm gaun awa' to seek my fortune.' Her mither did sae; and awa' she gaed to the auld wife, as her sister had dune. On the third day she looked out o' the back door, and saw a coach-and-four coming alang the road. 'Aweel,' quo' the auld wife, 'yon's for you.' Sae they took her in, and aff they set.

The third dochter says to her mither, 'Mither, bake me a bannock, and roast me a collop, for I'm gaun awa' to seek my fortune.' Her mither did sae; and awa' she gaed to the auld witch-wife. She bade her look out o' her back door, and see what she could see. She did sae; and when she came back said she saw nocht. The second day she did

24

the same, and saw nocht. The third day she looked again, and on coming back said to the auld wife she saw nocht but a muckle Black Bull coming roaring alang the road. 'Aweel,' quo' the auld wife, 'yon's for you.' On hearing this she was next to distracted wi' grief and terror; but she was lifted up and set on his back, and awa' they went.

Aye they travelled, and on they travelled, till the lady grew faint wi' hunger. 'Eat out o' my right lug,' says the Black Bull, 'and drink out o' my left lug, and set by your leavings.' Sae she did as he said, and was wonderfully refreshed. And lang they gaed, and sair they rade, till they came in sight o' a very big and bonny castle. 'Yonder we maun be this night,' quo' the bull; 'for my auld brither lives yonder;' and presently they were at the place. They lifted her aff his back, and took her in, and sent him away to a park for the night.

In the morning, when they brought the bull hame, they took the lady into a fine shining parlour, and gave her a beautiful apple, telling her no to break it till she was in the greatest strait ever mortal was in in the world, and that wad bring her out o't. Again she was lifted on the bull's back, and after she had ridden far, and farer than I can tell, they came in sight o' a far bonnier castle, and far farther awa' than the last. Says the bull to her, 'Yonder we maun be the night, for my second brither lives yonder;' and they were at the place directly. They lifted her down and took her in, and sent the bull to the field for the night.

In the morning they took the lady into a fine and rich room, and gave her the finest pear she had ever seen, bidding her no to break it till she was in the greatest strait ever mortal could be in, and that wad get her out o't. Again she was lifted and set on his back, and awa' they went. And lang they gaed, and sair they rade, till they came in sight o' the far biggest castle, and far farthest aff, they had yet seen. 'We maun be yonder the night,' says the bull, 'for my young brither lives yonder;' and they were there directly. They lifted her down, took her in, and sent the bull to the field for the night.

In the morning they took her into a room, the finest of a', and gave her a plum, telling her no to break it till she was in the greatest strait mortal could be in, and that wad get her out o't. Presently they brought hame the bull, set the lady on his back, and awa' they went.

And aye they gaed, and on they rade, till they came to a dark and ugsome glen, where they stopped, and the lady lighted down. Says the bull to her, 'Here ye maun stay till I gang and fight the deil. Ye maun seat yoursel' on that stane, and move neither hand nor foot till I come back, else I'll never find ye again. And if everything round about ye turns blue I hae beaten the deil; but should a' things turn red he'll hae conquered me.' She set hersel' down on the stane, and by-and-by a' round her turned blue. O'ercome wi' joy, she lifted the ae foot and crossed it owre the ither, sae glad was she that her companion was victorious. The bull returned and sought for but never could find her.

Lang she sat, and aye she grat, till she wearied. At last she rase and gaed awa', she kendna whaur to. On she wandered till she came to a great hill o' glass, that she tried a' she could to climb, but wasna able. Round the bottom o' the hill she gaed, sabbing and seeking a passage owre, till at last she came to a smith's house; and the smith promised, if she wad serve him seven years, he wad make her iron shoon, wherewi' she could climb owre the glassy hill. At seven years' end she got her iron shoon, clamb the glassy hill, and chanced to come to the habitation o' an auld washerwif.

There she was telled of a gallant young knight that had given in some bluidy sarks to wash, and whaever washed thae sarks was to be his wife. The auld wife had washed till she was tired, and then she set to her dochter, and baith washed, and they washed, and they better washed, in hopes of getting the young knight; but a' they could do they couldna bring out a stain. At length they set the stranger damosel to wark; and whenever she began the stains came out pure and clean, but the auld wife made the knight believe it was her dochter had washed the sarks. So the knight and the dochter were to be married, and the stranger damosel was distracted at the thought of it, for she was deeply in love wi' him. So she bethought her of her apple, and breaking it, found it filled with gold and precious jewellery, the richest she had ever seen. 'All these,' she said to the dochter, 'I will give you, on condition that you put off your marriage for ae day, and allow me to go into his room alone at night.' So the lady consented but meanwhile the auld wife had prepared a sleeping-drink, and given it to the knight, wha drank it, and never wakered till next morning. The lee-lang night the damosel sabbed and sang:

> 'Seven lang years I served for thee,
> The glassy hill I clamb for thee,
> The bluidy shirt I wrang for thee;
> And wilt thou no wauken and turn to me?'

Next day she kentna what to do for grief. She then brak the pear, and found it filled wi' jewellery far richer than the contents o' the apple. Wi' thae jewels she bargained for permission to be a second night in the young knight's chamber; but the auld wife gied him anither sleeping-drink, and he again sleepit till morning. A' night she kept sighing and singing as before:

> 'Seven lang years I served for thee,
> The glassy hill I clamb for thee,
> The bluidy shirt I wrang for thee;
> And wilt thou no wauken and turn to me?'

Still he sleepit, and she nearly lost hope a'thegither. But that day when he was out at the hunting, somebody asked him what noise and moaning was yon they heard all last night in his bedchamber. He said he heardna ony noise. But they assured him there was sae; and he resolved to keep waking that night to try what he could hear. That being the third night, and the damosel being between hope and despair, she brak her plum, and it held far the richest jewellery of the three. She bargained as before; and the auld wife, as before, took in the sleeping-drink to the young knight's chamber; but he telled her he couldna drink it that night without sweetening. And when she gaed awa' for some honey to sweeten it wi', he poured out the drink, and sae made the auld wife think he had drunk it. They a' went to bed again, and the damosel began, as before, singing:

> 'Seven lang years I served for thee,
> The glassy hill I clamb for thee,
> The bluidy shirt I wrang for thee;
> And wilt thou no wauken and turn to me?'

He heard, and turned to her. And she telled him a' that had befa'en her, and he telled her a' that had happened to him. And he caused the auld washerwife and her dochter to be burnt. And they were married, and he and she are living happy till this day, for aught I ken.

The Black Thief and Knight of the Glen

IN TIMES of yore there was a King and a Queen in the south of Ireland who had three sons, all beautiful children; but the Queen, their mother, sickened unto death when they were yet very young, which caused great grief throughout the Court, particularly to the King, her husband, who could in no wise be comforted. Seeing that death was drawing near her, she called the King to her and spoke as follows:

'I am now going to leave you, and as you are young and in your prime, of course after my death you will marry again. Now all the request I ask of you is that you will build a tower in an island in the sea, wherein you will keep your three sons until they are come of age and fit to do for themselves; so that they may not be under the power or jurisdiction of any other woman. Neglect not to give them education suitable to their birth, and let them be trained up to every exercise and pastime requisite for king's sons to learn. This is all I have to say, so farewell.'

The King had scarce time, with tears in his eyes, to assure her she should be obeyed in everything, when she, turning herself in her bed, with a smile gave up the ghost. Never was greater mourning seen than was throughout the Court and the whole kingdom; for a better woman than the Queen, to rich and poor, was not to be found in the world. She was interred with great pomp and magnificence, and the King, her husband, became in a manner inconsolable for the loss of her. However, he caused the tower to be built and his sons placed in it, under proper guardians, according to his promise.

In process of time the lords and knights of the kingdom counselled the King (as he was young) to live no longer as he had done, but to take a wife: which counsel prevailing, they chose him a rich and beautiful Princess to be his consort – a neighbouring King's daughter, of whom he was very fond. Not long after, the new Queen had a fine son, which caused great feasting and rejoicing at the Court, insomuch that the late Queen, in a manner, was entirely forgotten. That fared well, and King and Queen lived happy together for several years.

At length the Queen, having some business with the hen-wife, went herself to her, and, after a long conference passed, was taking leave of her, when the hen-wife prayed that if ever she should come back to her again she might break her neck. The Queen, greatly incensed at such a daring insult from one of her meanest subjects, demanded immediately the reason, or she would have her put to death.

'It was worth your while, madam,' says the hen-wife, 'to pay me well for it, for the reason I prayed so on you concerns you much.'

'What must I pay you?' asked the Queen.

'You must give me,' says she, 'the full of a pack of wool, and I have an ancient crock which you must fill with butter, likewise a barrel which you must fill for me full of wheat.'

'How much wool will it take to the pack?' says the Queen.

'It will take seven herds of sheep,' said she, 'and their increase for seven years.'

'How much butter will it take to fill your crock?'

'Seven dairies,' said she, 'and their increase for seven years.'

'And how much will it take to fill the barrel you have?' says the Queen.

'It will take the increase of seven barrels of wheat for seven years.'

'That is a great quantity,' says the Queen; 'but the reason must be extraordinary, and before I want it, I will give you all you demand.'

'Well,' says the hen-wife, 'it is because you are so stupid that you don't observe or find out those affairs that are so dangerous and hurtful to yourself and your child.'

'What is that?' says the Queen.

'Why,' says she, 'the King your husband has three fine sons he had by the late Queen, whom he keeps shut up in a tower until they come of age, intending to divide the kingdom between them, and let your son push his fortune; now, if you don't find some means of destroying them, your child and perhaps yourself will be left desolate in the end.'

'And what would you advise me to do?' said the Queen; 'I am wholly at a loss in what manner to act in this affair.'

'You must make known to the King,' says the hen-wife, 'that you heard of his sons, and wonder greatly that he concealed them all this time from you. Tell him you wish to see them, and that it is full time for them to be liberated, and that you would be desirous he would bring them to the Court. The King will then do so, and there will be a great feast prepared on that account, and also diversions of every sort to amuse the people; and in these sports,' said she, 'ask the King's sons to play a game at cards with you, which they will not refuse. Now,' says the hen-wife, 'you must make a bargain, that if you win they must do whatever you command them, and if they win, that you must do whatever they command you to do; this bargain must be made before the assembly, and here is a pack of cards,' says she, 'that I am thinking you will not lose by.'

The Queen immediately took the cards and, after returning the hen-wife thanks for her kind instruction, went back to the palace, where she was quite uneasy until she got speaking to the King in regard of his children; at last she broke it off to him in a very polite and engaging manner, so that he could see no muster or design in it. He readily consented to her desire, and his sons were sent for to the tower, who gladly came to Court, rejoicing that they were freed from such confinement. They were all very handsome, and very expert in all arts and exercises, so that they gained the love and esteem of all that had seen them.

The Queen, more jealous with them than ever, thought it an age until all the feasting and rejoicing was over, that she might get making her proposal, depending greatly on the power of the hen-wife's cards. At length this royal assembly began to sport and play at all kinds of diversions, and the Queen very cunningly challenged the three Princes to play at cards with her, making bargain with them as she had been instructed.

They accepted the challenge, and the eldest son and she played the first game, which she won; then the second son played, and she won that game likewise; the third son and she then played the last game, and he won it, which sorely grieved her that she had not him in her power as well as the rest, he being by far the handsomest and most beloved of the three.

However, everyone was anxious to hear the Queen's commands in regard to the two Princes, not thinking that she had any ill design in her head against them. Whether it was the hen-wife instructed her, or whether it was from her own knowledge, I cannot tell; but she gave out they must go and bring her the Knight of the Glen's wild Steed of Bells, or they should lose their heads.

The young Princes were not in the least concerned, not knowing what they had to do; but the whole Court was amazed at her demand, knowing very well that it was impossible for them ever to get the steed, as all that ever sought him perished in the attempt. However, they could not retract the bargain, and the youngest Prince was desired to tell what demand he had on the Queen, as he had won his game.

'My brothers,' says he, 'are now going to travel, and, as I under-stand, a perilous journey wherein they know not what road to take or what may happen them. I am resolved, therefore, not to stay here, but to go with them, let what will betide; and I request and command, according to my bargain, that the Queen shall stand on the highest tower of the palace until we come back (or until she finds out that we are certainly dead), with nothing but sheaf corn for her food and cold water for her drink, if it should be for seven years and longer.'

All things being now fixed, the three Princes departed the Court in search of the Knight of the Glen's palace, and travelling along the road they came up with a man who was a little lame, and seemed to be somewhat advanced in years; they soon fell into discourse, and the youngest of the Princes asked the stranger his name, and what was the reason he wore so remarkable a black cap as he saw on him.

'I am called,' said he, 'the Thief of Sloan, and sometimes the Black Thief from my cap;' and so telling the Prince the most of his adventures, he asked him again where they were bound for, or what they were about.

The Prince, willing to gratify his request, told him their affairs from the beginning to the end. 'And now,' said he, 'we are travelling, and do not know whether we are on the right road or not.'

'Ah! my brave fellows,' says the Black Thief, 'you little know the danger you run. I am after that steed myself these seven years, and can never steal him on account of a silk covering he has on him in the stable, with sixty bells fixed to it, and when ever you approach the place he quickly observes it and shakes himself; which, by the sound of the bells, not only alarms his master and the guards, but the whole country round, so that it is impossible ever to get him, and those that are so unfortunate as to be taken by the Knight of the Glen are boiled in a red-hot fiery furnace.'

'Bless me,' says the young Prince, 'what will we do? If we return without the steed we will lose our heads, so I see we are ill fixed on both sides.'

'Well,' says the Thief of Sloan, 'if it were my case I would rather die by the Knight than by the wicked Queen; besides, I will go with you myself and show you the road, and whatever fortune you will have, I will take chance of the same.'

They returned him sincere thanks for his kindness, and he, being well acquainted with the road, in a short time brought them within view of the Knight's castle.

'Now,' says he, 'we must stay here till night comes; for I know all the ways of the place, and if there be any chance for it, it is when they are all at rest; for the steed is all the watch the Knight keeps there.'

Accordingly, in the dead hour of the night, the King's three sons and the Thief of Sloan attempted the Steed of Bells in order to carry him away, but before they could reach the stables the steed neighed most terribly and shook himself so, and the bells rang with such noise, that the Knight and all his men were up in a moment.

The Black Thief and the King's sons thought to make their escape, but they were suddenly surrounded by the Knight's guards and taken prisoners; where they were brought into that dismal part of the palace where the Knight kept a furnace always boiling, in which he threw all offenders that ever came in his way, which in a few moments would entirely consume them.

'Audacious villains!' says the Knight of the Glen, 'how dare you attempt so bold an action as to steal my steed? See, now, the reward of your folly; for your greater punishment I will not boil you all together, but one after the other, so that he that survives may witness the dire afflictions of his unfortunate companions.'

So saying he ordered his servants to stir up the fire. 'We will boil the eldest-looking of these young men first,' said he, 'and so on to the last, which will be this old champion with the black cap. He seems to be the captain, and looks as if he had come through many toils.'

'I was as near death once as the Prince is yet,' says the Black Thief, 'and escaped; and so will he too.'

'No, you never were,' said the Knight; 'for he is within two or three minutes of his latter end.'

'But,' says the Black Thief, 'I was within one moment of my death, and I am here yet.'

'How was that?' says the Knight; 'I would be glad to hear it, for it seems impossible.'

'If you think, Sir Knight,' says the Black Thief, 'that the danger I was in surpasses that of this young man, will you pardon him his crime?'

'I will,' says the Knight, 'so go on with your story.'

'I was, sir,' says he, 'a very wild boy in my youth, and came through many distresses; once in particular, as I was on my rambling, I was benighted and could find no lodging. At length I came to an old kiln, and being much fatigued I went up and lay on the ribs. I had not been long there when I saw three witches coming in with three bags of gold. Each put their bags of gold under their heads, as if to sleep. I heard one of them say to the other that if the Black Thief came on them while they slept, he would not leave them a penny. I found by their discourse that everybody had got my name into their mouth, though I kept silent as death during their discourse. At length they fell fast asleep, and then I stole softly down, and seeing some turf convenient, I placed one under each of their heads, and off I went, with their gold, as fast as I could.

'I had not gone far,' continued the Thief of Sloan, 'before I saw a greyhound, a hare, and a hawk in pursuit of me, and began to think it must be the witches that had taken these shapes in order that I might not escape them unseen either by land or water. Seeing they did not appear in any formidable shape, I was more than once resolved to attack them, thinking that with my broad sword I could easily destroy them. But considering again that it was perhaps still in their power to become alive again, I gave over the attempt and climbed with difficulty up a tree, bringing my sword in my hand and all the gold along with me. However, when they came to the tree they found what I had done, and making further use of their hellish art, one of them was changed into a smith's anvil and another into a piece of iron, of which the third soon made a hatchet. Having the hatchet made, she fell to cutting down the tree, and in the course of an hour it began to shake

with me. At length it began to bend, and I found that one or two blows at the most would put it down. I then began to think that my death was inevitable, considering that those who were capable of doing so much would soon end my life, but just as she had the stroke drawn that would terminate my fate, the cock crew, and the witches disappeared, having resumed their natural shapes for fear of being known, and I got safe off with my bags of gold.

'Now, sir,' says he to the Knight of the Glen, 'if that be not as great an adventure as ever you heard, to be within one blow of a hatchet of my end, and that blow even drawn, and after all to escape, I leave it to yourself.'

'Well, I cannot say but it is very extraordinary,' says the Knight of the Glen, 'and on that account I pardon this young man his crime; so stir up the fire, till I boil this second one.'

'Indeed,' says the Black Thief, 'I would fain think he would not die this time either.'

'How so?' says the Knight; 'it is impossible for him to escape.'

'I escaped death more wonderfully myself,' says the Thief of Sloan, 'than if you had him ready to throw into the furnace, and I hope it will be the case with him likewise.'

'Why, have you been in another great danger?' says the Knight. 'I would be glad to hear the story too, and if it be as wonderful as the last, I will pardon this young man as I did the other.'

'My way of living, sir,' says the Black Thief, 'was not good, as I told you before; and being at a certain time fairly run out of cash, and meeting with no enterprise worthy of notice, I was reduced to great straits. At length a rich bishop died in the neighbourhood I was then in, and I heard he was interred with a great deal of jewels and rich robes upon him, all which I intended in a short time to be master of. Accordingly that very night I set about it, and coming to the place, I understood he was placed at the farther end of a long dark vault, which I slowly entered.

'I had not gone in far until I heard a foot coming towards me with a quick pace, and although naturally bold and daring, yet, thinking of the deceased bishop and the crime I was engaged in, I lost courage, and ran towards the entrance of the vault. I had retreated but a few paces when I observed, between me and the light, the figure of a tall black man standing in the entrance. Being in great fear and not knowing how to pass, I fired a pistol at him, and he immediately fell across the entrance. Perceiving he still retained the figure of a mortal man, I began to imagine that it could not be the bishop's ghost; recovering myself therefore from the fear I was in, I ventured to the upper end of the vault, where I found a large bundle, and upon further examination I found that the corpse was already rifled, and that which I had taken to be a ghost was no more than one of his own clergy. I was then very sorry that I had the misfortune to kill him, but it then could not be helped. I took up the bundle that contained everything belonging to the corpse that was valuable, intending to take my departure from this melancholy abode; but just as I came to the mouth of the entrance I saw the guards of the place coming towards me, and distinctly heard them saying that they would look in the vault, for that the Black Thief would think little of robbing the corpse if he was anywhere in the place.

'I did not then know in what manner to act, for if I was seen I would surely lose my life, as everybody had a look-out at that time, and because there was no person bold enough to come in on me. I knew very well on the first sight of me that could be got, I would be shot like a dog. However, I had not time to lose. I took and raised up the man which I had killed, as if he was standing on his feet, and I, crouching behind him, bore him up as well as I could, so that the guards readily saw him as they came up to the vault. Seeing the man in black, one of the men cried that was the Black Thief, and, presenting his piece, fired at the man, at which I let him fall, and crept into a little dark corner myself, that was at the entrance of the place. When they saw the man fall, they ran all into the vault, and never stopped until they were at the end of it, for fear, as I thought, that there might be some others along with him that was killed. But while they were busy inspecting the corpse and the vault to see what had been taken, I slipped out, and, once away, and still away; and they never had the Black Thief in their power since.'

'Well, my brave fellow,' says the Knight of the Glen, 'I see you have come through many dangers: you have freed these two Princes by your stories; but I am sorry myself that this youngest Prince has to suffer for all. Now, if you could tell me something as wonderful as you have told already, I would pardon him likewise; I pity the youth and would not want to put him to death if I could help it.'

'That happens well,' says the Thief of Sloan, 'for I like him best myself, and have reserved the most curious passage for the last on his account.'

'Well, then,' says the Knight, 'let us hear it.'

'I was one day on my travels,' says the Black Thief, 'and I came into a great forest, where I wandered a long time, and could not get out of it. At length I came to a large castle, and fatigue obliged me to call in the same, where I found a young woman and a child sitting on her knee, and she crying. I asked her what made her cry, and where the lord of the castle was, for I wondered greatly that I saw no stir of servants or any person about the place.

'"It is well for you," says the young woman, "that the lord of this castle is not at home at present; for he is a monstrous giant, with but one eye on his forehead, who lives on human flesh. He brought me this child," says she, "I do not know where he got it, and ordered me to make it into a pie, and I cannot help crying at the command."

'I told her that if she knew of any place convenient that I could leave the child safely I would do it, rather than it should be killed by such a monster.

'She told me of a house a distance off where I would get a woman who would take care of it. "But what will I do in regard of the pie?"

'"Cut a finger off it," said I, "and I will bring you in a young pig out of the forest, which you may dress as if it was the child, and put the finger in a certain place, that if the giant doubts anything about the pie you may know where to turn it over at the first, and when he sees it he will be fully satisfied that the pie is made of the child."

'She agreed to the scheme I proposed, and, cutting off the child's finger, by her direction I soon had it at the house she told me of, and brought her the little pig in the place of it. She then made ready the pie, and after eating and drinking heartily myself, I was just taking my leave of the young woman when we observed the giant coming through the castle gates.

'"Bless me," said she, "what will you do now? Run away and lie down among the dead bodies that he has in the room" (showing me the place), "and strip off your clothes that he may not know you from the rest if he has occasion to go that way."

'I took her advice, and laid myself down among the rest, as if dead, to see how he would behave. The first thing I heard was him calling for his pie. When she set it down before him he swore it smelt like swine's flesh, but knowing where to find the finger, she immediately turned it up, which fairly convinced him of the contrary. The pie only served to whet his appetite, and I heard him sharpening his knife and saying he must have a collop or two, for he was not near satisfied. But what was my terror when I heard the giant groping among the bodies, and, fancying myself, he cut the half of my hip off, and took it with him to be roasted. You may be certain I was in great pain, but the fear of being killed prevented me from making any complaint. However, when he had eaten all he began to drink hot liquors in great abundance, so that in a short time he could not hold up his head, but threw himself on a large creel he had made for the purpose, and fell fast asleep. When I heard him snoring, as I was I went up and caused the woman to bind my wound with a handkerchief; and, taking the giant's spit, reddened it in the fire, and ran it through the eye, but was not able to kill him.

'However, I left the spit sticking in his head, and took to my heels, but I soon found he was in pursuit of me, although blind, and having an enchanted ring he threw it at me, and it fell on my big toe and remained fastened to it.

'The giant then called to the ring, asking where it was, and to my great surprise it made him answer on my foot; and he, guided by the same, made a leap at me which I had the good luck to observe, and fortunately escaped the danger. However, I found running was of no use in saving me, as long as I had the ring on my foot; so I took my sword and cut off the toe it was fastened on, and threw both into a large fish-pond that was convenient. The giant called again to the ring, which by the power of enchantment always made him answer; but he, not knowing what I had done, imagined it was still on some part of me, and made a violent leap to seize me, when he went into the pond, over head and ears, and was drowned. Now, Sir Knight,' says the Thief of Sloan, 'you see what dangers I came through and always escaped; but, indeed I am lame for the want of my toe ever since.'

'My lord and master,' says an old woman that was listening all the time, 'that story is but too true, as I well know, for I am the very woman that was in the giant's castle, and you, my lord, the child that I was to make into a pie; and this is the very man that saved your life, which you may know by the want of your finger that was taken off, as you have heard, to deceive the giant.'

The Knight of the Glen, greatly surprised at what he had heard the old woman tell, and knowing he wanted his finger from his childhood, began to understand that the story was true enough.

'And is this my deliverer?' says he. 'O brave fellow, I not only pardon you all, but will keep you with myself while you live, where you shall feast like Princes, and have every attendance that I have myself.'

They all returned thanks on their knees, and the Black Thief told him the reason they attempted to steal the Steed of Bells, and the necessity they were under in going home.

'Well,' says the Knight of the Glen, 'if that's the case I bestow you my steed rather than this brave fellow should die; so you may go when you please, only remember to call and see me betimes, that we may come to know each other well.'

They promised they would, and with great joy they set off for the King their father's palace, and the Black Thief along with them.

The wicked Queen was standing all this time on the tower, and, hearing the bells ringing at a great distance off, knew very well it was the Princes coming home, and the steed with them, and through spite and vexation precipitated herself from the tower and was shattered to pieces.

The three Princes lived happy and well during their father's reign, and always keeping the Black Thief along with them; but how they did after the old King's death is not known.

The Caliph Stork

CALIPH CHASID, of Baghdad, was resting comfortably on his divan one fine afternoon. He was smoking a long pipe, and from time to time he sipped a little coffee which a slave handed to him, and after each sip he stroked his long beard with an air of enjoyment. In short, anyone could see that the Caliph was in an excellent humour. This was, in fact, the best time of day in which to approach him, for just now he was pretty sure to be both affable and in good spirits, and for this reason the Grand Vizier Mansor always chose this hour in which to pay his daily visit.

He arrived as usual this afternoon, but, contrary to his usual custom, with an anxious face. The Caliph withdrew his pipe for a moment from his lips and asked, 'Why do you look so anxious, Grand Vizier?'

The Grand Vizier crossed his arms on his breast and bent low before his master as he answered:

'O my Lord! Whether my countenance be anxious or not I know not, but down below, in the court of the palace, is a pedlar with such beautiful things that I cannot help feeling annoyed at having so little money to spare.'

The Caliph, who had wished for some time past to give his Grand Vizier a present, ordered his black slave to bring the pedlar before him at once. The slave soon returned, followed by the pedlar, a short stout man with a swarthy face, and dressed in very ragged clothes. He carried a box containing all manner of wares – strings of pearls, rings, richly mounted pistols, goblets, and combs. The Caliph and his Vizier inspected everything, and the Caliph chose some handsome pistols for himself and Mansor, and a jewelled comb for the Vizier's wife. Just as the pedlar was about to close his box, the Caliph noticed a small drawer, and asked if there was anything else in it for sale. The pedlar opened the drawer and showed them a box containing a black powder, and a scroll written in strange characters, which neither the Caliph nor the Vizier could read.

'I got these two articles from a merchant who had picked them up in the street at Mecca,' said the pedlar. 'I do not know what they may contain, but as they are of no use to me, you are welcome to have them for a trifle.'

The Caliph, who liked to have old manuscripts in his library, even though he could not read them, purchased the scroll and the box, and dismissed the pedlar. Then, being anxious to know what might be the contents of the scroll, he asked the Vizier if he did not know of anyone who might be able to decipher it.

'Most gracious Lord and master,' replied the Vizier, 'near the great Mosque lives a man called Selim the learned, who knows every language under the sun. Send for him; it may be that he will be able to interpret these mysterious characters.'

The learned Selim was summoned immediately.

'Selim,' said the Caliph, 'I hear you are a scholar. Look well at this scroll and see whether you can read it. If you can, I will give you a robe of honour; but if you fail, I will order you to receive twelve strokes on your cheeks, and five-and-twenty on the soles of your feet, because you have been falsely called Selim the learned.'

Selim prostrated himself and said, 'Be it according to your will, O master!' Then he gazed long at the scroll. Suddenly he exclaimed, 'May I die, O my Lord, if this isn't Latin!'

'Well,' said the Caliph, 'if it is Latin, let us hear what it means.'

So Selim began to translate. 'Thou who mayest find this, praise Allah for his mercy. Whoever shall snuff the powder in this box, and at the same time shall pronounce the word "Mutabor!" can transform himself into any creature he likes, and will understand the language of all animals. When he wishes to resume the human form, he has only to bow three times towards the east, and to repeat the same word. Be careful, however, when wearing the shape of some beast or bird, not to laugh, or thou wilt certainly forget the magic word and remain transformed for ever.'

When Selim the learned had read this, the Caliph was delighted. He made the wise man swear not to tell the matter to anyone, gave him a splendid robe, and dismissed him. Then he said to his Vizier, 'That's what I call a good bargain, Mansor. I am longing for the moment when I can become some animal. Tomorrow morning I shall expect you early; we will go into the country, take some snuff from my box, and then hear what is being said in air, earth, and water.'

Next morning Caliph Chasid had barely finished dressing and breakfasting, when the Grand Vizier arrived, according to orders, to accompany him on his expedition. The Caliph stuck the snuff-box in his girdle, and, having desired his servants to remain at home, started off with the Grand Vizier only in attendance. First they walked through the palace gardens, but they looked in vain for some creature which could tempt them to try their magic power. At length the Vizier suggested going farther on to a pond which lay beyond the town, and where he had often seen a variety of creatures, especially storks, whose grave, dignified appearance and constant chatter had often attracted his attention.

The Caliph consented, and they went straight to the pond. As soon as they arrived they remarked a stork strutting up and down with a stately air, hunting for frogs, and now and then muttering something to itself. At the same time they saw another stork far above in the sky flying towards the same spot.

'I would wager my bread, most gracious master,' said the Grand Vizier, 'that these two long legs will have a good chat together. How would it be if we turned ourselves into storks?'

'Well said,' replied the Caliph; 'but first let us remember carefully how we are to become men once more. We must bow three times towards the east and say "Mutabor!" and I shall be Caliph and you my Grand Vizier again. But for heavens' sake don't laugh or we are lost!'

As the Caliph spoke he saw the second stork circling round his head and gradually flying towards the earth. Quickly he drew the box from his girdle, took a good pinch of the snuff, and offered one to Mansor, who also took one, and both cried together 'Mutabor!'

Instantly their legs shrivelled up and grew thin and red; their smart yellow slippers turned to clumsy stork's feet, their arms to wings; their necks began to sprout from between their shoulders and grew a yard long; their beards disappeared, and their bodies were covered with feathers.

'You've got a fine long bill, Sir Vizier,' cried the Caliph, after standing for some time lost in astonishment. 'By the beard of the Prophet I never saw such a thing in all my life!'

'My very humble thanks,' replied the Grand Vizier, as he bent his long neck; 'but, if I may venture to say so, your Highness is even handsomer as a stork than as a Caliph. But come, if it so pleases you, let us go near our comrades there and find out whether we really do understand the language of storks.'

Meantime the second stork had reached the ground. It first scraped its bill with its claw, stroked down its feathers, and then advanced towards the first stork. The two newly-made storks lost no time in drawing near, and to their amazement overheard the following conversation:

'Good morning, Dame Longlegs. You are out early this morning!'

'Yes, indeed, dear Chatterbill! I am getting myself a morsel of breakfast. May I offer you a joint of lizard or a frog's thigh?'

'A thousand thanks, but I have really no appetite this morning. I am here for a very different purpose. I am to dance today before my father's guests, and I have come to the meadow for a little quiet practice.'

Thereupon the young stork began to move about with the most strange and wonderful steps. The Caliph and Mansor looked on in surprise for some time; but when at last she balanced herself in a picturesque attitude on one leg, and flapped her wings gracefully up and down, they could hold out no longer; a prolonged peal burst from each of their bills, and it was some time before they could recover their composure. The Caliph was the first to collect himself. 'That was the best joke,' said he, 'I've ever seen. It's a pity the stupid creatures were scared away by our laughter, or no doubt they would have sung next!'

Suddenly, however, the Vizier remembered how strictly they had been warned not to laugh during their transformation. He at once communicated his fears to the Caliph, who exclaimed, 'By Mecca and Medina! It would indeed prove but a poor joke if I had to remain a stork for the remainder of my days! Do just try and remember the stupid word, it has slipped my memory.'

'We must bow three times eastwards and say "Mu . . . mu . . . mu . . ."'

They turned to the east and fell to bowing till their bills touched the ground, but, oh horror – the magic word was quite forgotten, and however often the Caliph bowed and however touchingly his Vizier cried 'Mu . . . mu . . .' they could not recall it, and the unhappy Chasid and Mansor remained storks as they were.

The two enchanted birds wandered sadly on through the meadows. In their misery they could not think what to do next. They could not rid themselves of their new forms; there was no use in returning to the town and saying who they were; for who would believe a stork who announced that he was a Caliph; and even if they did believe him, would the people of Baghdad consent to let a stork rule over them?

So they lounged about for several days, supporting themselves on fruits, which, however, they found some difficulty in eating with their long bills. They did not much care to eat frogs or lizards. Their one comfort in their sad plight was the power of flying, and accordingly they often flew over the roofs of Baghdad to see what was going on there.

During the first few days they noticed signs of much disturbance and distress in the streets, but about the fourth day, as they sat on the roof of the palace, they perceived a splendid procession passing below them along the street. Drums and trumpets sounded, a man in a scarlet mantle, embroidered in gold, sat on a splendidly caparisoned horse surrounded by richly dressed slaves; half Baghdad crowded after him, and they all shouted, 'Hail, Mirza, the Lord of Baghdad!'

The two storks on the palace roof looked at each other, and Caliph Chasid said, 'Can you guess now, Grand Vizier, why I have been enchanted? This Mirza is the son of my deadly enemy, the mighty magician Kaschnur, who in an evil moment vowed vengeance on me. Still, I will not despair! Come with me, my faithful friend; we will go to the grave of the Prophet, and perhaps at that sacred spot the spell may be loosed.'

They rose from the palace roof, and spread their wings towards Medina.

But flying so great a distance was not quite an easy matter, for the two storks had had but little practice as yet.

'O my Lord!' gasped the Vizier, after a couple of hours, 'I can get on no longer; you really fly too quick for me. Besides, it is nearly evening, and we should do well to find some place in which to spend the night.'

Chasid listened with favour to his servant's suggestion, and perceiving in the valley beneath them a ruin which seemed to promise shelter they flew towards it. The building in which they proposed to pass the night had apparently been formerly a castle. Some handsome pillars still stood amongst the heaps of ruins, and several rooms, which yet remained in fair preservation, gave evidence of former splendour. Chasid and his companion wandered along the passages seeking a dry spot, when suddenly Mansor stood still.

'My Lord and master,' he whispered, 'if it were not absurd for a Grand Vizier, and still more for a stork, to be afraid of ghosts, I should feel quite nervous, for someone, or something close by me, has sighed and moaned quite audibly.'

The Caliph stood still and distinctly heard a low weeping sound which seemed to proceed from a human being rather than from any animal. Full of curiosity he was about to rush towards the spot from whence the sounds of woe came, when the Vizier caught him by the wing with his bill, and implored him not to expose himself to fresh and unknown dangers. The Caliph, however, under whose stork's breast a brave heart beat, tore himself away with the loss of a few feathers, and hurried down a dark passage. He saw a door which stood ajar, and through which he distinctly heard sighs, mingled with sobs. He pushed open the door with his bill, but remained on the threshold, astonished at the sight which met his eyes. On the floor of the ruined chamber – which was but scantily lighted by a small barred window – sat a large screech owl. Big tears rolled from its large round eyes, and in a hoarse voice it uttered its complaints through its crooked beak. As soon as it saw the Caliph and his Vizier – who had crept up meanwhile – it gave vent to a joyful cry. It gently wiped the tears from its eyes with its spotted brown wings, and to the great amazement of the two visitors, addressed them in good human Arabic.

'Welcome, ye storks! You are a good sign of my deliverance, for it was foretold me that a piece of good fortune should befall me through a stork.'

When the Caliph had recovered from his surprise, he drew up his feet into a graceful position, bent his long neck, and said, 'O screech owl! From your words I am led to believe that we see in you a companion in misfortune. But, alas! your hope that you may attain your deliverance through us is but a vain one. You will know our helplessness when you have heard our story.'

The screech owl begged him to relate it, and the Caliph accordingly told him what we already know.

When the Caliph had ended, the owl thanked him and said, 'You hear my story, and own that I am no less unfortunate than yourselves. My father is the King of the Indies. I, his only daughter, am named Lusa. That magician Kaschnur, who enchanted you, has been the cause of my misfortunes too. He came one day to my father and demanded my hand for his son Mirza. My father – who is rather hasty – ordered him to be thrown downstairs. The wretch not long after managed to approach me under another form, and one day, when I was in the garden, and asked for some refreshment, he brought me – in the disguise of a slave – a draught which changed me at once to this horrid shape. Whilst I was fainting with terror he transported me here, and cried to me with his awful voice, "There shall you remain, lonely and hideous, despised even by the brutes, till the end of your days, or till someone of his own free will asks you to be his wife. Thus do I avenge myself on you and your proud father."

'Since then many months have passed away. Sad and lonely do I live like any hermit within these walls, avoided by the world, and a terror even to animals; the beauties of nature are hidden from me, for

I am blind by day, and it is only when the moon sheds her pale light on this spot that the veil falls from my eyes and I can see.' The owl paused, and once more wiped her eyes with her wing, for the recital of her woes had drawn fresh tears from her.

The Caliph fell into deep thought on hearing this story of the Princess. 'If I am not much mistaken,' said he, 'there is some mysterious connection between our misfortunes, but how to find the key to the riddle is the question.'

The owl answered, 'O my Lord! I too felt sure of this, for in my earliest youth a wise woman foretold that a stork would bring me some great happiness, and I think I could tell you how we might save ourselves.' The Caliph was much surprised, and asked her what she meant.

'The Magician who has made us both miserable,' said she, 'comes once a month to these ruins. Not far from this room is a large hall where he is in the habit of feasting with his companions. I have often watched them. They tell each other all about their evil deeds, and possibly the magic word which you have forgotten may be mentioned.'

'O dearest Princess!' exclaimed the Caliph. 'Say, when does he come, and where is the hall?'

The owl paused a moment and then said, 'Do not think me unkind, but I can only grant your request on one condition.'

'Speak, speak!' cried Chasid. 'Command; I will gladly do whatever you wish!'

'Well,' replied the owl, 'you see I should like to be free too; but this can only be if one of you will offer me his hand in marriage.'

The storks seemed rather taken aback by this suggestion, and the Caliph beckoned to his Vizier to retire and consult with him.

When they were outside the door the Caliph said, 'Grand Vizier, this is a tiresome business. However, you can take her.'

'Indeed!' said the Vizier; 'so that when I go home my wife may scratch my eyes out! Besides, I am an old man, and your Highness is still young and unmarried, and a far more suitable match for a young and lovely Princess.'

'Ah, that's just it,' sighed the Caliph, whose wings drooped in a dejected manner. 'How do you know she is young and lovely? I call it buying a pig in a poke.'

They argued on for some time, but at length, when the Caliph saw plainly that his Vizier would rather remain a stork to the end of his days than marry the owl, he determined to fulfil the condition himself. The owl was delighted. She owned that they could not have arrived at a better time, as most probably the magicians would meet that very night.

She then proceeded to lead the two storks to the chamber. They passed through a long dark passage till at length a bright ray of light shone before them through the chinks of a half-ruined wall. When she reached it the owl advised them to keep very quiet. Through the gap near which they stood they could with ease survey the whole of the large hall. It was adorned with splendid carved pillars; a number of coloured lamps replaced the light of day. In the middle of the hall stood a round table covered with a variety of dishes, and round about the table were divans on which eight magicians were seated, and in one of them the two storks recognised the pedlar who had sold the magic powder. The man next him begged him to relate all his latest doings, and after other tales of wickedness he told the story of the Caliph and his Vizier.

'And what word did you give them?' asked another old sorcerer.

'A very difficult Latin word; it is "Mutabor".'

As soon as the storks heard this they were nearly beside themselves with joy. They ran at such a pace to the door of the ruined castle that the owl could scarcely keep up with them. When they reached it the Caliph turned to the owl, and said with much feeling, 'Deliverer of my friend and myself, as a proof of my eternal gratitude, accept me as your husband.' Then he turned towards the east. Three times the storks bowed their long necks to the sun, which was just rising over the mountains. 'Mutabor!' they both cried, and in an instant they were once more transformed. In the rapture of their newly-given lives master and servant fell laughing and weeping into each other's arms. Who shall describe their surprise when they at last turned round and beheld standing before them a beautiful lady exquisitely dressed!

With a smile she held out her hand to the Caliph, and asked, 'Do you not recognise your screech owl?'

It was indeed she! The Caliph was so enchanted by her grace and beauty, that he declared being turned into a stork had been the best piece of luck which had ever befallen him. The three set out at once for Baghdad. Fortunately, the Caliph found not only the box with the magic powder, but also his purse in his girdle; he was, therefore, able to buy in the nearest village all they required for their journey, and so at last they reached the gates of Baghdad.

Here the Caliph's arrival created the greatest sensation. He had been quite given up for dead, and the people were greatly rejoiced to see their beloved ruler again.

Their rage with the usurper Mirza, however, was great in proportion. They marched in force to the palace and took the old magician and his son prisoners. The Caliph sent the magician to the room where the Princess had lived as an owl, and there had him hanged. As the son, however, knew nothing of his father's acts, the Caliph gave him his choice between death and a pinch of the magic snuff. When he chose the latter, the Grand Vizier handed him the box. One good pinch, and the magic word transformed him to a stork. The Caliph ordered him to be confined in an iron cage, and placed in the palace gardens.

Caliph Chasid lived long and happily with his wife the Princess. His merriest time was when the Grand Vizier visited him in the afternoon; and when the Caliph was in particularly high spirits he would condescend to mimic the Vizier's appearance when he was a stork. He would strut gravely, and with well-stiffened legs, up and down the room, chattering, and showing how he had vainly bowed to the east and cried 'Mu . . . Mu . . .' The Princess and her children were always much entertained by this performance; but when the Caliph went on nodding and bowing, and calling 'Mu . . . mu . . .' too long, the Vizier would threaten laughingly to tell the Caliph's wife the subject of the discussion carried on that night in the ruined castle outside the door of Princess Screech Owl.

The Cats' Elopement

ONCE UPON a time there lived a cat of marvellous beauty, with a
skin as soft and shining as silk, and wise green eyes, that could see even
in the dark. His name was Gon, and he belonged to a music teacher,
who was so fond and proud of him that he would not have parted with
him for anything in the world.

Now not far from the music master's house there dwelt a lady who
possessed a most lovely little pussy cat called Koma. She was such a
dear, and blinked her eyes so daintily, and ate her supper so tidily, and
when she had finished she licked her pink nose so delicately with her
little tongue, that her mistress was never tired of saying, 'Koma,
Koma, what should I do without you?'

Well, it happened one day that these two cats, when out for an evening stroll, met under a cherry tree, and in one moment fell madly in
love with each other. Gon had long felt that it was time for him to find
a wife, for all the ladies in the neighbourhood paid him so much attention that it made him quite shy; but he was not easy to please, and did
not care about any of them. Now, before he had time to think, Cupid
had entangled him in his net, and he was filled with love towards
Koma. She fully returned his passion, but, like a woman, she saw the

51

difficulties in the way, and consulted sadly with Gon as to the means of overcoming them. Gon entreated his master to set matters right by buying Koma, but Koma's mistress would not part with her. Then the music master was asked to sell Gon to the lady, but he declined to listen to any such suggestion, so everything remained as before.

At length the love of the couple grew to such a pitch that they determined to please themselves, and to go off to seek their fortunes together. So one moonlight night they stole away, and ventured out into an unknown world. All day long they marched bravely on through the sunshine, till they had left their homes far behind them, and towards evening they found themselves in a large park. The wanderers by this time were hot and tired, and the grass looked very soft and inviting, and the trees cast cool deep shadows. Then suddenly an ogre appeared in this Paradise, in the shape of a dog! He came springing towards them showing all his teeth. Koma shrieked, and rushed up a cherry tree; Gon, however, stood his ground boldly, and prepared to give battle, for he felt that Koma's eyes were upon him, and that he must not run away. But, alas! his courage would have availed him nothing had his enemy once touched him, for the dog was large and powerful, and very fierce. From her perch in the tree Koma saw it all, and screamed with all her might, hoping that someone would hear, and come to help. Luckily a servant of the Princess to whom the park belonged was walking by, and he drove off the dog, and picking up the trembling Gon in his arms, carried him to his mistress.

So poor little Koma was left alone, while Gon was borne away full of trouble, not in the least knowing what to do. Even the attention paid him by the Princess, who was delighted with his beauty and pretty ways, did not console him, but there was no use in fighting against fate, and he could only wait and see what would turn up.

The Princess, Gon's new mistress, was so good and kind that everybody loved her, and she would have led a happy life, had it not been for a serpent who had fallen in love with her, and was constantly annoying her by his presence. Her servants had orders to drive him away as often as he appeared; but as they were careless, and the serpent very sly, it sometimes happened that he was able to slip past them, and to frighten the Princess by appearing before her. One day she was seated in her room, playing on her favourite musical instrument, when she felt something gliding up her sash, and saw her enemy making his way to kiss her cheek. She shrieked and threw herself backwards, and Gon, who had been curled up on a stool at her feet, understood her terror, and with one bound seized the snake by his neck. He gave him one bite and one shake, and flung him on the ground, where he lay, never to worry the Princess any more. Then she took Gon in her arms, and praised and caressed him, and saw that he had the nicest bits to eat, and the softest mats to lie on; and he would have had nothing in the world to wish for if only he could have found Koma again.

Time passed on, and one morning Gon lay before the house door, basking in the sun. He looked lazily at the world stretched out before him, and saw in the distance a big ruffian of a cat teasing and ill-treating quite a little one. He jumped up, full of rage, and chased away the big cat, and then he turned to comfort the little one, when his heart nearly burst with joy to find that it was Koma. At first Koma did not know him again, he had grown so large and stately; but when it dawned upon her who it was, her happiness knew no bounds. And they rubbed heads and noses again and again, while their purring might have been heard a mile off.

Paw in paw they appeared before the Princess, and told her the story of their life and its sorrows. The Princess wept for sympathy, and promised that they should never more be parted, but should live with her to the end of their days. By and by the Princess herself got married, and brought a Prince to dwell in the palace in the park. And she told him all about her two cats, and how brave Gon had been, and how he had delivered her from her enemy the serpent.

And when the Prince heard, he swore they should never leave them, but should go with the Princess wherever she went. So it all fell out as the Princess wished; and Gon and Koma had many children, and so had the Princess, and they all played together, and were friends to the end of their lives.

The Clever Weaver

ONCE UPON a time the King of a far country was sitting on his throne, listening to the complaints of his people, and judging between them. That morning there had been fewer cases than usual to deal with, and the King was about to rise and go into his gardens, when a sudden stir was heard outside, and the lord high chamberlain entered, and inquired if his majesty would be graciously pleased to receive the ambassador of a powerful Emperor who lived in the east, and was greatly feared by the neighbouring sovereigns. The King, who stood as much in dread of the Emperor as the rest, gave orders that the envoy should be admitted at once, and that a banquet should be prepared in his honour. Then he settled himself again on his throne, wondering what the envoy had to say.

The envoy said nothing. He advanced to the throne where the King was awaiting him, and stooping down, traced on the floor with a rod which he held in his hand a black circle all round it. Then he sat down on a seat that was near, and took no further notice of anyone.

The King and his courtiers were equally mystified and enraged at this strange behaviour, but the envoy sat as calm and still as an image, and it soon became plain that they would get no explanation from *him*. The ministers were hastily summoned to a council, but not one of them could throw any light upon the subject. This made the King more angry than ever, and he told them that unless before sunset they could find someone capable of solving the mystery he would hang them all.

The King was, as the ministers knew, a man of his word; and they quickly mapped out the city into districts, so that they might visit house by house, and question the occupants as to whether they could explain the action of the ambassador. Most of them received no reply except a puzzled stare; but, luckily, one of them was more observant than the rest, and on entering an empty cottage where a swing was swinging of itself, he began to think it might be worth while for him to see the owner. Opening a door leading into another room, he found

54

a second swing, swinging gently like the first, and from the window he beheld a patch of corn, and a willow pole which moved perpetually without any wind, in order to frighten away the sparrows. Feeling more and more curious, he descended the stairs and found himself in a large light workshop in which was seated a weaver at his loom. But all the weaver did was to guide his threads, for the machine that he had invented to set in motion the swings and the willow pole, made the loom work.

When he saw the great wheel standing in the corner, and had guessed the use of it, the minister heaved a sigh of relief. At any rate even if the weaver could not solve the riddle, he at least might put the minister on the right track. So without more ado he told the story of the envoy and the circle, and ended by declaring that the person who could explain the meaning of this riddle should be handsomely rewarded.

'Come with me at once,' said the minister. 'The sun is low in the heavens, and there is no time to lose.'

The weaver stood thinking for a moment and then walked across to a window, outside of which was a hen-coop with two knuckle-bones lying beside it. These he picked up, and taking the hen from the coop, he tucked it under his arm.

'I am ready,' he answered, turning to the minister.

In the hall the King still sat on his throne, and the envoy on his seat. Signing to the minister to remain where he was, the weaver advanced to the envoy, and placed the knuckle-bones on the floor beside him. For answer, the envoy took a handful of millet seed out of his pocket and scattered it round; upon which the weaver set down the hen, who ate it up in a moment. At that the envoy rose without a word, and took his departure.

As soon as he had left the hall, the King beckoned to the weaver.

'You alone seem to have guessed the riddle,' said he, 'and great shall be your reward. But tell me, I pray you, what it all means?'

'The meaning, O King,' replied the weaver, 'is this: the circle drawn by the envoy round your throne is the message of the Emperor, and signifies, "If I send an army and surround your capital, will you lay down your arms?" The knuckle-bones which I placed before him told him, "You are but children in comparison with us. Toys like

these are the only playthings you are fit for." The millet that he scattered was an emblem of the number of soldiers that his master can bring into the field; but by the hen which ate up the seed he understood that one of our men could destroy a host of theirs.

'I do not think,' he added, 'that the Emperor will declare war.'

'You have saved me and my honour,' cried the King, 'and wealth and glory shall be heaped upon you. Name your reward, and you shall have it even to the half of my kingdom.'

'The small farm outside the city gates, as a marriage portion for my daughter, is all I ask,' answered the weaver, and it was all he would accept. 'Only, O King,' were his parting words, 'I would beg of you to remember that weavers also are of value to a state, and that they are sometimes cleverer even than ministers!'

The Cottager and his Cat

ONCE UPON a time there lived an old man in a dirty, tumble-down cottage, not very many miles from the splendid palace where the King and Queen dwelt. In spite of the wretched state of the hut, which many people declared was too bad even for a pig to live in, the old man was very rich. He had been lucky in business dealings, but he was a great miser, and would often go without food all day sooner than change one of his beloved gold pieces. But after a while he found that he had starved himself once too often. He fell ill, and had no strength to get well again, and in a few days died, leaving his wife and one son behind him.

The night following his father's death, the son dreamed that an unknown man appeared to him and said, 'Listen to me; your father is dead and your mother will soon die, and all their riches will belong to you. Half of his wealth is ill-gotten, and this you must give back to the poor from whom he squeezed it. The other half you must throw into the sea. Watch, however, as the money sinks into the water, and if anything should swim, catch it and keep it, even if it is nothing more than a bit of paper.'

Then the man vanished, and the youth awoke.

The remembrance of his dream troubled him greatly. He did not want to part with the riches that his father had left him, for he had known all his life what it was to be cold and hungry, and now he had hoped for a little comfort and pleasure. Still, he was honest and good-hearted, and if his father had come wrongfully by his wealth he felt he could never enjoy it, and at last he made up his mind to do as he had been bidden. He found out who were the poorest people in the village, and spent half of his money in helping them, and the other half he put in his pocket. From a rock that jutted right out into the sea he flung it in. In a moment it was out of sight, and no man could have told the spot where it had sunk, except for a tiny scrap of paper floating on the water. He stretched down carefully and managed to reach it, and on opening it found six shillings wrapped inside. This was now all the money he had in the world.

The young man stood and looked at it thoughtfully. 'Well, I can't do much with this,' he said to himself; but, after all, six shillings were better than nothing, and he wrapped them up again and slipped them into his coat.

He worked in his garden for the next few weeks, and he and his mother contrived to live on the fruit and vegetables he got out of it, and then she too died suddenly. The poor fellow felt very sad when he had laid her in her grave, and with a heavy heart he wandered into the forest, not knowing where he was going. By and by he began to feel very hungry, and seeing a small hut in front of him, he knocked at the door and asked if they could give him some milk. The old woman who opened it begged him to come in, adding kindly, that if he wanted a night's lodging he might have it without its costing him anything.

Two women and three men were at supper when he entered, and silently made room for him to sit down by them. When he had eaten he began to look about him, and was surprised to see an animal sitting by the fire different from anything he had ever seen before. It was grey in colour, and not very big; but its eyes were large and very bright, and it seemed to be singing in an odd way, quite unlike any wild animal of the forest. 'What is the name of that strange little creature?' asked he. And they answered, 'We call it a cat.'

'I should like to buy it – if it is not too dear,' said the young man; 'it would be company for me.' And they told him that he might have it for six shillings, if he cared to give so much. The young man took out his precious bit of paper, handed them the six shillings, and the next morning bade them farewell, carrying the cat snugly in a fold of his cloak.

For the whole day he wandered through meadows and forests, till in the evening he reached a house. He knocked at the door and asked the old man who opened it if he could rest there that night, adding that he had no money to pay for it. 'Then I must give hospitality to you,' answered the man, and led him into a room where two women and two men were sitting at supper. One of the women was the old man's wife, the other his daughter. The young man placed the cat on the mantelshelf, and they all crowded round to examine this strange beast, and the cat rubbed itself against them, and held out its paw, and sang to them; and the women were delighted, and gave it everything that a cat could eat, and a great deal more besides.

After hearing the youth's story, and how he had nothing in the world left him except his cat, the old man advised him to go to the palace, which was only a few miles distant, and take counsel of the King, who was kind to everyone, and would certainly be his friend. The young man thanked him, and said he would gladly take his advice; and early next morning he set out for the royal palace.

He sent a message to the King to beg for an audience, and received a reply that he was to go into the great hall, where he would find his majesty.

The King was at dinner with his court when the young man entered, and he signed to him to come near. The youth bowed low, and then gazed in surprise at the crowd of little black creatures who were running about the floor, and even on the table itself. Indeed, they were so bold they snatched pieces of food from the King's own plate, and if he drove them away, tried to bite his hands, so that he could not eat his food, and his courtiers fared no better.

'What sort of animals are these?' asked the youth of one of the ladies sitting near him.

'They are called rats,' answered the King, who had overheard the question, 'and for years we have tried some way of putting an end to them, but it is impossible. They come into our very beds.'

At this moment something was seen flying through the air. The cat was on the table, and with two or three shakes a number of rats were lying dead round him. Then a great scuffling of feet was heard, and in a few minutes the hall was clear.

For some minutes the King and his courtiers only looked at each other in astonishment. 'What kind of animal is that which can work magic of this sort?' asked he. And the young man told him that it was called a cat, and that he had bought it for six shillings.

And the King answered, 'Because of the luck you have brought me, in freeing my palace from the plague which has tormented me for many years, I will give you the choice of two things. Either you shall be my Prime Minister, or else you shall marry my daughter and reign after me. Say, which shall it be?'

'The Princess and the kingdom,' said the young man.

And so it was.

The Death of Abu Nowas
and of his Wife

ONCE UPON a time there lived a man whose name was Abu Nowas, and he was a great favourite with the Sultan of the country, who had a palace in the same town where he dwelt. Now one day the wife of Abu Nowas died, and he came weeping into the hall of the palace where the Sultan was sitting, and said to him, 'O mighty Sultan, my wife is dead.'

'That is bad news,' replied the Sultan; 'I must get you another wife.' And he bade his Grand Vizier send for the Sultana.

'This poor Abu Nowas has lost his wife,' said he, when she entered the hall.

'Oh, then we must get him another,' answered the Sultana; 'I have a girl that will suit him exactly,' and clapped her hands loudly. At this signal a maiden appeared and stood before her.

'I have got a husband for you,' said the Sultana.

'Who is he?' asked the girl.

'Abu Nowas, the jester,' replied the Sultana.

'I will take him,' answered the maiden; and as Abu Nowas made no objection, it was all arranged. The Sultana had the most beautiful clothes made for the bride, and the Sultan gave the bridegroom his wedding suit, and a thousand gold pieces into the bargain, and soft carpets for the house.

So Abu Nowas took his wife home, and for some time they were very happy, and spent the money freely which the Sultan had given them, never thinking what they should do for more when that was gone. But come to an end it did, and they had to sell their fine things one by one, till at length nothing was left but a cloak apiece, and one blanket to cover them.

'We have run through our fortune,' said Abu Nowas, 'what are we to do now? I am afraid to go back to the Sultan, for he will command his servants to turn me from the door. But you shall return to your mistress, and throw yourself at her feet and weep, and perhaps she will help us.'

'Oh, you had much better go,' said the wife. 'I shall not know what to say.'

'Well, then, stay at home, if you like,' answered Abu Nowas, 'and I will ask to be admitted to the Sultan's presence, and will tell him, with sobs, that my wife is dead, and that I have no money for her burial. When he hears that perhaps he will give us something.'

'Yes, that is a good plan,' said the wife; and Abu Nowas set out.

The Sultan was sitting in the hall of justice when Abu Nowas entered, his eyes streaming with tears, for he had rubbed some pepper into them. They smarted dreadfully, and he could hardly see to walk straight, and everyone wondered what was the matter with him.

'Abu Nowas! What has happened?' cried the Sultan.

'O noble Sultan, my wife is dead,' wept he.

'We must all die,' answered the Sultan; but this was not the reply for which Abu Nowas had hoped.

'True, O Sultan, but I have neither shroud to wrap her in, nor money to bury her with,' went on Abu Nowas, in no way abashed by the way the Sultan had received his news.

'Well, give him a hundred pieces of gold,' said the Sultan, turning to the Grand Vizier. And when the money was counted out Abu Nowas bowed low, and left the hall, his tears still flowing, but with joy in his heart.

'Have you got anything?' cried his wife, who was waiting for him anxiously.

'Yes, a hundred gold pieces,' said he, throwing down the bag, 'but that will not last us any time. Now you must go to the Sultana, clothed in sackcloth and robes of mourning, and tell her that your husband, Abu Nowas, is dead, and you have no money for his burial. When she hears that, she will be sure to ask you what has become of the money and the fine clothes she gave us on our marriage, and you will answer, "before he died he sold everything".'

The wife did as she was told, and wrapping herself in sackcloth went up to the Sultana's own palace, and as she was known to have been one of Subida's favourite attendants, she was taken without difficulty into the private apartments.

'What is the matter?' inquired the Sultana, at the sight of the dismal figure.

'My husband lies dead at home, and he has spent all our money, and sold everything, and I have nothing left to bury him with,' sobbed the wife.

Then Subida took up a purse containing two hundred gold pieces, and said, 'Your husband served us long and faithfully. You must see that he has a fine funeral.'

The wife took the money, and, kissing the feet of the Sultana, she joyfully hastened home. They spent some happy hours planning how they should spend it, and thinking how clever they had been.

'When the Sultan goes this evening to Subida's palace,' said Abu Nowas, 'she will be sure to tell him that Abu Nowas is dead. "Not Abu Nowas, it is his wife," he will reply, and they will quarrel over it, and all the time we shall be sitting here enjoying ourselves. Oh, if they only knew, how angry they would be!'

As Abu Nowas had foreseen, the Sultan went, in the evening after his business was over, to pay his usual visit to the Sultana.

'Poor Abu Nowas is dead!' said Subida when he entered the room.

'It is not Abu Nowas, but his wife who is dead,' answered the Sultan.

'No; really you are quite wrong. She came to tell me herself only a couple of hours ago,' replied Subida, 'and as he had spent all their money, I gave her something to bury him with.'

'You must be dreaming,' exclaimed the Sultan. 'Soon after midday Abu Nowas came into the hall, his eyes streaming with tears, and when I asked him the reason he answered that his wife was dead, and they had sold everything they had, and he had nothing left, not so much as would buy her a shroud, far less pay for her burial.'

For a long time they talked, and neither would listen to the other, till the Sultan sent for the door-keeper and bade him go instantly to the house of Abu Nowas and see if it was the man or his wife who was dead. But Abu Nowas happened to be sitting with his wife behind the latticed window, which looked on the street, and he saw the man coming, and sprang up at once. 'There is the Sultan's door-keeper! They have sent him here to find out the truth. Quick! throw yourself on the bed and pretend that you are dead.' And in a moment the wife

was stretched out stiffly, with a linen sheet spread across her, like a corpse.

She was only just in time, for the sheet was hardly drawn across her when the door opened and the porter came in. 'Has anything happened?' asked he.

'My poor wife is dead,' replied Abu Nowas. 'Look! she is laid out here.' And the porter approached the bed, which was in a corner of the room, and saw the stiff form lying underneath.

'We must all die,' said he, and went back to the Sultan.

'Well, have you found out which of them is dead?' asked the Sultan.

'Yes, noble Sultan; it is the wife,' replied the porter.

'He only says that to please you,' cried Subida in a rage; and calling to her chamberlain, she ordered him to go at once to the dwelling of Abu Nowas and see which of the two was dead. 'And be sure you tell the truth about it,' added she, 'or it will be the worse for you.'

As her chamberlain drew near the house, Abu Nowas caught sight of him. 'There is the Sultana's chamberlain,' he exclaimed in a fright. 'Now it is my turn to die. Be quick and spread the sheet over me.' And he laid himself on the bed, and held his breath when the chamberlain came in. 'What are you weeping for?' asked the man, finding the wife in tears.

'My husband is dead,' answered she, pointing to the bed; and the chamberlain drew back the sheet and beheld Abu Nowas lying stiff and motionless. Then he gently replaced the sheet and returned to the palace.

'Well, have you found out this time?' asked the Sultan.

'My lord, it is the husband who is dead.'

'But I tell you he was with me only a few hours ago,' cried the Sultan angrily. 'I must get to the bottom of this before I sleep! Let my golden coach be brought round at once.'

The coach was before the door in another five minutes, and the Sultan and Sultana both got in. Abu Nowas had ceased being a dead man, and was looking into the street when he saw the coach coming. 'Quick! quick!' he called to his wife. 'The Sultan will be here directly, and we must both be dead to receive him.' So they lay down, pulled the sheet over themselves, and held their breath. At that instant the

Sultan entered, followed by the Sultana and the chamberlain, and he went up to the bed and found the bodies stiff and motionless. 'I would give a thousand gold pieces to anyone who would tell me the truth about this,' cried he. At these words Abu Nowas sat up. 'Give them to me, then,' said he, holding out his hand. 'You cannot give them to anyone who needs them more.'

'O Abu Nowas, you impudent dog!' exclaimed the Sultan, bursting into laughter, in which the Sultana joined. 'I might have known it was one of your tricks!' But he sent Abu Nowas the gold he had promised, and let us hope that it did not fly so fast as the first had done.

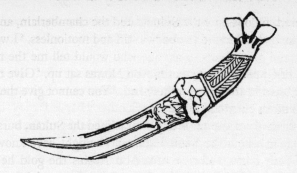

The Enchanted Knife

ONCE UPON a time there lived a young man who vowed he would never marry any girl who had not royal blood in her veins. One day he plucked up all his courage and went to the palace to ask the Emperor for his daughter. The Emperor was not much pleased at the thought of such a match for his only child, but being very polite, he only said:

'Very well, my son, if you can win the Princess you shall have her, and the conditions are these. In eight days you must manage to tame and bring to me three horses that have never felt a master. The first is pure white, the second foxy-red with a black head, the third coal black with white head and feet. And besides that, you must also bring as a present to the Empress, my wife, as much gold as the three horses can carry.'

The young man listened in dismay to these words, but with an effort he thanked the Emperor for his kindness and left the palace, wondering how he was to fulfil the task allotted to him. Luckily for him, the Emperor's daughter had overheard everything her father had said, and peeping through a curtain had seen the youth and thought him handsomer than anyone she had ever beheld. So returning hastily to her own room, she wrote him a letter which she gave to a trusty servant to deliver, begging him to come to her rooms early the next day, and to undertake nothing without her advice, if he ever wished her to be his wife.

That night, when her father was asleep, she crept softly into his chamber and took out an enchanted knife from the chest where he kept his treasures, and hid it carefully in a safe place before she went to bed.

The sun had hardly risen the following morning when the Princess's nurse brought the young man to her apartments. Neither spoke for some minutes, but stood holding each other's hands for joy, till at last they both cried out that nothing but death should part them. Then the maiden gave him the enchanted knife and said:

'Take also my horse, and ride straight through the wood towards the sunset till you come to a hill with three peaks. When you get there, turn first to the right and then to the left, and you will find yourself in a meadow where many horses are feeding. From these you must pick out the three described to you by my father. If they prove shy, and refuse to let you get near them, draw out your knife and let the sun shine on it so that the whole meadow is lit up by its rays, and the horses will then approach you of their own accord, and will let you lead them away. When you have them safely, look about till you see a cypress tree, whose roots are of brass, whose boughs are of silver, and whose leaves are of gold. Go to it, and cut away the roots with your knife, and you will come to countless bags of gold. Load the horses with all they can carry, and return to my father, and tell him that you have done your task, and can claim me for your wife.'

The Princess had finished all she had to say, and now it depended on the young man to do his part. He hid the knife in the folds of his girdle, mounted his horse, and rode off in search of the meadow. This he found without much difficulty, but the horses were all so shy that they galloped away directly he approached them. Then he drew the knife, and held it up towards the sun, and directly there shone such a glory that the whole meadow was bathed in it. From all sides the horses rushed pressing round, and each one that passed him fell on its knees to do him honour. But he chose from them all only the three that the Emperor had described. These he secured by a silken rope to his own horse, and then looked about for the cypress tree. It was standing by itself in one corner, and in a moment he was beside it, tearing away the earth with the knife. Deeper and deeper he dug, till far down, below the roots of brass, his knife struck upon the buried treasure, which lay heaped up in bags all around. With a great effort he lifted them from their hiding place, and laid them one by one on his horses' backs, and when they could carry no more he led them back to the Emperor. And when the Emperor saw him, he wondered, but never guessed how it was the young man had been too clever for him, till the betrothal ceremony was over. Then he asked his newly-made son-in-law what dowry he would require with his bride. To which the bridegroom made answer, 'Noble Emperor! All I desire is that I may have your daughter for my wife, and enjoy for ever the use of your enchanted knife.'

The Five Wise Words of the Guru

ONCE THERE lived a handsome young man named Ram Singh, who, though a favourite with everyone, was unhappy because he had a scold for a stepmother. All day long she went on talking, until the youth was driven so distracted that he determined to go away somewhere and seek his fortune. No sooner had he decided to leave his home than he made his plans, and the very next morning he started off with a few clothes in a bundle, and a little money in his pocket.

But there was one person in the village to whom he wished to say good-bye, and that was a wise old guru, or teacher, who had taught him much. So he turned his face first of all towards his master's hut, and before the sun was well up he was knocking at his door. The old man received his pupil affectionately; but he was wise in reading faces, and saw at once that the youth was in trouble.

'My son,' said he, 'what is the matter?'

'Nothing, father,' replied the young man, 'but I have determined to go into the world and seek my fortune.'

'Be advised,' returned the guru, 'and remain in your father's house; it is better to have half a loaf at home than to seek a whole in distant countries.'

But Ram Singh was in no mood to heed such counsel, and very soon the old man ceased to press him.

'Well,' said he at last, 'if your mind is made up I suppose you must have your way. But listen carefully, and remember these five rules which I will give you in parting; if you keep these no evil shall befall you. First – always obey without question the orders of him whose service you enter; second – never speak harshly or unkindly to anyone; third – never lie; fourth – never try to appear the equal of those above you in station; and fifth – wherever you go, if you meet those who read or teach from the holy books, stay and listen, if but for a few minutes, that you may be strengthened in the path of duty.'

Then Ram Singh started out upon his journey, promising to bear in mind the old man's words.

After some days he came to a great city. He had spent all the money which he had at starting, and therefore resolved to look for work, however humble it might be. Catching sight of a prosperous-looking merchant standing in front of a shop full of grain of all kinds, Ram Singh went up to him and asked whether he could give him anything to do. The merchant gazed at him so long that the young man began to lose heart, but at length he answered:

'Yes, of course; there is a place waiting for you.'

'What do you mean?' asked Ram Singh.

'Why,' replied the other, 'yesterday our Rajah's Chief Wazir dismissed his body servant and is wanting another. Now you are just the sort of person that he needs, for you are young and tall and handsome; I advise you to apply there.'

Thanking the merchant for this advice, the young man set out at once for the Wazir's house, and soon managed, thanks to his good looks and appearance, to be engaged as the great man's servant.

One day, soon after this, the Rajah of the place started on a journey and the Chief Wazir accompanied him. With them was an army of servants and attendants, soldiers, muleteers, camel-drivers, merchants with grain and stores for man and beast, singers to make entertainment by the way and musicians to accompany them, besides elephants, camels, horses, mules, ponies, donkeys, goats, and carts and wagons of every kind and description, so that it seemed more like a large town on the march than anything else.

Thus they travelled for several days, till they entered a country that was like a sea of sand, where the swirling dust floated in clouds, and men and beasts were half choked by it. Towards the close of that day they came to a village, and when the headmen hurried out to salute the Rajah and to pay him their respects, they began, with very long and serious faces, to explain that, whilst they and all that they had were of course at the disposal of the Rajah, the coming of so large a company had nevertheless put them into a dreadful difficulty because they had never a well nor spring of water in their country; and they had no water to give drink to such an army of men and beasts!

Great fear fell upon the host at the words of the headmen, but the Rajah merely told the Wazir that he must get water somehow, and that settled the matter so far as *he* was concerned. The Wazir sent off

in haste for all the oldest men in the place, and began to question them
as to whether there were no wells nearby.

They all looked helplessly at each other, and said nothing; but at
length one old grey-beard replied:

'Truly, Sir Wazir, there is, within a mile or two of this village, a
well which some former king made hundreds of years ago. It is, they
say, great and inexhaustible, covered in by heavy stone-work and with
a flight of steps leading down to the water in the very bowels of the
earth; but no man ever goes near it because it is haunted by evil
spirits, and it is known that whoso goes down the well shall never be
seen again.'

The Wazir stroked his beard and considered a moment. Then he
turned to Ram Singh who stood behind his chair.

'There is a proverb,' said he, 'that no man can be trusted until he
has been tried. Go you and get the Rajah and his people water from
this well.'

Then there flashed into Ram Singh's mind the first counsel of the
old guru – 'Always obey without question the orders of him whose
service you enter.' So he replied at once that he was ready, and left to
prepare for his adventure. Two great brazen vessels he fastened to a
mule, two lesser ones he bound upon his shoulders, and thus provided
he set out, with the old villager for his guide. In a short time they came
within sight of some big trees towering above the barren country,
whilst under their shadow lay the dome of an ancient building. This
the guide pointed out as the well, but excused himself from going
farther as he was an old man and tired, and it was already nearly sunset, so that he must be returning home. So Ram Singh bade him
farewell, and went on alone with the mule.

Arrived at the trees, Ram Singh tied up his beast, lifted the vessels
from his shoulder, and having found the opening of the well, descended by a flight of steps which led down into the darkness. The steps
were broad white slabs of alabaster which gleamed in the shadows as
he went lower and lower. All was very silent. Even the sound of his
bare feet upon the stone seemed to wake an echo in that lonely place,
and when one of the vessels which he carried slipped and fell upon the
steps it clanged so loudly that he jumped at the noise. Still he went on,
until at last he reached a wide pool of sweet water, and there he washed

his jars with care before he filled them, and began to remount the steps with the lighter vessels, as the big ones were so heavy he could only take up one at a time. Suddenly, something moved above him, and looking up he saw a great giant standing on the stairway! In one hand he held clasped to his heart a dreadful-looking mass of bones, in the other was a lamp which cast long shadows about the walls, and made him seem even more terrible than he really was.

'What think you, O mortal,' said the giant, 'of my fair and lovely wife?' And he held the light towards the bones in his arms and looked lovingly at them.

Now I must tell you that this poor giant had had a very beautiful wife, whom he had loved dearly; but, when she died, he refused to believe in her death, and always carried her about long after she had become nothing but bones. Ram Singh of course did not know of this, but there came to his mind the second wise saying of the guru, which forbade him to speak harshly or inconsiderately to others; so he replied:

'Truly, sir, I am sure you could find nowhere such another.'

'Ah, what eyes you have!' cried the delighted giant, 'you at least can see! I do not know how often I have slain those who insulted her by saying she was but dried bones! You are a fine young man, and I will help you.'

So saying, he laid down the bones with great tenderness, and snatching up the huge brass vessels, carried them up again, and replaced them with such ease that it was all done by the time that Ram Singh had reached the open air with the smaller ones.

'Now,' said the giant, 'you have pleased me, and you may ask of me one favour, and whatever you wish I will do it for you. Perhaps you would like me to show you where lies buried the treasure of dead kings?' he added eagerly.

But Ram Singh shook his head at the mention of buried wealth.

'The favour that I would ask,' said he, 'is that you will leave off haunting this well, so that men may go in and out and obtain water.'

Perhaps the giant expected some favour more difficult to grant, for his face brightened, and he promised to depart at once; and as Ram Singh went off through the gathering darkness with his precious burden of water, he beheld the giant striding away with the bones of his dead wife in his arms.

Great was the wonder and rejoicing in the camp when Ram Singh returned with the water. He never said anything, however, about his adventure with the giant, but merely told the Rajah that there was nothing to prevent the well being used; and used it was, and nobody ever saw any more of the giant.

The Rajah was so pleased with the bearing of Ram Singh that he ordered the Wazir to give the young man to him in exchange for one of his own servants. So Ram Singh became the Rajah's attendant; and as the days went by the Rajah became more and more delighted with the youth because, mindful of the old guru's third counsel, he was always honest and spoke the truth. He grew in favour rapidly, until at last the Rajah made him his treasurer, and thus he reached a high place in the court and had wealth and power in his hands. Unluckily the Rajah had a brother who was a very bad man; and this brother thought that if he could win the young treasurer over to himself he might by this means manage to steal little by little any of the Rajah's treasure which he needed. Then, with plenty of money, he could bribe the soldiers and some of the Rajah's counsellors, head a rebellion, dethrone and kill his brother, and reign himself instead. He was too wary, of course, to tell Ram Singh anything of these wicked plans; but he began by flattering him whenever he saw him, and at last offered him his daughter in marriage. But Ram Singh remembered the fourth counsel of the old guru – never to try to appear the equal of those above him in station – therefore he respectfully declined the great honour of marrying a Princess. Of course the Rajah's brother, rebuffed at the very beginning of his enterprise, was furious, and determined to work Ram Singh's ruin. So, entering the Rajah's presence, he told him a tissue of lies about Ram Singh: how he had spoken insultingly about his royal master and also about the Princess. What it was all about nobody knew, and, as it was not true, the wicked Prince did not know either; but the Rajah grew very angry and red in the face as he listened, and declared that until the treasurer's head was cut off neither he nor the Princess nor his brother would eat or drink.

'But,' added he, 'I do not wish anyone to know that this is done by my desire, and anyone who mentions the subject will be severely punished.' And with that the Prince was forced to be content.

Then the Rajah sent for an officer of his guard, and told him to take some soldiers and ride at once to a tower which was being erected just outside the town, and if anyone should come to inquire when the building was going to be finished, or should ask any other questions about it, the officer must chop his head off, and bring it to him. As for the body, that could be buried on the spot. The old officer thought these instructions rather odd, but it was no business of his, so he saluted, and went off to do his master's bidding.

Early in the morning the Rajah, who had not slept all night, sent for Ram Singh, and bade him go to the new hunting-tower, and ask the people there how it was getting on and when it was going to be finished, and to hurry back with the answer! Away went Ram Singh upon his errand, but, on the road, as he was passing a little temple on the outskirts of the city, he heard someone inside reading aloud; and, remembering the guru's fifth counsel, he just stepped inside and sat down to listen for a minute. He did not mean to stay longer, but became so deeply interested in the wisdom of the teacher, that he sat, and sat, and sat, while the sun rose higher and higher.

In the meantime, the wicked Prince, who dared not disobey the Rajah's command, was feeling very hungry; and as for the Princess, she was quietly crying in a corner waiting for the news of Ram Singh's death, so that she might eat her breakfast.

Hours passed, and stare as he might from the window no messenger could be seen.

At last the Prince could bear it no longer, and hastily disguising himself so that no one should recognise him, he jumped on a horse and galloped out to the hunting-tower, where the Rajah had told him that the execution was to take place. But, when he got there, there was no execution going on. There were only some men engaged in building, and a number of soldiers idly watching them. He forgot that he had disguised himself and that no one would know him, so, riding up, he cried out:

'Now then, you men, why are you idling about here instead of finishing what you came to do? When is it to be done?'

At his words the soldiers looked at the commanding officer, who was standing a little apart from the rest. Unperceived by the Prince he made a slight sign, a sword flashed in the sun, and off flew a head on the ground beneath!

As part of the Prince's disguise had been a thick beard, the men did not recognise the dead man as the Rajah's brother; but they wrapped the head in a cloth, and buried the body as their commander bade them. When this was ended, the officer took the cloth bundle, and rode off in the direction of the palace.

Meanwhile the Rajah came home from his council, and to his great surprise found neither head nor brother awaiting him; as time passed, he became uneasy, and thought that he had better go himself and see what the matter was. So ordering his horse he rode off alone.

It happened that, just as the Rajah came near to the temple where Ram Singh still sat, the young treasurer, hearing the sound of a horse's hoofs, looked over his shoulder and saw that the rider was the Rajah himself! Feeling much ashamed for having forgotten his errand, he jumped up and hurried out to meet his master, who reined up his horse, and seemed very surprised (as indeed he was) to see him. At that moment there arrived the officer of the guard carrying his parcel. He saluted the Rajah gravely, and, dismounting, laid the bundle in the road and began to undo the wrappings, whilst the Rajah watched him with wonder and interest. When the last string was undone, and the head of his brother was displayed to his view, the Rajah sprang from his horse and caught the soldier by the arm. As soon as he could speak he questioned the man as to what had occurred, and little by little a dark suspicion came to him. Then, briefly telling the soldier that he had done well, the Rajah drew Ram Singh to one side, and in a few minutes learned from him how, in attending to the guru's counsel, he had delayed to do the Rajah's message.

In the end the Rajah found from some papers the proofs of his dead brother's treachery; and Ram Singh easily established his innocence and integrity. He continued to serve the Rajah for many years with unswerving fidelity; and married a maiden of his own rank in life, with whom he lived happily, honoured and loved by all men. Sons were born to him; and, in time, to them also he taught the five wise sayings of the old guru.

The Fortunes of Moti

ONCE UPON a time there was a youth called Moti. He was very big and strong, but he was also the clumsiest creature you can imagine. So clumsy was he that he was always putting his great feet into the bowls of sweet milk or curds which his mother set out on the floor to cool, always smashing, upsetting, breaking, until at last his father said to him:

'Here, Moti, here are fifty silver pieces which are the savings of years: take them and go away from us and make your living or your fortune if you can.'

So Moti started off with his thick staff over his shoulder, singing gaily to himself as he walked along.

In one way and another he got along very well until a hot evening when he came to a certain city where he entered the travellers' 'serai' or inn to pass the night. Now a serai, you must know, is generally just a large square enclosed by a high wall with an open colonnade along the inside all round to accommodate both men and beasts, and with perhaps a few rooms in towers at the corners for those who are too rich or too proud to care about sleeping by their own camels and horses. Moti, of course, was a country lad and had lived with cattle all his life, and he wasn't rich and he wasn't proud, so he just borrowed a bed from the innkeeper, set it down beside an old buffalo who reminded him of home, and in five minutes was fast asleep.

In the middle of the night he woke, feeling that he had been disturbed, and putting his hand under his pillow found to his horror that his bag of money had been stolen. He jumped up quietly and began to prowl around to see whether anyone seemed to be awake, but, though he managed to arouse a few men and beasts by falling over them, he walked in the shadow of the archways round the whole serai without coming across a likely thief. He was just about to give it up when he overheard two men whispering, and one laughed softly, and, peering behind a pillar, he saw two Afghan horse-dealers counting out his bag of money! Then Moti went back to bed.

78

In the morning Moti followed the two Afghans outside the city to the horsemarket in which their horses were offered for sale. Choosing the best-looking horse amongst them he went up to it and asked:

'Is this horse for sale? may I try it?' and, the Afghans assenting, he scrambled up on its back, dug in his heels, and off they flew. Now Moti had never been on a horse in his life, and had so much ado to hold on with both hands as well as with both legs that the animal went just where it liked, and very soon broke into a break-neck gallop and made straight back to the serai where it had spent the last few nights.

'This will do very well,' thought Moti as they whirled in at the entrance. As soon as the horse arrived it stopped of its own accord and Moti immediately rolled off; but he jumped up at once, tethered the beast, and called for some breakfast. Presently the Afghans appeared, out of breath and furious, and claimed the horse.

'What do you mean?' cried Moti, with his mouth full of rice, 'it's my horse; I paid you fifty pieces of silver for it – quite a bargain, I'm sure!'

'Nonsense! it is *our* horse,' answered one of the Afghans, beginning to untie the bridle.

'Leave off!' shouted Moti, seizing his staff. 'If you don't let my horse alone I'll crack your skulls! You thieves! *I* know you! Last night you took *my* money, so today I took your horse; that's fair enough!'

Now the Afghans began to look a little uncomfortable, but Moti seemed so determined to keep the horse that they resolved to appeal to the law, so they went off and laid a complaint before the King that Moti had stolen one of their horses and would not give it up or pay for it.

Presently a soldier came to summon Moti to the King; and, when he arrived and made his obeisance, the King began to question him as to why he had galloped off with the horse in this fashion. But Moti declared that he had got the animal in exchange for fifty pieces of silver, whilst the horse merchants vowed that the money they had on them was what they had received for the sale of other horses; and in one way and another the dispute got so confusing that the King (who really thought that Moti had stolen the horse) said at last, 'Well, I tell you what I will do. I will lock something into this box before me, and if he guesses what it is, the horse is his, and if he doesn't, then it is yours.'

To this Moti agreed, and the King arose and went out alone by a little door at the back of the court, and presently came back clasping something wrapped up in a cloth under his robe, slipped it into the little box, locked the box, and set it up where all might see.

'Now,' said the King to Moti, 'guess!'

It happened that when the King had opened the door behind him, Moti noticed that there was a garden outside: without waiting for the King's return, he began to think what could be got out of the garden small enough to be shut in the box. 'Is it likely to be a fruit or a flower? No, not a flower this time, for he clasped it too tight. Then it must be a fruit or a stone. Yet not a stone, because he wouldn't wrap a dirty stone in his nice clean cloth. Then it is a fruit! And a fruit without much scent, or else he would be afraid that I might smell it. Now what fruit without much scent is in season just now? When I know that I shall have guessed the riddle!'

As has been said before, Moti was a country lad, and was accustomed to work in his father's garden. He knew all the common fruits, so he thought he ought to be able to guess right; but so as not to let it seem too easy, he gazed up at the ceiling with a puzzled expression, and looked down at the floor with an air of wisdom and his fingers pressed against his forehead, and then he said, slowly, with his eyes on the King:

'It is freshly picked! It is round and it is red! It is a pomegranate!'

Now the King knew nothing about fruits except that they were good to eat; and, as for seasons, he asked for whatever fruit he wanted whenever he wanted it, and saw that he got it; so to him Moti's guess was like a miracle, and clear proof not only of his wisdom but of his innocence, for it *was* a pomegranate that he had put into the box. Of course when the King marvelled and praised Moti's wisdom, everybody else did too; and, whilst the Afghans went off crestfallen, Moti took the horse and entered the King's service.

Very soon after this, Moti, who continued to live in the serai, came back one wet and stormy evening to find that his precious horse had strayed. Nothing remained of him but a broken halter cord, and no one knew what had become of him. After inquiring of everyone who

was likely to know, Moti seized the cord and his big staff and sallied out to look for him. Away and away he tramped out of the city and into the neighbouring forest, tracking hoof-marks in the mud. Presently it grew late, but still Moti wandered on until suddenly in the gathering darkness he came right upon a tiger who was contentedly eating his horse.

'You thief!' shrieked Moti, and ran up, and, just as the tiger, in astonishment, dropped a bone – whack! came Moti's staff on his head with such good will that the beast was half stunned and could hardly breathe or see. Then Moti continued to shower upon him blows and abuse until the poor tiger could hardly stand, whereupon Moti tied the end of the broken halter round his neck and dragged him back to the serai.

'If you had my horse,' he said, 'I will at least have you, that's fair enough!' And he tied him up securely by the head and feet, much as he used to tie the horse; then, the night being far gone, he flung himself beside the tiger and slept soundly.

You cannot imagine anything like the fright of the people in the serai, when they woke up and found a tiger – very battered but still a tiger – tethered amongst themselves and their beasts! Men gathered in groups talking and exclaiming, and finding fault with the innkeeper for allowing such a dangerous beast into the serai, and all the while

the innkeeper was just as troubled as the rest, and none dared go near
the place where the tiger stood blinking miserably on everyone, and
where Moti lay stretched out snoring like thunder.

At last news reached the King that Moti had exchanged his horse
for a live tiger; and the monarch himself came down, half disbelieving
the tale, to see if it were really true. Someone at last awakened Moti
with the news that his royal master was come; and he arose yawning,
and was soon delightedly explaining and showing off his new possession. The King, however, did not share his pleasure at all, but called
up a soldier to shoot the tiger, much to the relief of all the inmates of
the serai except Moti. If the King, however, was before convinced
that Moti was one of the wisest of men, he was now still more convinced that he was the bravest, and he increased his pay a hundred-
fold, so that our hero thought that he was the luckiest of men.

A week or two after this incident the King sent for Moti, who on
arrival found his master in despair. A neighbouring monarch, he
explained, who had many more soldiers than he, had declared war
against him, and he was at his wits' end, for he had neither money to
buy him off nor soldiers enough to fight him – what was he to do?

'If that is all, don't you trouble,' said Moti. 'Turn out your men,
and I'll go with them, and we'll soon bring this robber to reason.'

The King began to revive at these hopeful words, and took Moti
off to his stable where he bade him choose for himself any horse he
liked. There were plenty of fine horses in the stalls, but to the King's
astonishment Moti chose a poor little rat of a pony that was used to
carry grass and water for the rest of the stable.

'But why do you choose that beast?' said the King.

'Well, you see, your majesty,' replied Moti, 'there are so many
chances that I may fall off, and if I choose one of your fine big horses
I shall have so far to fall that I shall probably break my leg or my
arm, if not my neck, but if I fall off this little beast I can't hurt myself
much.'

A very comical sight was Moti when he rode out to the war. The
only weapon he carried was his staff, and to help him to keep his
balance on horseback he had tied to each of his ankles a big stone that
nearly touched the ground as he sat astride the little pony. The rest
of the King's cavalry were not very numerous, but they pranced along

in armour on fine horses. Behind them came a great rabble of men on foot armed with all sorts of weapons, and last of all was the King with his attendants, very nervous and ill at ease. So the army started.

They had not very far to go, but Moti's little pony, weighted with a heavy man and two big rocks, soon began to lag behind the cavalry, and would have lagged behind the infantry too, only they were not very anxious to be too early in the fight, and hung back so as to give Moti plenty of time. The young man jogged along more and more slowly for some time, until at last, getting impatient at the slowness of the pony, he gave him such a tremendous thwack with his staff that the pony completely lost his temper and bolted. First one stone became untied and rolled away in a cloud of dust to one side of the road, whilst Moti nearly rolled off too, but clasped his steed valiantly by its ragged mane, and, dropping his staff, held on for dear life. Then fortunately the other rock broke away from his other leg and rolled thunderously down a neighbouring ravine. Meanwhile the advanced cavalry had barely time to draw to one side when Moti came dashing by, yelling bloodthirsty threats to his pony:

'You wait till I get hold of you! I'll skin you alive! I'll wring your neck! I'll break every bone in your body!' The cavalry thought that this dreadful language was meant for the enemy, and were filled with admiration of his courage. Many of their horses too were quite upset by this whirlwind that galloped howling through their midst, and in a few minutes, after a little plunging and rearing and kicking, the whole troop were following on Moti's heels.

Far in advance, Moti continued his wild career. Presently in his course he came to a great field of castor-oil plants, ten or twelve feet high, big and bushy, but quite green and soft. Hoping to escape from the back of his fiery steed Moti grasped one in passing, but its roots gave way, and he dashed on, with the whole plant looking like a young tree flourishing in his grip.

The enemy were in battle array, advancing over the plain, their King with them, confident and cheerful, when suddenly from the front came a desperate rider at a furious gallop.

'Sire!' he cried, 'save yourself! The enemy are coming!'

'What *do* you mean?' said the King.

'Oh, sire!' panted the messenger, 'fly at once, there is no time to lose. Foremost of the enemy rides a mad giant at a furious gallop. He flourishes a tree for a club and is wild with anger, for as he goes he cries, "You wait till I get hold of you! I'll skin you alive! I'll wring your neck! I'll break every bone in your body!" Others ride behind, and you will do well to retire before this whirlwind of destruction comes upon you.'

Just then out of a cloud of dust in the distance the King saw Moti approaching at a hard gallop, looking indeed like a giant compared with the little beast he rode, whirling his castor-oil plant, which in the distance might have been an oak tree, and the sound of his revilings and shoutings came down upon the breeze! Behind him the dust cloud moved to the sound of the thunder of hoofs, whilst here and there flashed the glitter of steel. The sight and the sound struck terror into the King, and, turning his horse, he fled at top speed, thinking that a regiment of yelling giants was upon him; and all his force followed him as fast as they might go. One fat officer alone could not keep up on foot with that mad rush, and as Moti came galloping up he flung himself to the ground in abject fear. This was too much for Moti's excited pony, who shied so suddenly that Moti went flying over his head like a sky rocket, and alighted right on the top of his fat foe.

Quickly regaining his feet Moti began to swing his plant round his head and to shout:

'Where are your men? Bring them up and I'll kill them. My regiments! Come on, the whole lot of you! Where's your King? Bring him to me. Here are all my fine fellows coming up and we'll each pull up a tree by the roots and lay you all flat and your houses and towns and everything else! Come on!'

But the poor fat officer could do nothing but squat on his knees with his hands together, gasping. At last, when he got his breath, Moti sent him off to bring his King, and to tell him that if he was reasonable his life should be spared. Off the poor man went, and by the time the troops of Moti's side had come up and arranged themselves to look as formidable as possible, he returned with his King. The latter was very humble and apologetic, and promised never to make war any more, to pay a large sum of money, and altogether do whatever his conqueror wished.

So the armies on both sides went rejoicing home, and this was really the making of the fortune of clumsy Moti, who lived long and contrived always to be looked up to as a fountain of wisdom, valour, and discretion by all except his relations, who could never understand what he had done to be considered so much wiser than anyone else.

The Golden Goose

THERE WAS once a man who had three sons. The youngest of them was called Dullhead, and he was sneered and jeered at and snubbed on every possible occasion.

One day it happened that the eldest son wished to go into the forest to cut wood, and before he started his mother gave him a fine rich cake and a bottle of wine, so that he might be sure not to suffer from hunger or thirst.

When he reached the forest he met a little old grey man who wished him 'Good-morning' and said, 'Do give me a piece of your cake, and let me have a draught of your wine – I am so hungry and thirsty.'

But this clever son replied, 'If I give you my cake and wine I shall have none left for myself; you just go your own way;' and he left the little man standing there and went farther on into the forest. There he began to cut down a tree, but before long he made a false stroke with his axe, and cut his own arm so badly that he was obliged to go home and have it bound up.

Then the second son went to the forest, and his mother gave him a good cake and a bottle of wine as she had given his elder brother. He too met the little old grey man, who begged him for a morsel of cake and a draught of wine.

But the second son spoke most sensibly too, and said, 'Whatever I give to you I deprive myself of. Just go your own way, will you?' Not long after, his punishment overtook him, for no sooner had he struck a couple of blows on a tree with his axe, than he cut his leg so badly that he had to be carried home.

So then Dullhead said, 'Father, let me go out and cut wood.'

But his father answered, 'Both your brothers have injured themselves. You had better leave it alone; you know nothing about it.'

But Dullhead begged so hard to be allowed to go that at last his father said, 'Very well, then – go. Perhaps when you have hurt yourself, you may learn to know better.' His mother only gave him a very plain cake made with water and baked in the cinders, and a bottle of sour beer.

When he got to the forest, he too met the little grey old man, who greeted him and said, 'Give me a piece of your cake and a draught from your bottle; I am so hungry and thirsty.'

And Dullhead replied, 'I've only got a cinder-cake and some sour beer, but if you care to have that, let us sit down and eat.'

So they sat down, and when Dullhead brought out his cake he found it had turned into a fine rich cake, and the sour beer into excellent wine. Then they ate and drank, and when they had finished the little man said, 'Now I will bring you luck, because you have a kind heart and are willing to share what you have with others. There stands an old tree; cut it down, and amongst its roots you'll find something.' With that the little man took his leave.

Then Dullhead began at once to hew down the tree, and when it fell he found amongst its roots a goose, whose feathers were all of pure gold. He lifted it out, carried it off, and took it with him to an inn where he meant to spend the night.

Now the landlord of the inn had three daughters, and when they saw the goose they were filled with curiosity as to what this wonderful bird could be, and each longed to have one of its golden feathers.

The eldest thought to herself, 'No doubt I shall soon find a good opportunity to pluck out one of its feathers,' and the first time Dullhead happened to leave the room she caught hold of the goose by its wing. But, lo and behold! her fingers seemed to stick fast to the goose, and she could not take her hand away.

Soon after, the second daughter came in, and thought to pluck a golden feather for herself too; but hardly had she touched her sister than she stuck as well. At last the third daughter came with the same intention, but the other two cried out, 'Keep off! for Heaven's sake, keep off!'

The younger sister could not imagine why she was to keep off, and thought to herself, 'If they are both there, why should not I be there too?'

So she sprang to them; but no sooner had she touched one of her sisters than she stuck fast to her. So they all three had to spend the night with the goose.

Next morning Dullhead tucked the goose under his arm and went off, without in the least troubling himself about the three girls who were hanging on to it. They just had to run after him right or left as best they could. In the middle of a field they met the parson, and when he saw this procession he cried, 'For shame, you bold girls! What do you mean by running after a young fellow through the fields like that? Do you call that proper behaviour?' And with that he caught the youngest girl by the hand to try and draw her away. But directly he touched her he hung on himself, and had to run along with the rest of them.

Not long after the clerk came that way, and was much surprised to see the parson following the footsteps of three girls. 'Why, where is your reverence going so fast?' cried he; 'don't forget there is to be a christening today;' and he ran after him, caught him by the sleeve, and so was caught himself. As the five of them trotted along in this fashion one after the other, two peasants were coming from their work with their hoes. On seeing them the parson called out and begged them to come and rescue him and the clerk. But no sooner did they touch the clerk than they stuck on too, and so there were seven of them running after Dullhead and his goose.

After a time they all came to a town where a King reigned whose daughter was so serious and solemn that no one could ever manage to make her laugh. So the King had decreed that whoever should succeed in making her laugh should marry her.

When Dullhead heard this he marched before the Princess with his goose and its appendages, and as soon as she saw these seven people continually running after each other she burst out laughing, and could not stop herself. Then Dullhead claimed her as his bride, but the King, who did not much fancy him as a son-in-law, made all sorts of objections, and told him he must first find a man who could drink up a whole cellarful of wine.

Dullhead bethought him of the little grey man, who could, he felt sure, help him; so he went off to the forest, and on the very spot where he had cut down the tree he saw a man sitting with a most dismal expression of face.

Dullhead asked him what he was taking so much to heart, and the man answered, 'I don't know how I am ever to quench this terrible thirst I am suffering from. Cold water doesn't suit me at all. To be sure I've emptied a whole barrel of wine, but what is one drop on a hot stone?'

'I think I can help you,' said Dullhead. 'Come with me, and you shall drink to your heart's content.' So he took him to the King's cellar, and the man sat down before the huge casks and drank and drank till he drank up the whole contents of the cellar before the day closed.

Then Dullhead asked once more for his bride, but the King felt vexed at the idea of a stupid fellow whom people called 'Dullhead' carrying off his daughter, and he began to make fresh conditions. He required Dullhead to find a man who could eat a mountain of bread. Dullhead did not wait to consider long but went straight off to the forest, and there on the same spot sat a man who was drawing in a strap as tight as he could round his body, and making a most woeful face the while. Said he, 'I've eaten up a whole oven full of loaves, but what's the good of that to anyone who is as hungry as I am? I declare my stomach feels quite empty, and I must draw my belt tight if I'm not to die of starvation.'

Dullhead was delighted, and said, 'Get up and come with me, and you shall have plenty to eat,' and he brought him to the King's Court.

Now the King had given orders to have all the flour in his kingdom brought together, and to have a huge mountain baked of it. But the man from the wood just took up his stand before the mountain and began to eat, and in one day it had all vanished.

For the third time Dullhead asked for his bride, but again the King tried to make some evasion, and demanded a ship 'which could sail on land or water! When you come sailing in such a ship,' said he, 'you shall have my daughter without further delay.'

Again Dullhead started off to the forest, and there he found the little old grey man with whom he had shared his cake, and who said, 'I have eaten and I have drunk for you, and now I will give you the ship. I have done all this for you because you were kind and merciful to me.'

Then he gave Dullhead a ship which could sail on land or water, and when the King saw it he felt he could no longer refuse him his daughter.

So they celebrated the wedding with great rejoicings; and on the King's death Dullhead succeeded to the kingdom, and lived happily with his wife for many years after.

Grasp All, Lose All

ONCE, IN former times, there lived in a certain city in India a poor oil-seller, called Déna, who never could keep any money in his pockets; and when the story begins he had borrowed from a banker, of the name of Léna, the sum of one hundred rupees; which, with the interest Léna always charged, amounted to a debt of three hundred rupees.

Now business for Déna was very bad, and he had no money with which to pay his debt, so Léna was very angry, and used to come round to Déna's house every evening and abuse him until the poor man was nearly worried out of his life. Léna generally timed his visit just when Déna's wife was cooking the evening meal, and would make such a scene that the poor oil-seller and his wife and daughter quite lost their appetites and could eat nothing. This went on for some weeks, till, one day, Déna said to himself that he could stand it no longer, and that he had better run away; and, as a man cannot fly easily with a wife and daughter, he thought he must leave them behind. So that evening, instead of turning into his house as usual after his day's work, he just slipped out of the city and without knowing at all where he was going, began to walk through the forest.

At about ten o'clock that night Déna came to a well by the roadside, near which grew a giant peepul tree; and, as he was very tired, he determined to climb it, and rest for a little before continuing his journey in the morning. Up he went and curled himself so comfortably amongst the great branches that, overcome with weariness, he fell fast asleep. While he slept, some spirits, who roam about such places on certain nights, picked up the tree and flew away with it to a far-away shore where no creature lived, and there, long before the sun rose, they set it down. Just then the oil-seller awoke; but instead of finding himself in the midst of a forest, he was amazed to behold nothing but waste shore and wide sea, and was dumb with horror and astonishment.

While he sat up, trying to collect his senses, he began to catch sight here and there of twinkling, flashing lights, like little fires, that moved and sparkled all about, and he wondered what they were. Presently he saw one so close to him that he reached out his hand and grasped it, and found that it was a sparkling red stone, scarcely smaller than a walnut. He opened a corner of his loin-cloth and tied the stone in it; and by and by he got another, and then a third, and a fourth, all of which he tied up carefully in his cloth.

At last, just as day was breaking, the tree rose, and, flying rapidly through the air, came to rest once more by the well where it had stood the previous evening.

When Déna had recovered a little from the fright which the extraordinary antics of the tree had caused him, he began to thank Providence that he was alive, and, as his desire to wander had been quite cured, he made his way back to the city and to his own house. Here he was met and soundly scolded by his wife, who assailed him with a hundred questions and reproaches. As soon as she paused for breath, Déna replied:

'I have only this one thing to say, just look what I have got!' And after carefully shutting all the doors, he opened the corner of his loin-cloth and showed her the four stones, which glittered and flashed as he turned them over and over.

'Pooh!' said his wife, 'the silly pebbles! If it was something to eat, now, there'd be some sense in them: but what's the good of *such* things?' And she turned away with a sob, for it had happened that the night before, when Léna had come round as usual to storm at Déna, he had been rather disturbed to find that his victim was from home, and had frightened the poor woman by his threats. Directly, however, he heard that Déna had come back, Léna appeared in the doorway, and shouted at the oil-seller at the top of his voice, until he was tired; then Déna said:

'If your honour would deign to walk into my humble dwelling, I will speak.'

So Léna walked in, and the other, shutting as before all the doors, untied the corner of his loin-cloth and showed him the four great flashing stones.

'This is all that I have in the world,' he said, 'to set against my debt, for, as your honour knows, I haven't a penny, but the stones are pretty!'

Now Léna looked and saw at once that these were magnificent rubies, and his mouth watered for them; but as it would never do to show what was in his mind, he said:

'What do I care about your stupid stones? It is my money I want, my lawful debt which you owe me, and I shall get it out of you yet somehow or another or it will be the worse for you.'

To all reproaches Déna could answer nothing but sat with his hands joined together beseechingly, asking for patience and pity. At length Léna pretended that, rather than have a bad debt on his hand, he would be willing to lose by taking the stones in lieu of his money; and, while Déna nearly wept with gratitude, he wrote out a receipt for the three hundred rupees; and, wrapping the four stones in a cloth, he put them into his bosom, and went off to his house.

'How shall I turn these rubies into money?' thought Léna, as he walked along; 'I daren't keep them, for they are of great value, and if the Rajah heard that I had them he could probably put me into prison on some pretence and seize the stones and all else that I have as well. But what a bargain I have got! Four rubies worth a King's ransom, for one hundred rupees! Well, well, I must take heed not to betray my secret.' And he went on making plans. Presently he made up his mind what to do, and, putting on his cleanest clothes, he set off to the house of the Chief Wazir, whose name was Musli, and, after seeking a private audience, he brought out the four rubies and laid them before him.

The Wazir's eyes sparkled as he beheld the splendid gems.

'Fine, indeed,' murmured he. 'I can't buy them at their real value; but, if you like to take it, I will give you ten thousand rupees for the four.'

To this the banker consented gratefully; and, handing over the stones in exchange for the rupees, he hurried home, thanking his stars that he had driven such a reasonable bargain and obtained such an enormous profit.

After Léna had departed the Wazir began casting about in his mind what to do with the gems; and very soon determined that the best thing to do was to present them to the Rajah, whose name was Kahre. Without losing a moment, he went that very day to the palace, and sought a private interview with the Rajah; and when he found himself alone with his royal master, he brought the four jewels and laid them before him.

'Oh, ho!' said the Rajah, 'these are priceless gems, and you have done well to give them to me. In return I give you and your heirs the revenues of ten villages.'

Now the Wazir was overjoyed at these words, but only made his deepest obeisance; and, while the Rajah put the rubies into his turban, hurried away beaming with happiness at the thought that for ten thousand rupees he had become lord of ten villages. The Rajah was also equally pleased, and strolled off with his new purchases to the women's quarters and showed them to the Rani, who was nearly out of her mind with delight. Then, as she turned them over and over in her hands, she said, 'Ah! If I had eight more such gems, what a necklace they would make! Get me eight more of them or I shall die!'

'Most unreasonable of women,' cried the Rajah, 'where am I to get eight more such jewels as these? I gave ten villages for them, and yet you are not satisfied!'

'What does it matter?' said the Rani. 'Do you want me to die? Surely you can get some more where these came from?' And then she fell to weeping and wailing until the Rajah promised that in the morning he would make arrangements to get some more such rubies, and that if she would be patient she should have her desire.

In the morning the Rajah sent for the Wazir, and said that he must manage to get eight more rubies like those he had brought him the day before. 'And if you don't, I shall hang you,' cried the Rajah, for he was very cross. The poor Wazir protested in vain that he knew not where to seek them; his master would not listen to a word he said.

'You *must*,' said he. 'The Rani shall not die for the want of a few rubies! Get more where those came from.'

The Wazir left the palace, much troubled in mind, and bade his slaves bring Léna before him.

'Get me eight more such rubies as those you brought yesterday,' commanded the Wazir, directly the banker was shown into his presence. 'Eight more, and be quick, or I am a dead man.'

'But how can I?' wailed Léna. 'Rubies like those don't grow upon bushes!'

'Where did you get them from?' asked the Wazir.

'From Déna, the oil-seller,' said the banker.

'Well, send for him and ask him where *he* got them,' answered the Wazir. 'I am not going to hang for twenty Dénas!' And other slaves were sent to summon Déna.

When Déna arrived he was closely questioned, and then all three set out to see the Rajah, and to him Déna told the whole story.

'What night was it that you slept in the peepul tree?' demanded the Rajah.

'I can't remember,' said Déna; 'but my wife will know.'

Then Déna's wife was sent for, and she explained that it was on the last Sunday of the new moon.

Now everyone knows that it is on the Sunday of the new moon that spirits have special power to play pranks upon mortals. So the Rajah forbade them all, on pain of death, to say a word to anyone; and declared that, on the next Sunday of the new moon, they four – Kahre, Musli, Léna and Déna – would go and sit in the peepul tree and see what happened.

The days dragged on to the appointed Sunday, and that evening the four met secretly, and entered the forest. They had not far to go before they reached the peepul tree, into which they climbed as the Rajah had planned. At midnight the tree began to sway, and presently it moved through the air.

'See, sire,' whispered Déna. 'The tree is flying!'

'Yes, yes,' said the Rajah, 'you have told the truth. Now sit quiet, and we shall see what happens.'

Away and away flew the tree with the four men clinging tightly to its branches, until at last it was set down by the waste sea-shore where a great wide sea came tumbling in on a desert beach. Presently, as before, they began to see little points of light that glistened like fires all around them. Then Déna thought to himself:

'Think! Last time I only took four that came close to me, and I got rid of all my debt in return. This time I will take all I can get and be rich!'

'If I got ten thousand rupees for four stones,' thought Léna, 'I will gather forty now for myself, and become so wealthy that they will probably make me a Wazir at least!'

'For four stones I received ten villages,' Musli was silently

thinking; 'now I will get stones enough to purchase a kingdom, become a Rajah, and employ wazirs of my own!'

And Kahre thought, 'What is the good of only getting eight stones? Why, here are enough to make twenty necklaces; and wealth means power!'

Full of avarice and desire, each scrambled down from the tree, spread his cloth, and darted hither and thither picking up the precious jewels, looking the while over his shoulder to see whether his neighbour fared better than he. So engrossed were they in the business of gathering wealth that the dawn came upon them unawares; and suddenly the tree rose up again and flew away, leaving them upon the sea-shore staring after it, each with his cloth heavy with priceless jewels.

Morning broke in the city, and great was the consternation in the palace when the chamberlains declared that the Rajah had gone out the evening before and had not returned.

'Ah!' said one. 'It is all right! Musli Wazir will know where he is, for it was he who was the King's companion.'

Then they went to the Wazir's house, and there they learnt that the Wazir had left it the evening before and had not returned. 'But,' said a servant, 'Léna the banker will know where he is, for it was with him that Musli went.'

Then they visited the house of Léna, and there they learnt that the banker had gone out the evening before, and that he too had not returned; but the porter told them that he was accompanied by Déna the oil-seller, so he would know where they were.

So they departed to Déna's house, and Déna's wife met them with a torrent of reproaches and wailings, for Déna too had gone off the evening before to Léna's house and had not returned.

In vain they waited, and searched – never did any of the hapless four return to their homes; and the confused tale which was told by Déna's wife was the only clue to their fate.

To this day, in that country, when a greedy man has over-reached himself, and lost all in grasping at too much, folks say:

'All has he lost! Neither Déna, or Léna, nor Musli, nor Kahre remain.' And not five men in a hundred know how the proverb began, nor what it really signifies.

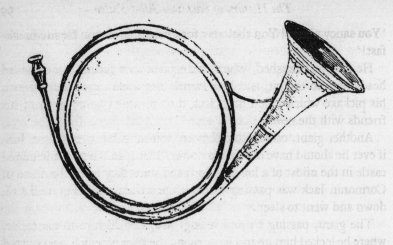

The History of
Jack the Giant-Killer

IN THE reign of the famous King Arthur there lived in Cornwall a lad named Jack, who was a boy of a bold temper, and took delight in hearing or reading of conjurers, giants, and fairies; and used to listen eagerly to the deeds of the knights of King Arthur's Round Table.

In those days there lived on St Michael's Mount, off Cornwall, a huge giant called Cormoran. He was eighteen feet high and nine feet round, and his fierce and savage looks were the terror of all who beheld him.

He dwelt in a gloomy cavern on the top of the mountain, and used to wade over to the mainland in search of prey; when he would throw half-a-dozen oxen upon his back, and tie three times as many sheep and hogs round his waist, and march back to his own abode.

The giant had done this for many years when Jack resolved to destroy him.

Jack took a horn, a shovel, a pickaxe, his armour, and a dark lantern, and one winter's evening he went to the mount. There he dug a pit twenty-two feet deep and twenty broad. He covered the top over so as to make it look like solid ground. He then blew such a tantivy on the horn that the giant awoke and came out of his den, crying out,

'You saucy villain! You shall pay for this. I'll broil you for my breakfast!'

He had just finished, when, taking one step farther, he tumbled headlong into the pit, and Jack struck him a blow on the head with his pickaxe which killed him. Jack then returned home to cheer his friends with the news.

Another giant, called Blunderbore, vowed to be revenged on Jack if ever he should have him in his power. This giant kept an enchanted castle in the midst of a lonely wood; and some time after the death of Cormoran Jack was passing through the wood, and being weary sat down and went to sleep.

The giant, passing by and seeing Jack, carried him to his castle, where he locked him up in a large room, the floor of which was covered with the bodies, skulls, and bones of men and women.

Soon after the giant went to fetch his brother, who was likewise a giant, to take a meal off his flesh; and Jack saw with terror through the bars of his prison the two giants approaching.

Jack, perceiving in one corner of the room a strong cord, took courage, and making a slip-knot at each end, he threw it over their heads, and tied it to the window-bars; he then pulled till he had choked them. When they were black in the face he slid down the rope and stabbed them to the heart.

Jack next took a great bunch of keys from the pocket of Blunderbore, and went into the castle again. He made a strict search through all the rooms, and in one of them found three ladies tied up by the hair of their heads, and almost starved to death. They told him that their husbands had been killed by the giants, who had then condemned them to be starved to death, because they would not eat the flesh of their own dead husbands.

'Ladies,' said Jack, 'I have put an end to the monster and his wicked brother; and I give you this castle and all the riches it contains, to make some amends for the dreadful pains you have felt.' He then very politely gave them the keys of the castle, and went farther on his journey to Wales.

As Jack had but little money, he went on as fast as possible. At length he came to a handsome house. Jack knocked at the door, when there came forth a Welsh giant. Jack said he was a traveller who had lost his way, on which the giant made him welcome, and let him into a room where there was a good bed to sleep in.

Jack took off his clothes quickly, but though he was weary he could not go to sleep. Soon after this he heard the giant walking backward and forward in the next room, and saying to himself:

> 'Though here you lodge with me this night,
> You shall not see the morning light;
> My club shall dash your brains out quite.'

'Say you so?' thought Jack. 'Are these your tricks upon travellers? But I hope to prove as cunning as you are.' Then, getting out of bed, he groped about the room, and at last found a large thick billet of wood. He laid it in his own place in the bed, and then hid himself in a dark corner of the room.

The giant, about midnight, entered the apartment, and with his bludgeon struck many blows on the bed, in the very place where Jack had laid the log; and then he went back to his own room, thinking he had broken all Jack's bones.

Early in the morning Jack put a bold face upon the matter, and walked into the giant's room to thank him for his lodging. The giant started when he saw him, and began to stammer out, 'Oh! dear me; is it you? Pray how did you sleep last night? Did you hear or see anything in the dead of the night?'

'Nothing worth speaking of,' said Jack carelessly. 'A rat, I believe, gave me three or four slaps with its tail, and disturbed me a little; but I soon went to sleep again.'

The giant wondered more and more at this: yet he did not answer a word, but went to bring two great bowls of hasty-pudding for their breakfast. Jack wanted to make the giant believe that he could eat as much as himself, so he contrived to button a leathern bag inside his coat, and slip the hasty-pudding into this bag, while he seemed to put it into his mouth.

When breakfast was over he said to the giant, 'Now I will show you a fine trick. I can cure all wounds with a touch: I could cut off my head in one minute, and the next put it sound again on my shoulders. You shall see an example.' He then took hold of the knife, ripped up the leathern bag, and all the hasty-pudding tumbled out upon the floor.

'Ods splutter hur nails!' cried the Welsh giant, who was ashamed to be outdone by such a little fellow as Jack, 'hur can do that hurself;' so he snatched up the knife, plunged it into his own stomach, and in a moment dropped down dead.

Jack, having hitherto been successful in all his undertakings, resolved not to be idle in future; he therefore furnished himself with a horse, a cap of knowledge, a sword of sharpness, shoes of swiftness, and an invisible coat, the better to perform the wonderful enterprises that lay before him.

He travelled over high hills, and on the third day he came to a large and spacious forest through which his road lay. Scarcely had he entered the forest when he beheld a monstrous giant dragging along by the hair of their heads a handsome knight and his lady. Jack alighted from his horse, and tying him to an oak tree, put on his invisible coat, under which he carried his sword of sharpness.

When he came up to the giant he made several strokes at him, but could not reach his body, but wounded his thighs in several places; and at length putting both hands to his sword and aiming with all his might, he cut off both his legs. Then Jack, setting his foot upon his neck, plunged his sword into the giant's body, when the monster gave a groan and expired.

The knight and his lady thanked Jack for their deliverance, and invited him to their house, to receive a proper reward for his services. 'No,' said Jack, 'I cannot be easy till I find out this monster's habitation.' So taking the knight's directions, he mounted his horse, and soon came in sight of another giant, who was sitting on a block of timber waiting for his brother's return.

Jack alighted from his horse, and, putting on his invisible coat, approached and aimed a blow at the giant's head, but missing his aim he only cut off his nose. On this the giant seized his club and laid about him most unmercifully.

'Nay,' said Jack, 'if this be the case I'd better dispatch you!' So jumping upon the block, he stabbed him in the back, whereupon the giant dropped down dead.

Jack then proceeded on his journey, and travelled over hills and dales, till arriving at the foot of a high mountain he knocked at the door of a lonely house, when an old man let him in.

When Jack was seated the hermit thus addressed him:

'My son, on the top of this mountain is an enchanted castle, kept by the giant Galligantus and a vile magician. I lament the fate of a duke's daughter, whom they seized as she was walking in her father's garden, and brought hither transformed into a deer.'

Jack promised that in the morning, at the risk of his life, he would break the enchantment; and after a sound sleep he rose early, put on his invisible coat, and got ready for the attempt.

When he had climbed to the top of the mountain, he saw two fiery griffins; but he passed between them without the least fear of danger, for they could not see him because of his invisible coat. On the castle gate he found a golden trumpet, under which were written these lines:

> Whoever can this trumpet blow
> Shall cause the giant's overthrow.

As soon as Jack had read this he seized the trumpet and blew a shrill blast, which made the gates fly open and the very castle itself tremble.

The giant and the conjurer now knew that their wicked course was at an end, and they stood biting their thumbs and shaking with fear. Jack, with his sword of sharpness, soon killed the giant, and the magician was then carried away by a whirlwind; and every knight and beautiful lady who had been changed into birds and beasts returned to their proper shapes. The castle vanished away like smoke, and the head of the giant Galligantus was then sent to King Arthur.

The knights and ladies rested that night at the old man's hermitage, and the next day they set out for the Court of King Arthur. Jack then went up to the King, and gave his Majesty an account of all his fierce battles.

Jack's fame had now spread through the whole country, and at the King's desire the duke gave him his daughter in marriage, to the joy of all his kingdom. After this the King gave him a large estate, on which he and his lady lived the rest of their days in joy and contentment.

Hok Lee and the Dwarfs

THERE ONCE lived in a small town in China a man named Hok Lee. He was a steady industrious man, who not only worked hard at his trade, but did all his own house-work as well, for he had no wife to do it for him. 'What an excellent industrious man is this Hok Lee!' said his neighbours; 'how hard he works: he never leaves his house to amuse himself or to take a holiday as others do!'

But Hok Lee was by no means the virtuous person his neighbours thought him. True, he worked hard enough by day, but at night, when all respectable folk were fast asleep, he used to steal out and join a dangerous band of robbers, who broke into rich people's houses and carried off all they could lay hands on.

This state of things went on for some time, and, although now and then one of the band of robbers was caught and punished, no suspicion ever fell on Hok Lee, he was such a *very* respectable, hard-working man.

Hok Lee had already amassed a good store of money as his share of the proceeds of these robberies when it happened one morning on going to market that a neighbour said to him:

'Why, Hok Lee, what is the matter with your face? One side of it is all swelled up.'

True enough, Hok Lee's right cheek was twice the size of his left, and it soon began to feel very uncomfortable.

'I will bind up my face,' said Hok Lee; 'doubtless the warmth will cure the swelling.' But no such thing. Next day it was worse, and day by day it grew bigger till it was nearly as large as his head, and became very painful.

Hok Lee was at his wits' end to know what to do. Not only was his cheek unsightly and painful, but his neighbours began to jeer and make fun of him, which hurt his feelings very much as well.

One day, as luck would have it, a travelling doctor came to the town. He sold not only all kinds of medicine, but also dealt in many strange charms against witches and evil spirits.

Hok Lee determined to consult him, and asked him into his house. After the doctor had examined him carefully, he spoke thus:

'This, O Hok Lee, is no ordinary swelled face. I strongly suspect you have been guilty of some wrong deed, and this has called down the anger of the spirits on you. None of my drugs will avail, but, if you are willing to pay me handsomely, I can tell you how you may be cured.'

Then Hok Lee and the doctor began to bargain together, and it was a long time before they could come to terms. However, the doctor got the better of it in the end, for he was determined not to part with his secret under a certain price, and Hok Lee had no mind to carry his huge cheek about with him to the end of his days. So he was obliged to give up the greater portion of his ill-gotten gains.

When the doctor had pocketed the money, he told Hok Lee to go on the first night of the full moon to a certain wood and there to watch by a particular tree. After a time he would see the dwarfs and little sprites who live underground come out to dance. When they saw him they would be sure to make him dance too. 'And mind you dance your very best,' added the doctor. 'If you dance well and please them they will grant you a petition and you can then beg to be cured; but if you dance badly they will most likely do you some mischief out of spite.' With that he took leave and departed.

Happily the first night of the full moon was near, and at the proper time Hok Lee set out for the wood. With little trouble he found the tree the doctor had described, and, feeling nervous, he climbed up into it.

He had hardly settled himself on a branch when he saw the little dwarfs assembling in the moonlight. They came from all sides, till at length there appeared to be hundreds of them. They seemed in high glee, and danced and skipped and capered about, whilst Hok Lee grew so eager watching them that he crept farther and farther along his branch till at length it gave a loud crack. All the dwarfs stood still, and Hok Lee felt as if his heart stood still also.

Then one of the dwarfs called out, 'Someone is up that tree. Come down at once, whoever you are, or we must come and fetch you.'

In great terror, Hok Lee proceeded to come down; but he was so nervous that he tripped near the ground and came rolling down in the most absurd manner. When he had picked himself up, he came forward with a low bow, and the dwarf who had first spoken and who appeared to be the leader, said, 'Now, then, who art thou, and what brings thee here?'

So Hok Lee told him the sad story of his swelled cheek, and how he had been advised to come to the forest and beg the dwarfs to cure him.

'It is well,' replied the dwarf. 'We will see about that. First, however, thou must dance before us. Should thy dancing please us, perhaps we may be able to do something; but shouldst thou dance badly, we shall assuredly punish thee, so now take warning and dance away.'

With that, he and all the other dwarfs sat down in a large ring, leaving Hok Lee to dance alone in the middle. He felt half frightened to death, and besides was a good deal shaken by his fall from the tree and did not feel at all inclined to dance. But the dwarfs were not to be trifled with.

'Begin!' cried their leader, and 'Begin!' shouted the rest in chorus.

So in despair Hok Lee began. First he hopped on one foot and then on the other, but he was so stiff and so nervous that he made but a poor attempt, and after a time sank down on the ground and vowed he could dance no more.

The dwarfs were very angry. They crowded round Hok Lee and abused him. 'Thou to come here to be cured, indeed!' they cried. 'Thou hast brought one big cheek with thee, but thou shalt take away two.' And with that they ran off and disappeared, leaving Hok Lee to find his way home as best he might.

He hobbled away, weary and depressed, and not a little anxious on account of the dwarfs' threat.

Nor were his fears unfounded, for when he rose next morning his left cheek was swelled up as big as his right, and he could hardly see out of his eyes. Hok Lee felt in despair, and his neighbours jeered at him more than ever. The doctor, too, had disappeared, so there was nothing for it but to try the dwarfs once more.

He waited a month till the first night of the full moon came round again, and then he trudged back to the forest, and sat down under the tree from which he had fallen. He had not long to wait. Ere long the dwarfs came trooping out till all were assembled.

'I don't feel quite easy,' said one; 'I feel as if some horrid human were near us.'

When Hok Lee heard this he came forward and bent down to the ground before the dwarfs, who came crowding round, and laughed heartily at his comical appearance with his two big cheeks.

'What dost thou want?' they asked; and Hok Lee proceeded to tell them of his fresh misfortunes, and begged so hard to be allowed one more trial at dancing that the dwarfs consented, for there is nothing they love so much as being amused.

Now, Hok Lee knew how much depended on his dancing well, so he put his heart into it and began, first quite slowly, and faster by degrees, and he danced so well and so vigorously and with such new and wonderful steps, that the dwarfs were quite delighted with him.

They clapped their tiny hands, and shouted, 'Well done, Hok Lee, well done; go on, dance more, for we are pleased.'

And Hok Lee danced on and on, till he really could dance no more, and was obliged to stop from very exhaustion.

Then the leader of the dwarfs said, 'We are well pleased, Hok Lee, and as a recompense for thy dancing thy face shall be cured. Farewell.'

With these words he and the other dwarfs vanished, and Hok Lee, putting his hands to his face, found to his great joy that his cheeks were reduced to their natural size. The way home seemed short and easy to him, and he went to bed happy, and resolved never to go out with the robber band again.

Next day the whole town was full of the news of Hok's sudden cure. His neighbours questioned him, but could get nothing from him, except the fact that he had discovered a wonderful cure for all kinds of diseases.

After a time a rich neighbour, who had been ill for some years, came, and offered to give Hok Lee a large sum of money if he would tell him how he might get cured. Hok Lee consented on condition that he swore to keep the secret. He did so, and Hok Lee told him of the dwarfs and their dances.

The neighbour went off, carefully obeyed Hok Lee's directions, and was duly cured by the dwarfs. Then another and another came to Hok Lee to beg his secret, and from each he extracted a vow of secrecy and a large sum of money. This went on for some years, so that at length Hok Lee became a very wealthy man, and ended his days in peace and prosperity.

Jack and the Beanstalk

ONCE UPON a time there was a poor widow who lived in a little cottage with her only son Jack.

Jack was a giddy, thoughtless boy, but very kindhearted and affectionate. There had been a hard winter, and after it the poor woman had suffered from fever and ague. Jack did no work as yet, and by degrees they grew dreadfully poor. The widow saw that there was no means of keeping Jack and herself from starvation but by selling her cow; so one morning she said to her son, 'I am too weak to go myself, Jack, so you must take the cow to market for me, and sell her.'

Jack liked going to market to sell the cow very much; but as he was on the way, he met a butcher who had some beautiful beans in his hand. Jack stopped to look at them, and the butcher told the boy that they were of great value, and persuaded the silly lad to sell the cow for these beans.

When he brought them home to his mother instead of the money she expected for her nice cow, she was very vexed and shed many tears, scolding Jack for his folly. He was very sorry, and mother and son went to bed very sadly that night; their last hope seemed gone.

At daybreak Jack rose and went out into the garden.

'At least,' he thought, 'I will sow the wonderful beans. Mother says that they are just common scarlet-runners, and nothing else; but I may as well sow them.'

So he took a piece of stick, and made some holes in the ground, and put in the beans.

That day they had very little dinner, and went sadly to bed, knowing that for the next day there would be none, and Jack, unable to sleep from grief and vexation got up at day-dawn and went out into the garden.

What was his amazement to find that the beans had grown up in the night, and climbed up and up till they covered the high cliff that sheltered the cottage, and disappeared above it! The stalks had twined and twisted themselves together till they formed quite a ladder.

'It would be easy to climb it,' thought Jack.

And, having thought of the experiment, he at once resolved to carry it out, for Jack was a good climber. However, after his late mistake about the cow, he thought he had better consult his mother first. So Jack called his mother, and they both gazed in silent wonder at the beanstalk, which was not only of great height, but was thick enough to bear Jack's weight.

'I wonder where it ends,' said Jack to his mother; 'I think I will climb up and see.'

His mother wished him not to venture up this strange ladder, but Jack coaxed her to give her consent to the attempt, for he was certain there must be something wonderful in the beanstalk; so at last she yielded to his wishes.

Jack instantly began to climb, and went up and up on the ladder-like bean till everything he had left behind him – the cottage, the village, and even the tall church tower – looked quite little, and still he could not see the top of the beanstalk. Jack felt a little tired, and thought for a moment that he would go back again; but he was a very persevering boy, and he knew that the way to succeed in anything is not to give up. So after resting for a moment he went on.

After climbing higher and higher, till he grew afraid to look down for fear he should be giddy, Jack at last reached the top of the bean-stalk, and found himself in a beautiful country, finely wooded, and with beautiful meadows covered with sheep. A crystal stream ran through the pastures; not far from the place where he had got off the beanstalk stood a fine, strong castle. Jack wondered very much that he had never heard of or seen this castle before; but when he reflected on the subject, he saw that it was as much separated from the village by the perpendicular rock on which it stood as if it were in another land.

While Jack was standing looking at the castle, a very strange-looking woman came out of the wood, and advanced towards him. She wore a pointed cap of quilted red satin turned up with ermine, her hair streamed loose over her shoulders, and she walked with a staff Jack took off his cap and made her a bow.

'If you please, ma'am,' said he, 'is this your house?'

'No,' said the old lady. 'Listen, and I will tell you the story of that castle.

'Once upon a time there was a noble knight, who lived in this castle, which is on the borders of fairyland. He had a fair and beloved wife and several lovely children: and as his neighbours, the little people, were very friendly towards him, they bestowed on him many excellent and precious gifts. Rumour whispered of these treasures; and a monstrous giant, who lived at no great distance, and who was a very wicked being, resolved to obtain possession of them.

'So he bribed a false servant to let him inside the castle, when the knight was in bed and asleep, and he killed him as he lay. Then he went to the part of the castle which was the nursery, and also killed all the poor little ones he found there. Happily for her, the lady was not to be found. She had gone with her infant son, who was only two or three months old, to visit her old nurse, who lived in the valley; and she had been detained all night there by a storm.

'The next morning, as soon as it was light, one of the servants at the castle, who had managed to escape, came to tell the poor lady of the sad fate of her husband and her pretty babes. She could scarcely believe him at first, and was eager at once to go back and share the fate of her dear ones; but the old nurse, with many tears, besought her to remember that she had still a child, and that it was her duty to preserve her life for the sake of the poor innocent.

'The lady yielded to this reasoning, and consented to remain at her nurse's house as the best place of concealment; for her servant told her that the giant had vowed, if he could find her, he would kill both her and her baby.

'Years rolled on. The old nurse died, leaving her cottage and the few articles of furniture it contained to her poor lady, who dwelt in it, working as a peasant for her daily bread. Her spinning-wheel and the milk of a cow, which she had purchased with the little money she had with her, sufficed for the scanty subsistence of herself and her little son. There was a nice little garden attached to the cottage, in which they cultivated peas, beans, and cabbages, and the lady was not ashamed to go out at harvest time, and glean in the fields to supply her little son's wants.

'Jack, that poor lady is your mother. This castle was once your father's, and must again be yours.'

Jack uttered a cry of surprise.

'My mother! Oh, madam, what ought I to do? My poor father! My dear mother!'

'Your duty requires you to win it back for your mother. But the task is a very difficult one, and full of peril, Jack. Have you courage to undertake it?'

'I fear nothing when I am doing right,' said Jack.

'Then,' said the lady in the red cap, 'you are one of those who slay giants. You must get into the castle, and if possible possess yourself of a hen that lays golden eggs, and a harp that talks. Remember, all the giant possesses is really yours.' As she ceased speaking, the lady of the red hat suddenly disappeared, and of course Jack knew she was a fairy.

Jack determined at once to attempt the adventure; so he advanced, and blew the horn which hung at the castle portal. The door was opened in a minute or two by a frightful giantess, with one great eye in the middle of her forehead. As soon as Jack saw her he turned to run away, but she caught him, and dragged him into the castle.

'Ho, ho!' she laughed terribly. 'You didn't expect to see *me* here, that is clear! No, I shan't let you go again. I am weary of my life. I am so overworked, and I don't see why I should not have a page as well as other ladies. And you shall be my boy. You shall clean the knives, and black the boots, and make the fires, and help me generally when the giant is out. When he is at home I must hide you, for he has eaten up all my pages hitherto, and you would be a dainty morsel, my little lad.'

While she spoke she dragged Jack right into the castle. The poor boy was very much frightened, as I am sure you and I would have been in his place. But he remembered that fear disgraces a man; so he struggled to be brave and make the best of things.

'I am quite ready to help you, and do all I can to serve you, madam,' he said, 'only I beg you will be good enough to hide me from your husband, for I should not like to be eaten at all.'

'That's a good boy,' said the giantess, nodding her head; 'it is lucky for you that you did not scream out when you saw me, as the other boys who have been here did, for if you had done so my husband would have awakened and have eaten you, as he did them, for breakfast. Come here, child; go into my wardrobe: he never ventures to open *that*; you will be safe there.'

And she opened a huge wardrobe which stood in the great hall, and shut him into it. But the keyhole was so large that it admitted plenty of air, and he could see everything that took place through it. By and by he heard a heavy tramp on the stairs, like the lumbering along of a great cannon, and then a voice like thunder cried out:

'Fe, fa, fi-fo-fum,
I smell the breath of an Englishman.
Let him be alive or let him be dead,
I'll grind his bones to make my bread.'

'Wife,' cried the giant, 'there is a man in the castle. Let me have him for breakfast.'

'You are grown old and stupid,' cried the lady in her loud tones. 'It is only a nice fresh steak off an elephant, that I have cooked for you, which you smell. There, sit down and make a good breakfast.'

And she placed a huge dish before him of savoury steaming meat, which greatly pleased him, and made him forget his idea of an Englishman being in the castle. When he had breakfasted he went out for a walk; and then the giantess opened the door, and made Jack come out to help her. He helped her all day. She fed him well, and when evening came put him back in the wardrobe.

The giant came in to supper. Jack watched him through the keyhole, and was amazed to see him pick a wolf's bone, and put half a fowl at a time into his capacious mouth. When the supper was ended he bade his wife bring him his hen that laid the golden eggs.

'It lays as well as it did when it belonged to that paltry knight,' he said; 'indeed I think the eggs are heavier than ever.'

The giantess went away, and soon returned with a little brown hen, which she placed on the table before her husband. 'And now, my dear,' she said, 'I am going for a walk, if you don't want me any longer.'

'Go,' said the giant; 'I shall be glad to have a nap by and by.'

Then he took up the brown hen and said to her:

'Lay!' And she instantly laid a golden egg.

'Lay!' said the giant again. And she laid another.

'Lay!' he repeated the third time. And again a golden egg lay on the table.

Now Jack was sure this hen was that of which the fairy had spoken. By and by the giant put the hen on the floor, and soon after went fast asleep, snoring so loud that it sounded like thunder. Directly Jack perceived that the giant was fast asleep, he pushed open the door of the wardrobe and crept out; very softly he stole across the room, and, picking up the hen, made haste to quit the apartment. He knew the way to the kitchen, the door of which he found was left ajar; he opened it, shut and locked it after him, and flew back to the beanstalk, which he descended as fast as his feet would move.

When his mother saw him enter the house she wept for joy, for she had feared that the fairies had carried him away, or that the giant had found him. But Jack put the brown hen down before her, and told her how he had been in the giant's castle, and all his adventures. She was very glad to see the hen, which would make them rich once more.

Jack made another journey up the beanstalk to the giant's castle one day while his mother had gone to market; but first he dyed his hair, and disguised himself. The old woman did not know him again, and dragged him in as she had done before, to help her to do the work; but she heard her husband coming, and hid him in the wardrobe, not thinking that it was the same boy who had stolen the hen. She bade him stay still there, or the giant would eat him.

Then the giant came in saying:

> 'Fe, fa, fi-fo-fum,
> I smell the breath of an Englishman.
> Let him be alive or let him be dead,
> I'll grind his bones to make my bread.'

'Nonsense!' said the wife, 'it is only a roasted bullock that I thought would be a tit-bit for your supper; sit down and I will bring it up at once.' The giant sat down, and soon his wife brought up a roasted bullock on a large dish, and they began their supper. Jack was amazed to see them pick the bones of the bullock as if it had been a lark. As soon as they had finished their meal, the giantess rose and said:

'Now, my dear, with your leave I am going up to my room to finish the story I am reading. If you want me call for me.'

'First,' answered the giant, 'bring me my money bags, that I may count my golden pieces before I sleep.' The giantess obeyed. She went and soon returned with two large bags over her shoulders, which she put down by her husband.

'There,' she said; 'that is all that is left of the knight's money. When you have spent it you must go and take another baron's castle.'

'That he shan't, if I can help it,' thought Jack.

The giant, when his wife was gone, took out heaps and heaps of golden pieces, and counted them, and put them in piles, till he was tired of the amusement. Then he swept them all back into their bags, and leaning back in his chair fell fast asleep, snoring so loud that no other sound was audible.

Jack stole softly out of the wardrobe, and taking up the bags of money (which were his very own, because the giant had stolen them from his father), he ran off, and with great difficulty descending the beanstalk, laid the bags of gold on his mother's table. She had just returned from town and was crying at not finding Jack.

'There, mother, I have brought you the gold that my father lost.'

'Oh, Jack! you are a very good boy, but I wish you would not risk your precious life in the giant's castle. Tell me how you came to go there again.'

And Jack told her all about it.

Jack's mother was very glad to get the money, but she did not like him to run any risk for her. But after a time Jack made up his mind to go again to the giant's castle, so he climbed the beanstalk once more, and blew the horn at the giant's gate. The giantess soon opened the door; she was very stupid, and did not know him again, but she stopped a minute before she took him in. She feared another robbery; but Jack's fresh face looked so innocent that she could not resist him, and so she bade him come in, and again hid him away in the wardrobe.

By and by the giant came home, and as soon as he had crossed the threshold he roared out:

> 'Fe, fa, fi-fo-fum,
> I smell the breath of an Englishman.
> Let him be alive or let him be dead,
> I'll grind his bones to make my bread.'

'You stupid old giant,' said his wife, 'you only smell a nice sheep, which I have grilled for your dinner.'

And the giant sat down, and his wife brought up a whole sheep for his dinner. When he had eaten it all up, he said:

'Now bring me my harp, and I will have a little music while you take your walk.'

The giantess obeyed, and returned with a beautiful harp. The framework was all sparkling with diamonds and rubies, and the strings were all of gold.

'This is one of the nicest things I took from the knight,' said the giant. 'I am very fond of music, and my harp is a faithful servant.'

So he drew the harp towards him, and said:

'Play!' And the harp played a very soft, sad air.

'Play something merrier!' said the giant. And the harp played a merry tune.

'Now play me a lullaby,' roared the giant; and the harp played a sweet lullaby, to the sound of which its master fell asleep.

Then Jack stole softly out of the wardrobe, and went into the huge kitchen to see if the giantess had gone out; he found no one there, so he went to the door and opened it softly, for he thought he could not do so with the harp in his hand.

Then he entered the giant's room and seized the harp and ran away with it; but as he jumped over the threshold the harp called out: 'MASTER! MASTER!'

And the giant woke up. With a tremendous roar he sprang from his seat, and in two strides had reached the door.

But Jack was very nimble. He fled like lightning with the harp, talking to it as he went (for he saw it was a fairy), and telling it he was the son of its old master, the knight.

Still the giant came on so fast that he was quite close to poor Jack, and had stretched out his great hand to catch him. But, luckily, just at that moment he stepped upon a loose stone, stumbled, and fell flat on the ground, where he lay at his full length.

This accident gave Jack time to get on the beanstalk and hasten down it; but just as he reached their own garden he beheld the giant descending after him.

'Mother! mother!' cried Jack, 'make haste and give me the axe.'

His mother ran to him with a hatchet in her hand, and Jack with one tremendous blow cut through all the beanstalks except one.

'Now, mother, stand out of the way!' said he.

Jack's mother shrank back, and it was well she did so, for just as the giant took hold of the last branch of the beanstalk, Jack cut the stem quite through and darted from the spot. Down came the giant with a terrible crash, and as he fell on his head, he broke his neck, and lay dead at the feet of the woman he had so much injured.

Before Jack and his mother had recovered from their alarm and agitation, a beautiful lady stood before them.

'Jack,' said she, 'you have acted like a brave knight's son, and deserve to have your inheritance restored to you. Dig a grave and bury the giant, and then go and kill the giantess.'

'But,' said Jack, 'I could not kill anyone unless I were fighting with him; and I could not draw my sword upon a woman. Moreover, the giantess was very kind to me.'

The fairy smiled on Jack.

'I am very much pleased with your generous feeling,' she said. 'Nevertheless, return to the castle, and act as you will find needful.'

Jack asked the fairy if she would show him the way to the castle, as the beanstalk was now down. She told him that she would drive him there in her chariot, which was drawn by two peacocks. Jack thanked her, and sat down in the chariot with her. The fairy drove him a long distance round, till they reached a village which lay at the bottom of the hill. Here they found a number of miserable-looking men assembled. The fairy stopped her carriage and addressed them.

'My friends,' said she, 'the cruel giant who oppressed you and ate up all your flocks and herds is dead, and this young gentleman was the means of your being delivered from him, and is the son of your kind old master, the knight.'

The men gave a loud cheer at these words, and pressed forward to say that they would serve Jack as faithfully as they had served his father. The fairy bade them follow her to the castle, and they marched thither in a body, and Jack blew the horn and demanded admittance.

The old giantess saw them coming from the turret loop-hole. She was very much frightened, for she guessed that something had happened to her husband; and as she came downstairs very fast she caught her foot in her dress, and fell from the top to the bottom and broke her neck. When the people outside found that the door was not opened to them, they took crowbars and forced the portal. Nobody was to be seen, but on leaving the hall they found the body of the giantess at the foot of the stairs.

Thus Jack took possession of the castle. The fairy went and brought his mother to him, with the hen and the harp. He had the giantess buried, and endeavoured as much as lay in his power to do right to those whom the giant had robbed.

Before her departure for fairyland, the fairy explained to Jack that she had sent the butcher to meet him with the beans, in order to try what sort of lad he was.

'If you had looked at the gigantic beanstalk and only stupidly wondered about it,' she said, 'I should have left you where misfortune had placed you, only restoring her cow to your mother. But you showed an inquiring mind, and great courage and enterprise, therefore you deserve to rise; and when you mounted the beanstalk you climbed the Ladder of Fortune.'

She then took her leave of Jack and his mother.

Lucky Luck

ONCE UPON a time there was an arrogant and selfish King who did not wish his only son to marry, for it was the law of the land that once the Prince had a wife the crown would pass to him.

Time went by, and the Prince himself determined to seek a bride. The King was very angry. 'You may go where you please,' he said, 'but none of my courtiers will accompany you.'

Only one servant refused to be parted from the Prince, and so the two set out on their travels. They journeyed over hill and dale till they came to a place called Goldtown. The King of Goldtown had a lovely daughter, and the Prince, who soon heard about her beauty, could not rest till he saw her.

He was very kindly received, for he was extremely good-looking and had charming manners, so he lost no time in asking for her hand and her parents gave her to him with joy. The wedding took place at once, and the feasting and rejoicings went on for a whole month. At the end of the month they set off for home, but as the journey was a long one they spent the first evening at an inn. Everyone in the house slept, and only the faithful servant kept watch. About midnight he heard three crows, who had flown to the roof, talking together.

'That's a handsome couple which arrived here tonight. It seems quite a pity they should lose their lives so soon.'

'Truly,' said the second crow; 'for tomorrow, when midday strikes, the bridge over the Gold Stream will break just as they are driving over it. But, listen; whoever overhears and tells what we have said will be turned to stone up to his knees.'

The crows had hardly done speaking when away they flew. And close upon them followed three pigeons.

'Even if the Prince and Princess get safely over the bridge they will perish,' said they; 'for the King is going to send a carriage to meet them which looks as new as paint. But when they are seated in it a raging wind will rise and whirl the carriage away into the clouds. Then it will fall suddenly to earth, and they will be killed. But anyone who hears and betrays what we have said will be turned to stone up to his waist.'

With that the pigeons flew off and three eagles took their places, and this is what they said:

'If the young couple do manage to escape the dangers of the bridge and the carriage, the King means to send them each a splendid gold embroidered robe. When they put these on they will be burnt up at once. But whoever hears and repeats this will turn to stone from head to foot.'

Early next morning the travellers got up and breakfasted. They began to tell each other their dreams. At last the servant said:

'Gracious Prince, I dreamt that if your Royal Highness would grant all I asked we should get home safe and sound; but if you did not we should certainly be lost. My dreams never deceive me, so I entreat you to follow my advice during the rest of the journey.'

'Don't make such a fuss about a dream,' said the Prince; 'dreams are but clouds. Still, to prevent your being anxious I will promise to do as you wish.'

With that they set out on the next stage of their journey.

At midday they reached the Gold Stream. When they got to the bridge the servant said, 'Let us leave the carriage here, my Prince, and walk a little way. The town is not far off and we can easily get another carriage there, for the wheels of this one are bad and will not hold out much longer.'

The Prince looked well at the carriage. He did not think it looked so unsafe as his servant said; but he had given his word and he held to it.

They got down and loaded the horses with the luggage. The Prince and his bride walked over the bridge, but the servant said he would ride the horses through the stream so as to water and bathe them.

They reached the other side without harm, and bought a new carriage in the town, which was quite near, and set off once more on their travels; but they had not gone far when they met a messenger from the King who said to the Prince, 'His Majesty has sent your Royal Highness this beautiful carriage so that you may make a fitting entry into your own country and amongst your own people.'

The Prince was so delighted that he could not speak. But the servant said, 'My lord, let me examine this carriage first and then you can get in if I find it is all right; otherwise we had better stay in our own.'

The Prince made no objections, and after looking the carriage well over the servant said, 'It is as bad as it is smart'; and with that he knocked it all to pieces, and they went on in the one that they had bought.

At last they reached the frontier; there another messenger was waiting for them, who said that the King had sent two splendid robes for the Prince and his bride, and begged that they would wear them for their state entry. But the servant implored the Prince to have nothing to do with them, and never gave him any peace till he had obtained leave to destroy the robes.

The old King was furious when he found that all his plots had failed – for now he would have to give up the crown to his son. He longed to know how the Prince had escaped, and said, 'My dear son, I do indeed rejoice to have you safely back, but I cannot imagine why the beautiful carriage and the splendid robes I sent did not please you; why you had them destroyed.'

'Indeed, sire,' said the Prince, 'I was myself much annoyed at their destruction; but my servant had begged to direct everything on the journey and I had promised him that he should do so. He declared that we could not possibly get home safely unless I did as he told me.'

The old King fell into a tremendous rage. He called his Council together and condemned the servant to death.

The gallows was put up in the square in front of the palace. The servant was led out and his sentence read to him.

The rope was being placed round his neck, when he begged to be allowed a few last words. 'On our journey home,' he said, 'we spent the first night at an inn. I did not sleep but kept watch all night.' And then he went on to tell what the crows had said, and as he spoke he turned to stone up to his knees. The Prince called to him to say no more as he had proved his innocence. But the servant paid no heed to him, and by the time his story was done he had turned to stone from head to foot.

Oh! how grieved the Prince was to lose his faithful servant! And what pained him most was the thought that he was lost through his

very faithfulness, and he determined to travel all over the world and
never rest till he found some means of restoring him to life.

Now there lived at Court an old woman who had been the Prince's
nurse. To her he confided all his plans, and left his wife, the Princess,
in her care. 'You have a long way before you, my son,' said the old
woman; 'you must never return till you have met with Lucky Luck.
If he cannot help you no one on earth can!'

So the Prince set off to try to find Lucky Luck. He walked and
walked till he got beyond his own country, and he wandered through
a wood for three days but did not meet a living being in it. At the end
of the third day he came to a river near which stood a large mill. Here
he spent the night. When he was leaving next morning the miller
asked him, 'My gracious lord, where are you going all alone?'

And the Prince told him.

'Then I beg your Highness to ask Lucky Luck this question: Why
is it that though I have an excellent mill, with all its machinery com-
plete, and get plenty of grain to grind, I am so poor that I hardly
know how to live from one day to another?'

The Prince promised to inquire, and went on his way. He wandered
about for three days more, and at the end of the third day saw a little
town. It was quite late when he reached it, but he could discover no
light anywhere, and walked almost right through it without finding a
house where he could turn in. But far away at the end of the town
he saw a light in a window. He went straight to it and in the house
were three girls playing a game together. The Prince asked for a
night's lodging and they took him in, gave him some supper and got
a room ready for him, where he slept.

Next morning when he was leaving they asked where he was going
and he told them his story. 'Gracious Prince,' said the maidens, 'do
ask Lucky Luck how it happens that here we are over thirty years old
and no lover has come to woo us, though we are good, pretty, and
very industrious.'

The Prince promised to inquire, and went on his way.

Then he came to a great forest and wandered about in it from
morning to night and from night to morning before he got near the
other end. Here he found a pretty stream which was different from
the other streams as, instead of flowing, it stood still and began to

talk. 'Sir Prince, tell me what brings you into these wilds? I must have been flowing here a hundred years and more and no one has ever yet come by.'

'I will tell you,' answered the Prince, 'if you will divide yourself so that I may walk through.'

The stream parted at once, and the Prince walked through without wetting his feet; and directly he got to the other side he told his story as he had promised.

'Oh, do ask Lucky Luck,' cried the brook, 'why, though I am such a clear, bright, rapid stream I never have a fish or any living creature in my waters.'

The Prince said he would do so, and continued his journey. When he got quite clear of the forest he walked on through a lovely valley till he reached a little house thatched with rushes, and he went in to rest, for he was very tired.

Everything in the house was beautifully clean and tidy, and a cheerful honest-looking old woman was sitting by the fire.

'Good-morning, mother,' said the Prince.

'May luck be with you, my son. What brings you into these parts?'

'I am looking for Lucky Luck,' replied the Prince.

'Then you have come to the right place, my son, for I am his mother. He is not at home just now, he is out digging in the vineyard. Do you go too. Here are two spades. When you find him begin to dig, but don't speak a word to him. It is now eleven o'clock. When he sits down to eat his dinner sit beside him and eat with him. After dinner he will question you, and then tell him all your troubles freely. He will answer whatever you may ask.'

With that she showed him the way, and the Prince went and did just as she had told him. After dinner they lay down to rest.

All of a sudden Lucky Luck began to speak and said, 'Tell me, what sort of man are you, for since you came here you have not spoken a word?'

'I am not dumb,' replied the young man, 'but I am that unhappy Prince whose faithful servant has been turned to stone, and I want to know how to help him.'

'And you do well, for he deserves everything. Go back, and when you get home your wife will just have had a little boy. Take three

drops of blood from the child's little finger, rub them on your servant's wrists with a blade of grass and he will return to life.'

'I have another thing to ask,' said the Prince, when he had thanked him. 'In the forest near here is a fine stream but not a fish or other living creature in it. Why is this?'

'Because no one has ever been drowned in the stream. But take care, in crossing, to get as near the other side as you can before you say so, or you may be the first victim yourself.'

'Another question, please, before I go. On my way here I lodged one night in the house of three maidens. All were well-mannered, hard-working, and pretty, and yet none has had a wooer. Why was this ?'

'Because they always throw out their sweepings in the face of the sun.'

'And why is it that a miller, who has a large mill with all the best machinery and gets plenty of corn to grind, is so poor that he can hardly live from day to day ?'

'Because the miller keeps everything for himself, and does not give to those who need it.'

The Prince wrote down the answers to his questions, took a friendly leave of Lucky Luck, and set off for home.

When he reached the stream it asked if he brought it any good news. 'When I get across I will tell you,' said he. So the stream parted; he walked through and on to the highest part of the bank. He stopped and shouted out:

'Listen, O stream! Lucky Luck says you will never have any living creature in your waters until someone is drowned in you.'

The words were hardly out of his mouth when the stream swelled and overflowed till it reached the rock up which he had climbed, and dashed so far up it that the spray flew over him. But he clung on tight, and after failing to reach him three times the stream returned to its proper course. Then the Prince climbed down, dried himself in the sun, and set out on his march home.

He spent the night once more at the mill and gave the miller his answer, and by and by he told the three sisters not to throw out all their sweepings in the face of the sun.

The Prince had hardly arrived at home when some thieves tried to ford the stream with a fine horse they had stolen. When they were half-way across, the stream rose so suddenly that it swept them all away. From that time it became the best fishing stream in the country-side.

The miller, too, began to give alms and became a very good man, and in time grew so rich that he hardly knew how much he had.

And the three sisters, now that they no longer insulted the sun, had each a wooer within a week.

When the Prince got home he found that his wife had just got a fine little boy. He did not lose a moment in pricking the baby's finger till the blood ran, and he brushed it on the wrists of the stone figure, which shuddered all over and split with a loud noise in seven parts, and there was the faithful servant alive and well.

When the old King saw this he foamed with rage, and fell down in a fit and died.

The servant stayed on with his royal master and served him faithfully all the rest of his life; and, if neither of them is dead, he is serving him still.

The Magic Kettle

RIGHT IN the middle of Japan, high up among the mountains, there once lived a good old man. He loved his little house and garden, was very proud of it, and never tired of admiring the whiteness of his straw mats, and the pretty papered walls of his room, which in warm weather he always slid back, so that the smell of the trees and flowers might come in.

One day he was standing looking at the mountain opposite, when he heard a kind of rumbling noise in the room behind him. He turned round, and in the corner he beheld a rusty old iron kettle, which could not have seen the light of day for many years. How the kettle got there the old man did not know, but he took it up and looked it over carefully, and when he found that it was quite whole he cleaned the dust off it and carried it into his kitchen.

'That was a piece of luck,' he said, smiling to himself. 'A good kettle costs money, and it is as well to have a second one at hand in case of need; mine, in any case, is wearing out, and is beginning to leak.'

Then he took the old kettle off the fire, filled the new one with water, and put it in its place.

No sooner was the water in the kettle getting warm than a strange thing happened, and the old man, who was standing by, thought he must be dreaming. First the handle of the kettle gradually changed its shape and became a head, and the spout grew into a tail, while out of the body sprang four paws, and in a few minutes the man found himself watching, not a kettle, but a kind of badger, a tanuki! The creature jumped off the fire, and bounded about the room like a kitten, running up the walls and over the ceiling, till the old man was in an agony lest his pretty room should be spoilt. He cried to a neighbour for help, and between them they managed to catch the tanuki, and shut him up safely in a wooden chest. Then, quite exhausted, they sat down on the mats, and consulted together what they should do with this troublesome beast. At length they decided to sell him,

127

and bade a child who was passing send them a certain tradesman called Jimmu.

When Jimmu arrived, the old man told him that he had something which he wished to get rid of, and lifted the lid of the wooden chest, where he had shut up the tanuki. But, to his surprise, no tanuki was there, nothing but the kettle he had found in the corner. It was certainly very odd, but the man remembered what had taken place on the fire, and did not want to keep the kettle any more, so after a little bargaining about the price, Jimmu went away carrying the kettle with him.

Now Jimmu had not gone very far before he felt that the kettle was getting heavier and heavier, and by the time he reached home he was so tired that he was thankful to put it down in the corner of his room, and then he forgot all about it. In the middle of the night, however, he was awakened by a loud noise in the corner where the kettle stood, and raised himself up in bed to see what it was. But nothing was there except the kettle which seemed quiet enough. He thought that he must have been dreaming, and fell asleep again, only to be roused a second time by the same disturbance. He jumped up and went to the corner, and by the light of the lamp that he always kept burning he saw that the kettle had become a tanuki, which was running round after his tail. After he grew weary of that, he ran on the balcony, where he turned several somersaults, from pure gladness of heart. Jimmu was much troubled as to what to do with the animal, and it was only towards morning that he managed to get any sleep; but when he opened his eyes again there was no tanuki, only the old kettle he had left there the night before.

As soon as he had tidied his house, Jimmu set off to tell his story to a neighbour. His friend listened quietly, and was not so surprised as Jimmu expected him to be, for he recollected having heard, in his youth, something about a wonder-working kettle. 'Go and travel with it, and show it off,' said he, 'and you will become a rich man; but be careful first to ask the tanuki's leave.'

Jimmu thanked his friend for his counsel, which he followed exactly. The tanuki's consent was obtained, a booth was built, and a notice was hung up outside it inviting the people to come and witness the most wonderful transformation that ever was seen.

They came in crowds, and the kettle was passed from hand to hand, and they were allowed to examine it all over, and even to look inside. Then Jimmu took it back, and setting it on the platform, commanded it to become a tanuki. In an instant the handle began to change into a head, and the spout into a tail, while the four paws appeared at the sides. 'Dance,' said Jimmu, and the tanuki did his steps, and moved first on one side and then on the other, till the people could not stand still any longer, and began to dance too. Gracefully the tanuki led the fan dance, and glided without a pause into the shadow dance and the umbrella dance, and it seemed as if he might go on dancing for ever. And so very likely he would, if Jimmu had not declared he had danced enough, and that the booth must now be closed.

Day after day the booth was so full it was hardly possible to enter it, and what the neighbour foretold had come to pass, and Jimmu was a rich man. Yet he did not feel happy. He was an honest man, and he thought that he owed some of his wealth to the good old man from whom he had bought the kettle. So, one morning, he put a hundred gold pieces into it, and hanging the kettle once more on his arm, he climbed the mountain and returned to the seller of it. 'I have no right to keep it any longer,' he added when he had ended his tale, 'so I have brought it back to you, and inside you will find a hundred gold pieces as the price of its hire.'

The man thanked Jimmu, and said that few people would have been as honest as he. And the kettle brought them both luck, and everything went well with them till they died, which they did when they were very, very old, respected by everyone.

The Maiden with the Wooden Helmet

IN A little village in the country of Japan there lived long, long ago a man and his wife. They had one child, a little girl who was as lovely as the morning. For some years they were happy and prosperous, but bad times came, and at last nothing was left to them but their daughter. The neighbours were very kind, and would have done anything they could to help their poor friends, but the old couple felt that since everything had changed they would rather go elsewhere, so one day they set off to bury themselves in another part of the country, taking their daughter with them.

Now the mother and daughter had plenty to do in keeping the house clean and looking after the garden, but the man would sit for hours together gazing straight in front of him, and thinking of the riches that had once been his. Each day he grew more and more wretched, till at length he took to his bed and never got up again.

His wife and his daughter wept bitterly for his loss, and it was many months before they could take pleasure in anything. Then one morning the mother suddenly looked at the girl, and found that she had grown still more lovely, and was now a very beautiful young woman. Once her heart would have been glad at the sight, but now that they two were alone in the world she feared some harm might come of it. So, like a good mother, she tried to teach her daughter all she knew, and to bring her up to be always busy, so that she would have no time to think about herself. And the girl was a good girl, and listened to all her mother's lessons, and so the years passed.

At last one wet spring the mother caught cold, and though in the beginning she did not pay much attention to it, she gradually grew more and more ill, and knew that she had not long to live. Then she called her daughter and told her that very soon she would be alone in the world; that she must look to herself, as there would be no one to take care of her. And because it was more difficult for beautiful women to pass unheeded than for others, she bade her fetch a wooden helmet out of the next room, and put it on her head, and pull it low over her

131

brows, so that nearly the whole of her face should lie in its shadow. The girl did as she was bid, and her beauty was so hidden beneath the wooden cap, which covered up all her hair, that she might have gone through any crowd, and no one would have looked twice at her. And when she saw this the heart of the mother was at rest, and she lay back in her bed and died.

The girl wept for many days, but by and by she felt that, being alone in the world, she must go and get work, for she had only herself to depend upon. There was none to be got by staying where she was, so she made her clothes into a bundle, and walked over the hills till she reached the house of the man who owned the fields in that part of the country. And she took service with him and laboured for him early and late, and every night when she went to bed she was at peace, for she had not forgotten one thing that she had promised her mother; and, however hot the sun might be, she always kept the wooden helmet on her head, and the people gave her the nickname of Hatschihime.

In spite, however, of all her care the fame of her beauty spread abroad: and often impudent young men (they are always to be found in the world) stole softly up behind her while she was at work, and tried to lift off the wooden helmet. But the girl would have nothing to do with them, and only bade them be off; then they began to talk to her, but she never answered them, and went on with what she was doing. And though her wages were low and food not very plentiful, still she could manage to live, and that was enough.

One day her master happened to pass through the field where she was working, and was struck by her industry and stopped to watch her. After a while he put one or two questions to her, and then led her into his house, and told her that henceforward her only duty should be to tend his sick wife. From this time the girl felt as if all her troubles were ended, but the worst of them was yet to come.

Not very long after Hatschihime had become maid to the sick woman, the eldest son of the house returned from Kioto, where he had been studying all sorts of things. He was tired of the splendours of the town and its pleasures, and was glad enough to be back in the green country, among the peach-blossoms and sweet flowers. Strolling about in the early morning, he caught sight of the girl with the odd wooden helmet on her head, and immediately he went to his mother to ask who she was, and where she came from, and why she wore that strange thing over her face. His mother answered that it was a whim, and nobody could persuade her to lay it aside; whereat the young man laughed, but kept his thoughts to himself.

One hot day, however, he happened to be going towards home when he caught sight of his mother's waiting-maid kneeling by a little stream that flowed through the garden, splashing water over her face. The helmet was pushed on one side, and as the youth stood watching from behind a tree he had a glimpse of the girl's great beauty; and he determined that no one else should be his wife. But when he told his family of his resolve to marry her they were very angry, and made up all sorts of wicked stories about her. However, they might have spared themselves the trouble, as he knew it was only idle talk. 'I have merely to remain firm,' thought he, 'and they will have to give in.' It was such a good match for the girl that it never occurred to anyone that she would refuse the young man, but so it was. It would not be right, she felt, to make a quarrel in the house, and though in secret she wept bitterly, for a long while, nothing would make her change her mind. At length one night her mother appeared to her in a dream, and bade her marry the young man. So the next time he asked her – as he did nearly every day – to his surprise and joy she consented. The parents then saw they had better make the best of a bad business, and set about making the grand preparations suitable to the occasion. Of course the neighbours said a great many ill-natured things about Hatschihime but the bridegroom was too happy to care, and only laughed at them.

When everything was ready for the feast, and the bride was dressed in the most beautiful embroidered dress to be found in Japan, the maids took hold of the helmet to lift it off her head, so that they might do her hair in the latest fashion. But the helmet would not come, and the harder they pulled, the faster it seemed to be, till the poor girl cried aloud with pain. Hearing her cries the bridegroom ran in and soothed her, and declared that she should be married in the helmet, as she could not be married without. Then the ceremonies began, and the bridal pair sat together, and the cup of wine was brought them, out of which they had to drink. And when they had drunk it all, and the cup was empty, a wonderful thing happened. The helmet suddenly burst with a loud noise, and fell in pieces on the ground; and as they all turned to look they found the floor covered with precious stones which had fallen out of it. But the guests were less astonished at the brilliance of the diamonds than at the beauty of the bride, which was beyond anything they had ever seen or heard of. The night was passed in singing and dancing, and then the bride and bridegroom went to their own house, where they lived till they died, and had many children, who were famous throughout Japan for their goodness and beauty.

The Nine Pea-Hens and the
Golden Apples

ONCE UPON a time there stood before the palace of an Emperor a golden apple tree, which blossomed and bore fruit each night. But every morning the fruit was gone, and the boughs were bare of blossom, without anyone being able to discover who was the thief.

At last the Emperor said to his eldest son, 'If only I could prevent those robbers from stealing my fruit, how happy I should be!'

And his son replied, 'I will sit up tonight and watch the tree, and I shall soon see who it is!'

So directly it grew dark the young man went and hid himself near the apple tree to begin his watch, but the apples had scarcely begun to ripen before he fell asleep, and when he awoke at sunrise the apples were gone. He felt much ashamed of himself, and went with lagging feet to tell his father.

Of course, though the eldest son had failed, the second made sure that he would do better, and set out gaily at nightfall to watch the apple tree. But no sooner had he lain himself down than his eyes grew heavy, and when the sunbeams roused him from his slumbers there was not an apple left on the tree.

Next came the turn of the youngest son, who made himself a comfortable bed under the apple tree, and prepared himself to sleep. Towards midnight he awoke, and sat up to look at the tree. And behold! The apples were beginning to ripen, and lit up the whole palace with their brightness. At the same moment nine golden pea-hens flew swiftly through the air, and while eight alighted upon the boughs laden with fruit, the ninth fluttered to the ground where the Prince lay, and instantly was changed into a beautiful maiden, more beautiful by far than any lady in the Emperor's court. The Prince at once fell in love with her, and they talked together for some time, till the maiden and her sisters had finished plucking the apples, and now they must all go home again. The Prince, however, begged her so hard

to leave him a little of the fruit that the maiden gave him two apples, one for himself and one for his father. Then she changed herself back into a pea-hen, and the whole nine flew away.

As soon as the sun rose the Prince entered the palace, and held out the apple to his father, who was rejoiced to see it, and praised his youngest son heartily for his cleverness. That evening the Prince returned to the apple tree, and everything passed as before, and so it happened for several nights. At length the other brothers grew angry at seeing that he never came back without bringing two golden apples with him, and they went to consult an old witch, who promised to spy after him, and discover how he managed to get the apples. So, when the evening came, the old woman hid herself under the tree and waited for the Prince. Before long he arrived, and lay down on his bed, and was soon fast asleep. Towards midnight there was a rush of wings, and the eight pea-hens settled on the tree, while the ninth became a maiden, and ran to greet the Prince. Then the witch stretched out her hand, and cut off a lock of the maiden's hair, and in an instant the girl sprang up, a pea-hen once more, spread her wings and flew away, while her sisters, who were busily stripping the boughs, flew after her.

When he had recovered from his surprise at the unexpected disappearance of the maiden, the Prince exclaimed, 'What can be the matter?' and, looking about him, discovered the old witch in her hiding place. He dragged her out, and in his fury called his guards, and ordered them to put her to death at once. But that did no good as far as the pea-hens went. They came back no more, though the Prince returned to the tree every night, and wept his heart out for his lost love. This went on for some time, till the Prince could bear it no longer, and made up his mind he would search the world through for her. In vain his father tried to persuade him that his task was hopeless, and that other girls were to be found as beautiful as this one. The Prince would listen to nothing, and, accompanied by only one servant, set out on his quest.

After travelling for many days, he arrived at length before a large gate, and through the bars he could see the streets of a town, and even the palace. The Prince tried to pass in, but the way was barred by the keeper of the gate, who wanted to know who he was, why he was there, and how he had learnt the way, for he was not allowed to enter unless the Empress herself came and gave him leave. A message was sent to her, and when she stood at the gate the Prince thought he had lost his wits, for there was the maiden he had left his home to seek. And she hastened to him, and took his hand, and drew him into the palace. In a few days they were married, and the Prince forgot his father and his brothers, and made up his mind that he would live and die in the castle.

One morning the Empress told him that she was going to take a walk by herself, and that she would leave the keys of twelve cellars to his care. 'If you wish to enter the first eleven cellars,' said she, 'you can; but beware of even unlocking the door of the twelfth, or it will fare badly with you.'

The Prince, who was thus left alone in the castle, soon got tired of being by himself, and began to look for something to amuse him.

'What *can* there be in that twelfth cellar,' he thought to himself, 'which I must not see?' And he went downstairs and unlocked the doors, one after the other. When he got to the twelfth he paused, but his curiosity was too much for him, and in another instant the key was turned and the cellar lay open before him. It was empty, save for a large cask, bound with iron hoops, and out of the cask a voice was saying entreatingly, 'For pity's sake, brother, fetch me some water; I am dying of thirst!'

The Prince, who was very tender-hearted, brought some water at once, and poured it through a hole in the barrel; and as he did so one of the iron hoops burst.

He was turning away, when a voice cried the second time, 'Brother, for pity's sake fetch me some water; I'm dying of thirst!'

So the Prince went back, and brought some more water, and again a hoop sprang.

And for the third time the voice still called for water; and when water was given it the last hoop was rent, the cask fell in pieces, and out flew a dragon, who snatched up the Empress just as she was returning from her walk, and carried her off. Some servants who saw what had happened came rushing to the Prince, and the poor young man went nearly mad when he heard the result of his own folly, and could only cry out that he would follow the dragon to the ends of the earth, until he got his wife again.

For months and months he wandered about, first in this direction and then in that, without finding any traces of the dragon or his captive. At last he came to a stream, and as he stopped for a moment to look at it he noticed a little fish lying on the bank beating its tail convulsively, in a vain effort to get back into the water.

'Oh, for pity's sake, my brother,' shrieked the little creature, 'help me, and put me back into the river, and I will repay you some day. Take one of my scales, and when you are in danger twist it in your fingers, and I will come!'

The Prince picked up the fish and threw it into the water; then he took off one of its scales, as he had been told, and put it in his pocket, carefully wrapped in a cloth. Then he went on his way till, some miles farther down the road, he found a fox caught in a trap.

'Oh! Be a brother to me!' called the fox, 'and free me from this trap, and I will help you when you are in need. Pull out one of my hairs, and when you are in danger twist it in your fingers, and I will come.'

So the Prince unfastened the trap, pulled out one of the fox's hairs, and continued his journey. And as he was going over the mountain he passed a wolf entangled in a snare, who begged to be set at liberty.

'Only deliver me from death,' he said, 'and you will never be sorry for it. Take a lock of my fur, and when you need me twist it in your fingers.' And the Prince undid the snare and let the wolf go.

For a long time he walked on, without having any more adventures, till at length he met a man travelling on the same road.

'Oh, brother!' asked the Prince. 'Tell me, if you can, where the dragon-emperor lives?'

The man told him where he would find the palace, and how long it would take him to get there, and the Prince thanked him, and followed his directions, till that same evening he reached the town where the dragon-emperor lived. When he entered the palace, to his great joy he found his wife sitting alone in a vast hall, and they began hastily to invent plans for her escape. There was no time to waste, as the dragon might return directly, so they took two horses out of the stable, and rode away at lightning speed. Hardly were they out of sight of the palace than the dragon came home and found that his prisoner had flown.

He sent at once for his talking horse, and said to him:

'Give me your advice; what shall I do – have my supper as usual, or set out in pursuit of them?'

'Eat your supper with a free mind first,' answered the horse, 'and follow them afterwards.'

So the dragon ate till it was past mid-day, and when he could eat no more he mounted his horse and set out after the fugitives. In a short time he had come up with them, and as he snatched the Empress out of her saddle he said to the Prince:

'This time I will forgive you, because you brought me the water when I was in the cask; but beware how you return here, or you will pay for it with your life.'

Half mad with grief, the Prince rode sadly on a little farther, hardly knowing what he was doing. Then he could bear it no longer and turned back to the palace, in spite of the dragon's threats. Again the Empress was sitting alone, and once more they began to think of a scheme by which they could escape the dragon's power.

'Ask the dragon when he comes home,' said the Prince, 'where he got that wonderful horse from, and then you can tell me, and I will try to find another like it.'

Then fearing to meet his enemy, he stole out of the castle.

Soon after the dragon came home, and the Empress sat down near him, and began to coax and flatter him into a good humour, and at last she said:

'But tell me about that wonderful horse you were riding yesterday. There cannot be another like it in the whole world. Where *did* you get it from?'

And he answered:

'The way I got it is a way which no one else can take. On the top of a high mountain dwells an old witch, who has in her stables twelve horses, each one more beautiful than the other. And in one corner is a thin, wretched-looking animal whom no one would glance at a second time, but he is in reality the best of the lot. He is twin brother to my own horse, and can fly as high as the clouds themselves. But no one can ever see this horse without first serving the old woman for three whole days. And besides the horses she has a foal and its mother, and the man who serves her must look after them for three days and nights, and if he does not let them run away he will in the end get the choice of any horse as a present from the old woman. But if he fails to keep the foal and its mother safe on any one of the three nights his head will pay the price!'

The next day the Prince watched till the dragon left the house, and then he crept in to the Empress, who told him all she had learnt from her gaoler. The Prince at once determined to seek the old woman on the top of the mountain, and lost no time in setting out. It was a long and steep climb, but at last he found her, and with a low bow he began:

'Good greeting to you, little mother!'

'Good greeting to you, my son! What are you doing here?'

'I wish to become your servant,' answered he.

'So you shall,' said the old woman. 'If you can take care of my mare for three days I will give you a horse for wages, but if you let her stray you will lose your head;' and as she spoke she led him into a courtyard surrounded with palings, and on every post a man's head was stuck.

One post only was empty, and as they passed it cried out:

'Woman, give me the head I am waiting for!'

The old woman made no answer, but turned to the Prince and said:

'Look! All those men took service with me, on the same conditions as you, but not one was able to guard the mare!'

But the Prince did not waver, and declared he would abide by his words.

When evening came he led the mare out of the stable and mounted her, and the colt ran behind. He managed to keep his seat for a long time, in spite of all her efforts to throw him, but at length he grew so weary that he fell fast asleep, and when he woke he found himself sitting on a log, with the halter in his hands. He jumped up in terror, but the mare was nowhere to be seen, and he started with a beating heart in search of her. He had gone some way without a single trace to guide him, when he came to a little river. The sight of the water brought back to his mind the fish whom he had saved from death, and he hastily drew the scale from his pocket. It had hardly touched his fingers when the fish appeared in the stream beside him.

'What is it, my brother?' asked the fish anxiously.

'The old woman's mare strayed last night, and I don't know where to look for her.'

'Oh, I can tell you that: she has changed herself into a big fish, and her foal into a little one. But strike the water with the halter and say, "Come here, O mare of the mountain witch!" and she will come.'

The Prince did as he was bid, and the mare and her foal stood before him. Then he put the halter round her neck, and rode her home, the foal always trotting behind them. The old woman was at the door to receive them, and gave the Prince some food while she led the mare back to the stable.

'You should have gone among the fishes,' cried the old woman, striking the animal with a stick.

'I did go among the fishes,' replied the mare; 'but they are no friends of mine, for they betrayed me at once.'

'Well, go among the foxes next time,' said she, and returned to the house, not knowing that the Prince had overheard her.

When it began to grow dark the Prince mounted the mare for the second time and rode into the meadows, and the foal trotted behind its mother. Again he managed to stick on till midnight; then a sleep overtook him that he could not battle against, and when he woke up he found himself, as before, sitting on the log, with the halter in his hands. He gave a shriek of dismay, and sprang up in search of the wanderers. Then he suddenly remembered the words that the old woman had said to the mare, and he drew out the fox hair and twisted it in his fingers.

'What is it, my brother?' asked the fox, who instantly appeared before him.

'The old witch's mare has run away from me, and I do not know where to look for her.'

'She is with us,' replied the fox, 'and has changed herself into a big fox, and her foal into a little one; but strike the ground with the halter and say, "Come here, O mare of the mountain witch!"'

The Prince did so, and in a moment the mare stood before him, with the little foal at her heels. He mounted and rode back, and the old woman placed food on the table, and led the mare back to the stable.

'You should have gone to the foxes, as I told you,' said she, striking the mare with a stick.

'I did go to the foxes,' replied the mare, 'but they are no friends of mine and betrayed me.'

'Well, this time you had better go to the wolves,' said she, not knowing that the Prince had heard all she had been saying.

So for the third night the Prince mounted the mare and rode her out to the meadows, with the foal trotting after. He tried hard to keep awake, but it was of no use, and in the morning there he was again on the log, grasping the halter. He started to his feet, and then stopped, for he remembered what the old woman had said, and pulled out the wolf's grey lock.

'What is it, my brother?' asked the wolf as it stood before him.

'The old witch's mare has run away from me,' replied the Prince, 'and I don't know where to find her.'

'Oh, she is with us,' answered the wolf, 'and she has changed herself into a she-wolf, and the foal into a cub; but strike the earth here with the halter, and cry, "Come to me, O mare of the mountain witch!"'

The Prince did as he was bid, and the she-wolf changed back into a mare, with the foal beside her. And when he had mounted and ridden her home the old woman was on the steps to receive them, and she set some food before the Prince, but led the mare back to her stable.

'You should have gone among the wolves,' said she, striking her with a stick.

'So I did,' replied the mare, 'but they are no friends of mine and betrayed me.'

The old woman made no answer, and left the stable, but the Prince was at the door waiting for her.

'I have served you well,' said he, 'and now for my reward.'

'What I promised, that will I perform,' answered she. 'Choose one of these twelve horses; you can have which you like.'

'Give me, instead, that half-starved creature in the corner,' asked the Prince. 'I prefer him to all those beautiful animals.'

'You can't really mean what you say?' replied the woman.

'Yes, I do,' said the Prince, and the old woman was forced to let him have his way. So he took leave of her, and put the halter round his horse's neck and led him into the forest, where he rubbed him down till his skin was shining like gold. Then he mounted, and they flew straight through the air to the dragon's palace. The Empress had been looking for him night and day, and stole out to meet him, and he swung her on to his saddle, and the horse flew off again.

Not long after the dragon came home, and when he found the Empress was missing he said to his horse, 'What shall we do? Shall we eat and drink, or shall we follow the runaways?' and the horse replied, 'Whether you eat or don't eat, drink or don't drink, follow them or stay at home, matters nothing now, for you can never, never catch them.'

But the dragon paid no heed to the horse's words, but sprang on his back and set off in chase of the fugitives. And when they saw him coming they were frightened, and urged the Prince's horse faster and faster, till he said, 'Fear nothing; no harm can happen to us,' and their hearts grew calm, for they trusted his wisdom.

Soon the dragon's horse was heard panting behind, and he cried out, 'Oh, my brother, do not go so fast! I shall sink to the earth if I try to keep up with you.'

And the Prince's horse answered, 'Why do you serve a monster like that? Kick him off, and let him fall to the ground, and come and join us.'

And the dragon's horse plunged and reared, and shook off the dragon – who, in falling on a rock, was broken into a hundred pieces. Then the Empress mounted his horse, and rode back with her husband to her kingdom, over which they ruled for many years.

The Prince and the Dragon

ONCE UPON a time there lived an Emperor who had three sons. They were all fine young men, and fond of hunting, and scarcely a day passed without one or other of them going out to look for game.

One morning the eldest of the three Princes mounted his horse and set out for a neighbouring forest, where wild animals of all sorts were to be found. He had not long left the castle, when a hare sprang out of a thicket and dashed across the road in front of him. The young man gave chase at once, and pursued it over hill and dale, till at last the hare took refuge in a mill which was standing by the side of a river. The Prince followed and entered the mill, but stopped in terror by the door, for, instead of a hare, before him stood a dragon, breathing fire and flame. At this fearful sight the Prince turned to fly, but a fiery tongue coiled round his waist, and drew him into the dragon's mouth, and he was seen no more.

A week passed away, and when the Prince did not come back everyone in the town began to grow uneasy. At last his next brother told the Emperor that he likewise would go out to hunt, and that perhaps he would find some clue to his brother's disappearance. But hardly had the castle gates closed on the Prince than the hare sprang out of the bushes as before, and led the huntsman up hill and down dale, till they reached the mill. Into this the hare flew with the Prince at his heels, when, lo! instead of the hare, there stood a dragon breathing fire and flame; and out shot a fiery tongue which coiled round the Prince's waist, and lifted him straight into the dragon's mouth, and he was seen no more.

Days went by, and the Emperor waited and waited for the sons who never came, and could not sleep at night for wondering where they were and what had become of them. His youngest son wished to go in search of his brothers, but for long the Emperor refused to listen to him, lest he should lose him also. But the Prince prayed so hard for leave to make the search, and promised so often that he would be

very cautious and careful, that at length the Emperor gave him permission, and ordered the best horse in the stables to be saddled for him.

Full of hope the young Prince started on his way, but no sooner was he outside the city walls than a hare sprang out of the bushes and ran before him, till they reached the mill. As before, the animal dashed in through the open door, but this time he was not followed by the Prince. Wiser than his brothers, the young man turned away, saying to himself, 'There are as good hares in the forest as any that have come out of it, and when I have caught them, I can come back and look for you.'

For many hours he rode up and down the mountain, but saw nothing, and at last, tired of waiting, he went back to the mill. Here he found an old woman sitting, whom he greeted pleasantly.

'Good morning to you, little mother,' he said; and the old woman answered, 'Good morning, my son.'

'Tell me, little mother,' went on the Prince, 'where shall I find my hare?'

'My son,' replied the old woman, 'that was no hare, but a dragon who has led many men hither, and then has eaten them all.' At these words the Prince's heart grew heavy, and he cried, 'Then my brothers must have come here, and have been eaten by the dragon!'

'You have guessed right,' answered the old woman; 'and I can give you no better counsel than to go home at once, before the same fate overtakes you.'

'Will you not come with me out of this dreadful place?' said the young man.

'He took me prisoner, too,' answered she, 'and I cannot shake off his chains.'

'Then listen to me,' cried the Prince. 'When the dragon comes back, ask him where he always goes when he leaves here, and what makes him so strong; and when you have coaxed the secret from him, tell me the next time I come.'

So the Prince went home, and the old woman remained in the mill, and as soon as the dragon returned she said to him, 'Where have you been all this time – you must have travelled far?'

'Yes, little mother, I have indeed travelled far,' answered he. Then the old woman began to flatter him, and to praise his cleverness; and when she thought she had got him into a good temper, she said, 'I have wondered so often where you get your strength from; I do wish you would tell me. I would stoop and kiss the place out of pure love!' The dragon laughed at this, and answered:

'In the hearthstone yonder lies the secret of my strength.'

Then the old woman jumped up and kissed the hearth; whereat the dragon laughed the more, and said:

'You foolish creature! I was only jesting. It is not in the hearth-stone, but in that tall tree that lies the secret of my strength.' Then the old woman jumped up again and put her arms round the tree, and kissed it heartily. Loudly laughed the dragon when he saw what she was doing.

'Old fool,' he cried, as soon as he could speak, 'did you really believe that my strength came from that tree?'

'Where is it then?' asked the old woman, rather crossly, for she did not like being made fun of.

'My strength,' replied the dragon, 'lies far away; so far that you could never reach it. Far, far from here is a kingdom, and by its capital city is a lake, and in the lake is a dragon, and inside the dragon is a wild boar, and inside the wild boar is a hare, and inside the hare is a pigeon, and inside the pigeon a sparrow, and inside the sparrow is my strength.' And when the old woman heard this, she thought it was no use flattering him any longer, for never, never, could she take his strength from him.

The following morning, when the dragon had left the mill, the Prince came back, and the old woman told him all that the creature had said. He listened in silence, and then returned to the castle, where he put on a suit of shepherd's clothes, and taking a staff in his hand, he went forth to seek work as tender of sheep.

And in this manner he wandered from village to village and from town to town, till he came at length to a large city in a distant kingdom, surrounded on three sides by a great lake, which happened to be the very lake in which the dragon lived. As was his custom, he stopped everybody whom he met in the streets that looked likely to want a shepherd and begged them to engage him, but they all seemed to have shepherds of their own, or else not to need any. The Prince was beginning to lose heart, when a man who had overheard his question turned round and said that he had better go and ask the Emperor, as he was in search of someone to see after his flocks.

'Will you take care of my sheep?' said the Emperor, when the young man knelt before him.

'Most willingly, your Majesty,' answered the young man, and he listened obediently while the Emperor told him what he was to do.

'Outside the city walls,' went on the Emperor, 'you will find a large lake, and by its banks lie the richest meadows in my kingdom. When you are leading out your flocks to pasture, they will all run straight to these meadows, and none that have gone there have ever been known to come back. Take heed, therefore, my son, not to suffer your sheep to go where they will, but drive them to the spot that you think best.'

With a low bow the Prince thanked the Emperor for his warning, and promised to do his best to keep the sheep safe. Then he left the palace and went to the market-place, where he bought two greyhounds, a hawk, and a set of pipes; after that he took the sheep out to pasture. The instant the animals caught sight of the lake lying before them, they trotted off as fast as their legs would go towards the green meadows lying round it. The Prince did not try to stop them; he only placed his hawk on the branch of a tree, laid his pipes on the grass, and bade the greyhounds sit still; then, rolling up his sleeves and trousers, he waded into the water crying as he did so:

'Dragon! Dragon! If you are not a coward, come out and fight with me!'

And a voice answered from the depths of the lake:

'I am waiting for you, O Prince;' and the next minute the dragon reared himself out of the water, huge and horrible to see. The Prince sprang upon him and they grappled with each other and fought together till the sun was high, and it was noonday. Then the dragon gasped:

'O Prince, let me but dip my burning head once into the lake, and I will hurl you up to the top of the sky.' But the Prince answered, 'Oh, ho! my good dragon, do not crow too soon! If the Emperor's daughter were only here, and would kiss me on the forehead, I would throw you up higher still!' And suddenly the dragon's hold loosened, and he fell back into the lake.

As soon as it was evening, the Prince washed away all signs of the fight, took his hawk upon his shoulder, and his pipes under his arm, and with his greyhounds in front and his flock following after him he set out for the city. As they all passed through the streets the people stared in wonder, for never before had any flock returned from the lake.

The next morning he rose early, and led his sheep down the road to the lake. This time, however, the Emperor sent two men on horseback to ride behind him, with orders to watch the Prince all day long. The horsemen kept the Prince and his sheep in sight, without being seen themselves. As soon as they beheld the sheep running towards the meadows, they turned aside up a steep hill, which overhung the lake. When the shepherd reached the place, he laid, as before, his pipes on the grass and bade the greyhounds sit beside them, while the hawk he perched on the branch of the tree. Then he rolled up his trousers and his sleeves, and waded into the water crying:

'Dragon! Dragon! If you are not a coward, come out and fight with me!' And the dragon answered:

'I am waiting for you, O Prince,' and the next minute he reared himself out of the water, huge and horrible to see. Again they clasped each other tight round the body and fought till it was noon, and when the sun was at its hottest, the dragon gasped:

'O Prince, let me but dip my burning head once in the lake, and I will hurl you up to the top of the sky.' But the Prince answered:

'Oh, ho! my good dragon, do not crow too soon! If the Emperor's daughter were only here, and would kiss me on the forehead, I would throw you up higher still!' And suddenly the dragon's hold loosened, and he fell back into the lake.

As soon as it was evening the Prince again collected his sheep, and playing on his pipes he marched before them into the city. When he passed through the gates all the people came out of their houses to stare in wonder, for never before had any flock returned from the lake.

Meanwhile the two horsemen had ridden quickly back, and told the Emperor all that they had seen and heard. The Emperor listened eagerly to their tale, then called his daughter to him and repeated it to her.

'Tomorrow,' he said, when he had finished, 'you shall go with the shepherd to the lake, and then you shall kiss him on the forehead as he wishes.'

But when the Princess heard these words, she burst into tears, and sobbed out:

'Will you really send me, your only child, to that dreadful place, from which most likely I shall never come back?'

'Fear nothing, my little daughter, all will be well. Many shepherds have gone to that lake and none have ever returned; but this one has in these two days fought twice with the dragon and has escaped without a wound. So I hope tomorrow he will kill the dragon altogether, and deliver this land from the monster who has slain so many of our bravest men.'

Scarcely had the sun begun to peep over the hills next morning, when the Princess stood by the shepherd's side, ready to go to the lake. The shepherd was brimming over with joy, but the Princess only wept bitterly.

'Dry your tears, I implore you,' said he. 'If you will just do what I ask you, and when the time comes, run and kiss my forehead, you have nothing to fear.'

Merrily the shepherd blew on his pipes as he marched at the head of his flock, only stopping every now and then to say to the weeping girl at his side, 'Do not cry so, Heart of Gold; trust me and fear nothing.' And so they reached the lake.

In an instant the sheep were scattered all over the meadows, and the Prince placed his hawk on the tree, and his pipes on the grass, while he bade his greyhounds lie beside them. Then he rolled up his trousers and his sleeves, and waded into the water, calling:

'Dragon! Dragon! If you are not a coward, come forth, and let us have one more fight together.' And the dragon answered:

'I am waiting for you, O Prince,' and the next minute he reared himself out of the water, huge and horrible to see. Swiftly he drew near to the bank, and the Prince sprang to meet him, and they grasped each other round the body and fought till it was noon. And when the sun was at its hottest, the dragon cried:

'O Prince, let me but dip my burning head in the lake, and I will hurl you to the top of the sky.' But the Prince answered:

'Oh, ho! my good dragon, do not crow too soon! If the Emperor's daughter were only here, and she would kiss my forehead, I would throw you higher still.'

Hardly had he spoken, when the Princess, who had been listening, ran up and kissed him on the forehead. Then the Prince swung the dragon straight up into the clouds, and when he touched the earth again, he broke into a thousand pieces. Out of the pieces there sprang a wild boar and galloped away, but the Prince called his hounds to give chase, and they caught the boar and tore it to bits. Out of the pieces of the boar there sprang a hare, and in a moment the greyhounds were after it, and they caught it and killed it; and out of the hare there came a pigeon. Quickly the Prince let loose his hawk, which soared straight into the air, then swooped upon the bird and brought it to his master. The Prince cut open its body and found the sparrow inside, as the old woman had said.

'Now,' cried the Prince, holding the sparrow in his hand, 'now you shall tell me where I can find my brothers.'

'Do not hurt me,' answered the sparrow, 'and I will tell you with all my heart. Behind your father's castle stands a mill, and in the mill are three slender twigs. Cut off these twigs and strike their roots with them, and the iron door of a cellar will open. In the cellar you will find as many people, young and old, women and children, as would fill a kingdom, and among them are your brothers.'

By this time twilight had fallen, so the Prince washed himself in the lake, took the hawk on his shoulder and the pipes under his arm, and with his greyhounds before him and his flock behind him, marched gaily into the town, the Princess following them all, still trembling with fright. And so they passed through the streets, thronged with a wondering crowd, till they reached the castle.

Unknown to anyone, the Emperor had stolen out on horseback, and had hidden himself on the hill, where he could see all that happened. When all was over, and the power of the dragon was broken for ever, he rode quickly back to the castle, and was ready to receive the Prince with open arms, and to promise him his daughter to wife. The wedding took place with great splendour, and for a whole week the town was hung with coloured lamps, and tables were spread in the hall of the castle for all who chose to come and eat. And when the feast was over, the Prince told the Emperor and the people who he really was, and at this everyone rejoiced still more, and preparations were made for the Prince and Princess to return to their own kingdom, for the Prince was impatient to set his brothers free.

The first thing he did when he reached his native country was to hasten to the mill, where he found the three twigs as the sparrow had told him. The moment that he struck the root the iron door flew open, and from the cellar a countless multitude of men and women streamed forth. He bade them go one by one wheresoever they would, while he himself waited by the door till his brothers passed through. How delighted they were to meet again, and to hear all that the Prince had done to deliver them from their enchantment. And they went home with him and served him all the days of their lives, for they said that he only who had proved himself brave and faithful was fit to be a King.

Puddocky

THERE WAS once upon a time a poor woman who had one child, a fair young daughter, who was very fond of broccoli. Indeed, she would hardly eat anything else. Her poor mother hadn't enough money always to be buying this for her, but the child was so beautiful that she could refuse her nothing, and so she went every night to the garden of an old witch who lived near and stole great branches of the coveted vegetable, in order to satisfy her daughter.

This remarkable taste of the girl soon became known, and the theft was discovered. The witch called the girl's mother to her, and proposed that she should let her daughter come and live with her, and then she could eat as much broccoli as she liked. The mother was quite pleased with this suggestion, and so the girl took up her abode with the old witch.

One day three Princes, whom their father had sent abroad to travel, came to the town and perceived the beautiful girl combing and plaiting her long black hair at the window. In one moment each fell hopelessly in love with her, and longed ardently to have her for his wife; but hardly had they with one breath expressed their desire than, mad with jealousy, they drew their swords and all three set upon each other. The struggle was so violent and the noise so loud that the old witch heard it, and said at once, 'Of course that girl is at the bottom of all this.'

And when she had convinced herself that this was so, she stepped forward, and, full of wrath over the quarrels and feuds the maiden's beauty gave rise to, she cursed her and said, 'I wish you were an ugly toad, sitting under a bridge at the other end of the world.'

Hardly were the words out of her mouth than the girl was changed into a toad and vanished from their sight. The Princes, now that the cause of their dispute was removed, put up their swords, kissed each other affectionately, and returned to their father.

The King was growing old and feeble, and wished to yield his sceptre and crown in favour of one of his sons, but he couldn't make

up his mind which of the three he should appoint as his successor. He determined that fate should decide for him. So he called his three children to him and said, 'My dear sons, I am growing old, and am weary of reigning, but I can't make up my mind to which of you three I should yield my crown, for I love you all equally. At the same time I would like the best and cleverest of you to rule over my people. I have, therefore, determined to set you three tasks to do, and the one that performs them best shall be my heir. The first thing I shall ask you to do is to bring me a piece of linen a hundred yards long, so fine that it will go through a gold ring.' The sons bowed low, and, promising to do their best, they started on their journey without further delay.

The two elder brothers took many servants and carriages with them, but the youngest set out quite alone. In a short time they came to three cross-roads; two of them were gay and crowded, but the third was dark and lonely.

The two elder brothers chose the more frequented ways, but the youngest, bidding them farewell, set out on the lonely road.

Wherever fine linen was to be bought, there the two elder brothers hastened. They loaded their carriages with bales of the finest linen they could find and then returned home.

The youngest brother, on the other hand, went on his weary way for many days, and nowhere did he come across any linen that would have done. So he journeyed on, and his spirits sank with every step. At last he came to a bridge which stretched over a deep river flowing through a flat and marshy land. Before crossing the bridge he sat down on the banks of the stream and sighed dismally over his sad fate. Suddenly a misshapen toad crawled out of the swamp, and, sitting down opposite him, asked, 'What's the matter with you, my dear Prince?'

The Prince answered impatiently, 'There's not much good telling you, Puddocky, for you couldn't help me if I did.'

'Don't be too sure of that,' replied the toad; 'tell me your trouble and we'll see.'

Then the Prince became most confidential and told the little creature why he had been sent out of his father's kingdom.

'Prince, I will certainly help you,' said the toad, and, crawling back into her swamp, she returned dragging after her a piece of linen not bigger than a finger, which she laid before the Prince, saying, 'Take this home, and you'll see it will help you.'

The Prince had no wish to take such an insignificant bundle with him; but he didn't like to hurt Puddocky's feelings by refusing it, so he took up the packet, put it in his pocket, and bade the little toad farewell. Puddocky watched the Prince till he was out of sight and then crept back into the water.

The farther the Prince went the more he noticed that the pocket in which the little roll of linen lay became heavier, and in proportion his heart grew lighter. And so, greatly comforted, he returned to the Court of his father, and arrived home just at the same time as his brothers with their caravans. The King was so delighted to see them all again, and at once drew the ring from his finger and the trial began. In all the wagon-loads there was not one piece of linen the tenth part of which would go through the ring, and the two elder brothers, who had at first sneered at their youngest brother for return-ing with no baggage, began to feel rather small. But what were their feelings when he drew a bale of linen out of his pocket which in fineness, softness, and purity of colour was unsurpassable! The threads were hardly visible, and it went through the ring without the smallest difficulty, at the same time measuring a hundred yards quite correctly.

The father embraced his fortunate son, and commanded the rest of the linen to be thrown into the water; then, turning to his children, he said, 'Now, dear Princes, prepare yourselves for the second task. You must bring back a little dog that will go comfortably into a wal-nut-shell.'

The sons were all in despair over this demand, but as they each wished to win the crown, they determined to do their best, and after a very few days set out on their travels again.

At the cross-roads they separated once more. The youngest went by himself along his lonely way, but this time he felt much more cheerful. Hardly had he sat down under the bridge and heaved a sigh than Puddocky came out; and, sitting down opposite him, asked, 'What's wrong with you now, dear Prince?'

The Prince, who this time did not doubt the little toad's power to help him, told her his difficulty at once. 'Prince, I will help you,' said the toad again, and crawled back into her swamp as fast as her short little legs would carry her. She returned, dragging a hazel-nut behind her, which she laid at the Prince's feet and said, 'Take this nut home with you and tell your father to crack it very carefully, and you'll see then what will happen.' The Prince thanked her heartily and went back on his way in the best of spirits while the little puddock crept slowly back into the water.

When the youngest son got home he found his brothers had just arrived with great wagon-loads of little dogs of all sorts. The King had a walnut-shell ready, and the trial began; but not one of the dogs the two eldest sons had brought with them would in the least fit into the shell. When they had tried all their little dogs, the youngest son handed his father the hazel-nut, with a modest bow, and begged him to crack it carefully. Hardly had the old King done so than a lovely tiny dog sprang out of the nutshell, and ran about on the King's hand, wagging its tail and barking lustily at all the other little dogs. The joy of the Court was great. The father again embraced his fortunate son, commanded the rest of the small dogs to be disposed of, and once more addressed his sons. 'The two most difficult tasks have been performed. Now listen to the third and last: whoever brings the fairest wife home with him shall be my heir.'

This demand seemed so easy and agreeable and the reward was so great, that the Princes lost no time in setting forth on their travels. At the cross-roads the two elder brothers debated if they should go the same way as the youngest, but when they saw how dreary and deserted it looked they made up their minds that it would be impossible to find what they sought in these wilds, and so they stuck to their former paths.

The youngest was very depressed this time and said to himself, 'Anything else Puddocky could have helped me in, but this task is quite beyond her power. How could she ever find a beautiful wife for me? Her swamps are wide and empty, and no human beings dwell there; only frogs and toads and other creatures of that sort.' However, he sat down as usual under the bridge, and this time he sighed from the bottom of his heart.

In a few minutes the toad stood in front of him and asked, 'What's the matter with you now, my dear Prince?'

'Oh, Puddocky, this time you can't help me, for the task is beyond even your power,' replied the Prince.

'Still,' answered the toad, 'you may as well tell me your difficulty, for who knows but I mayn't be able to help you this time also.'

The Prince then told her the task they had been set to do. 'I'll help you right enough, my dear Prince,' said the little toad; 'just you go home, and I'll soon follow you.' With these words, Puddocky, with a spring quite unlike her usual slow movements, jumped into the water and disappeared.

The Prince rose up and went sadly on his way, for he didn't believe it possible that the little toad could really help him in his present difficulty. He had hardly gone a few steps when he heard a sound behind him, and, looking round, he saw a carriage made of cardboard, drawn by six big rats, coming towards him. Two hedgehogs rode in front as outriders, and on the box sat a fat mouse as coachman, and behind stood two little frogs as footmen. In the carriage itself sat Puddocky, who kissed her hand to the Prince out of the window as she passed by.

Sunk deep in thought over the fickleness of fortune that had granted him two of his wishes and now seemed about to deny him the last and best, the Prince hardly noticed the absurd equipage, and still less did he feel inclined to laugh at its comic appearance.

The carriage drove on in front of him for some time and then turned a corner. But what was his joy and surprise when suddenly, round the same corner, but coming towards him, there appeared a grand coach drawn by six splendid horses, with outriders, coachmen, footmen and other servants all in the most gorgeous liveries, and seated in the carriage was the most beautiful woman the Prince had ever seen, and in whom he at once recognised the dark-haired girl for whom his heart had formerly burned. The carriage stopped when it reached him, and the footmen sprang down and opened the door for him. He got in and sat down beside Puddocky, now the beautiful maiden, and told her how much he loved her.

And so he arrived at his father's capital, at the same moment as his brothers who had returned with many carriage-loads of beautiful women. But when they were all led before the King, the whole Court with one consent awarded the prize of beauty to Puddocky.

The old King was delighted, and embraced his thrice fortunate son and his new daughter-in-law tenderly, and appointed them as his successors to the throne. But he commanded the other women to be sent from the Court, except for the two his other sons chose as their brides. The youngest Prince then married Puddocky and took over the kingdom. He reigned long and happily with her, and if they aren't dead I suppose they are living still.

Rumpelstiltskin

THERE WAS once upon a time a poor miller who had a very beautiful daughter. Now it happened one day that he had an audience with the King, and in order to appear a person of some importance he told him that he had a daughter who could spin straw into gold.

'Now that's a talent worth having,' said the King to the miller. 'If your daughter is as clever as you say, bring her to my palace tomorrow, and I'll put her to the test.'

When the girl was brought to him he led her into a room full of straw, gave her a spinning-wheel and spindle, and said, 'Now set to work and spin all night till early dawn, and if by that time you haven't spun the straw into gold you shall die.' Then he closed the door behind him and left her alone inside.

So the poor miller's daughter sat down, and didn't know what in the world she was to do. She hadn't the least idea of how to spin straw into gold, and became at last so miserable that she began to cry.

Suddenly the door opened, and in stepped a tiny little man and said, 'Good-evening, Miss Miller-maid; why are you crying so bitterly?'

'Oh!' answered the girl, 'I have to spin straw into gold, and haven't a notion how it's done.'

'What will you give me if I spin it for you?' asked the manikin.

'My necklace,' replied the girl.

The little man took the necklace, sat himself down at the wheel, and whir, whir, whir, the wheel went round three times, and the bobbin was full. Then he put on another, and whir, whir, whir, the wheel went round three times, and the second too was full; and so it went on till the morning, when all the straw was spun away, and all the bobbins were full of gold.

As soon as the sun rose the King came, and when he perceived the gold he was astonished and delighted, but his heart was only the more filled with greed. He had the miller's daughter put into another room, much bigger than the first, and full of straw. He bade her, if she

valued her life, spin it all into gold before the following morning.

The girl didn't know what to do, and began to cry; then the door opened as before, and the tiny little man appeared and said, 'What'll you give me if I spin the straw into gold for you?'

'The ring from my finger,' answered the girl.

The manikin took the ring, and whir! round went the spinning-wheel again, and when morning broke he had spun all the straw into glittering gold.

The King was pleased beyond measure at the sight, but his greed for gold was still not satisfied, and he had the miller's daughter brought into a yet bigger room full of straw, and said, 'You must spin all this away in the night; but if you succeed this time you shall become my wife.'

'She's only a miller's daughter, it's true,' he thought; 'but I couldn't find a richer wife if I were to search the whole world over.'

When the girl was alone the little man appeared for the third time, and said, 'What'll you give me if I spin the straw for you once again?'

'I've nothing more to give,' answered the girl.

'Then promise me when you are Queen to give me your first child.'

'Who knows what mayn't happen before that?' thought the miller's daughter; and besides, she saw no other way out of it, so she promised the manikin what he demanded, and he set to work once more and spun the straw into gold. When the King came in the morning, and found everything as he had desired, he straightway made her his wife, and the miller's daughter became a Queen.

When a year had passed a beautiful son was born to her, and she thought no more of the little man, till all of a sudden one day he stepped into her room and said, 'Now give me what you promised.'

The Queen was in a great state, and offered the little man all the riches in her kingdom if he would only leave her the child. But the manikin said, 'No, a living creature is dearer to me than all the treasures in the world.'

Then the Queen began to cry and sob so bitterly that the little man was sorry for her, and said, 'I'll give you three days to guess my name, and if you find out in that time you may keep your child.'

Then the Queen pondered the whole night over all the names she had ever heard, and sent a messenger to scour the land, and to pick up far and near all the names he should come across. When the little man arrived on the following day she began with Kasper, Melchior, Belshazzar, and all the other names she knew, in a string, but at each one the manikin called out, 'That's not my name.'

The next day she sent to inquire the names of all the people in the neighbourhood, and had a long list of the most uncommon and extraordinary for the little man when he made his appearance. 'Is your name, perhaps Sheepshanks, Cruickshanks, Spindleshanks?' but he always replied, 'That's not my name.'

On the third day the messenger returned and announced, 'I have not been able to find any new names, but as I came upon a high hill round the corner of the wood, where the foxes and hares bid each other good night, I saw a little house, and in front of the house burned a fire, and round the fire danced the most grotesque little man, hopping on one leg and crying:

> "Tomorrow I brew, today I bake,
> And then the child away I'll take;
> For little deems my royal dame
> That Rumpelstiltskin is my name!" '

You may imagine the Queen's delight at hearing the name, and when the little man stepped in shortly afterwards and asked, 'Now my lady Queen, what's my name?' she asked first, 'Is your name Conrad?'

'No.'

'Is your name Harry?'

'No.'

'Is your name, perhaps, Rumpelstiltskin?'

'Some demon has told you that, some demon has told you that,' screamed the little man, and in his rage drove his right foot so far into the ground that it sank in up to his waist; then in a passion he seized the left foot with both hands and tore himself in two.

The Story of Hassebu

ONCE UPON a time there lived a poor woman who had only one child, a little son called Hassebu, who had a strange little birthmark on his chest. When he ceased to be a baby, and his mother thought it was time for him to learn to read, she sent him to school. And, after he had done with school, he was put into a shop to learn how to make clothes, and did not learn; and he was put to do silversmith's work, and did not learn; and whatsoever he was taught, he did not learn it. His mother never wished him to do anything he did not like, so she said, 'Well, stay at home, my son.' And he stayed at home, eating and sleeping.

One day the boy said to his mother, 'What was my father's business?'

'He was a very learned doctor,' answered she.

'Where, then, are his books?' asked Hassebu.

'Many, many days have passed, and I have thought nothing of them. But look inside and see if they are there.' So Hassebu looked, and saw they were eaten by insects, all but one book, which he took away to read.

He was sitting at home one morning poring over the medicine book, when some neighbours came by and said to his mother, 'Give us this boy, that we may go together to cut wood.' For wood-cutting was their trade, and they would load several donkeys with firewood, to sell in the town.

And his mother answered, 'Very well; tomorrow I will buy him a donkey, and you can all go together.'

So the donkey was bought, and the neighbours came, and they worked hard all day, and in the evening they brought the wood back into the town, and sold it for a good sum of money. And for six days they went and did the like, but on the seventh it rained, and the wood-cutters ran and took shelter in the rocks, all but Hassebu, who did not mind getting wet, and stayed where he was.

While he was sitting in the place where the wood-cutters had left

164

him, he took up a stone that lay near him, and idly dropped it on the ground. It rang with a hollow sound, and he called to his companions, and said, 'Come here and listen; the ground seems hollow!'

'Knock again!' cried they. And he knocked and listened.

'Let us dig,' said the boy. And they dug, and found a large pit like a well, filled with honey up to the brim.

'This is better than firewood,' said they; 'it will bring us more money. And as you have found it, Hassebu, it is you who must dip out the honey and give to us, and we will take it to the town and sell it, and will divide the money with you.'

The following day each man brought every bowl and vessel he could find at home, and Hassebu filled them all with honey. And this he did every day for three months.

At the end of that time the honey was very nearly finished, and there was only a little left, quite at the bottom, and that was very deep down, so deep that it seemed as if it must be right in the middle of the earth. Seeing this, the men said to Hassebu, 'We will put a rope under your arms, and let you down, so that you may scrape up all the honey that is left, and when you have done we will lower the rope again, and you shall make it fast, and we will draw you up.'

'Very well,' answered the boy, and he went down, and he scraped and scraped till there was not so much honey left as would cover the point of a needle. 'Now I am ready!' he cried; but they consulted together and said, 'Let us leave him there inside the pit, and take his share of the money, and we will tell his mother, "Your son was caught by a lion and carried off into the forest, and we tried to follow him, but could not." '

Then they arose and went into the town and told his mother as they had agreed, and she wept much and made her mourning for many months. And when the men were dividing the money, one said, 'Let us send a little to our friend's mother,' and they sent some to her; and every day one took her rice, and one oil; one took her meat, and one took her cloth, every day.

It did not take long for Hassebu to find out that his companions had left him to die in the pit, but he had a brave heart, and hoped that he might be able to find a way out for himself. So he at once began to explore the pit and found it ran back a long way underground.

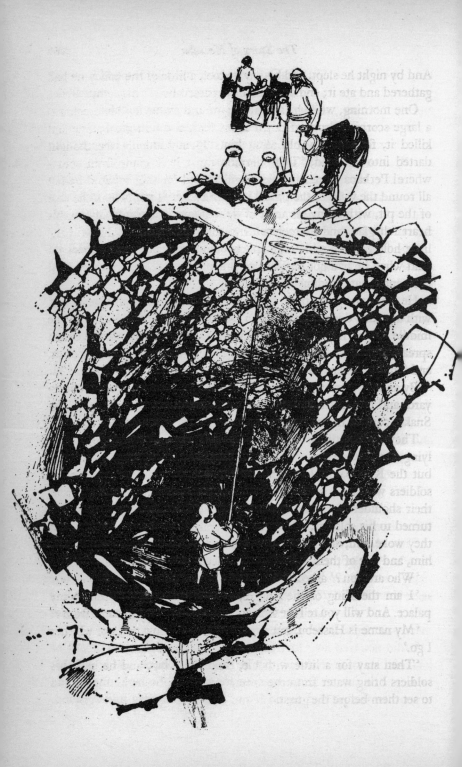

And by night he slept, and by day he took a little of the honey he had gathered and ate it; and so many days passed by.

One morning, while he was sitting on a rock having his breakfast, a large scorpion dropped down at his feet, and he took a stone and killed it, fearing it would sting him. Then suddenly the thought darted into his head, 'This scorpion must have come from somewhere! Perhaps there is a hole. I will go and look for it.' And he felt all round the walls of the pit till he found a very little hole in the roof of the pit, with a tiny glimmer of light at the far end of it. Then his heart felt glad, and he took out his knife and dug and dug, till the little hole became a big one, and he could wriggle himself through. And when he had got outside, he saw a large open space in front of him, and a path leading out of it.

He went along the path, on and on, till he reached a large house, with a golden door standing open. Inside was a great hall, and in the middle of the hall a throne set with precious stones and a couch spread with the softest cushions. And he went in and lay down on it, and fell fast asleep, for he had wandered far.

By and by there was a sound of people coming through the courtyard, and the measured tramp of soldiers. This was the King of the Snakes coming in state to his palace.

They entered the hall, but all stopped in surprise at finding a man lying on the King's own bed. The soldiers wished to kill him at once, but the King said, 'Leave him alone, put me on a chair,' and the soldiers who were carrying him knelt on the floor, and he slid from their shoulders on to a chair. When he was comfortably seated, he turned to his soldiers, and bade them wake the stranger gently. And they woke him, and Hassebu sat up and saw many snakes all round him, and one of them very beautiful, decked in royal robes.

'Who are you?' asked Hassebu.

'I am the King of the Snakes,' was the reply, 'and this is my palace. And will you tell me who you are, and where you come from?'

'My name is Hassebu, but whence I come I know not, nor whither I go.'

'Then stay for a little with me,' said the King, and he bade his soldiers bring water from the spring and fruits from the forest, and to set them before the guest.

For some weeks Hassebu rested and feasted in the palace of the King of the Snakes, and then he began to long for his mother and his own country. So he said to the King of the Snakes, 'Send me home, I pray.'

But the King of the Snakes answered, 'When you go home, you will do me evil!'

'I will do you no evil,' replied Hassebu; 'send me home, I pray.'

But the King said, 'I know it. If I send you home, you will come back and kill. I dare not do it.' But Hassebu begged so hard that at last the King said, 'Swear that when you get home you will not go to bathe where many people are gathered.' And Hassebu swore, and the King ordered his soldiers to take Hassebu in sight of his native city. Then he went straight to his mother's house, and the heart of his mother was glad.

Now the Sultan of the city was very ill, and all the wise men said that the only thing to cure him was the flesh of the King of the Snakes, and that the only man who could get it was a man with a strange mark on his chest. So the Vizier had set people to watch at the public baths, to see if such a man came there.

For three days Hassebu remembered his promise to the King of the Snakes, and did not go near the baths; then came a morning so hot he could hardly breathe, and he forgot all about it.

The moment he had slipped off his robe he was taken before the Vizier, who said to him, 'Lead us to the place where the King of the Snakes lives.'

'I do not know it!' answered he, but the Vizier did not believe him, and had him bound and beaten till his back was all torn.

Then Hassebu cried, 'Loose me, that I may take you.'

They went together a long way, till they reached the palace of the King of the Snakes.

And Hassebu said to the King, 'It was not I: look at my back and you will see how they drove me to it.'

'Who has beaten you like this?' asked the King.

'It was the Vizier,' replied Hassebu.

'Then I am already dead,' said the King sadly, 'but you must carry me there yourself.'

So Hassebu carried him. And on the way the King said, 'When I arrive, I shall be killed, and my flesh will be cooked. But take some of the water that I am boiled in, and put it in a bottle and lay it on one side. The Vizier will tell you to drink it, but be careful not to do so. Then take some more of the water, and drink it, and you will become a great physician, and the third supply you will give to the Sultan, and when the Vizier comes to you and asks, "Did you drink what I gave you?" you must answer, "I did, and this is for you," and he will drink it and die, and your soul will rest.'

And they went their way into the town, and all happened as the King of the Snakes had said.

And the Sultan loved Hassebu, who became a great physician, and cured many sick people. But all his life Hassebu kept in his heart the memory of the King of the Snakes.

The Three Brothers

THERE WAS once a man who had three sons, and no other possessions beyond the house in which he lived. Now the father loved his three sons equally, so that he could not make up his mind which of them should have the house after his death, because he did not wish to favour any one more than the others. And he did not want to sell the house, because it had belonged to his family for generations; otherwise he could have divided the money equally amongst them. At last an idea struck him, and he said to his sons, 'You must all go out into the world, and look about you, and each learn a trade, and then, when you return, whoever can produce the best masterpiece shall have the house.'

The sons were quite satisfied. The eldest wished to be a blacksmith, the second a barber, and the third a fencing-master. They appointed a time when they were to return home, and then they all set out.

It so happened that each found a good master, where he learnt all that was nececessary for his trade in the best possible way. The blacksmith had to shoe the King's horses, and thought to himself, 'Without doubt the house will be yours!' The barber shaved the highest in the kingdom, and he, too, made sure that the house would be his. The fencing-master received many a blow, but he set his teeth, and would not allow himself to be troubled by them, for he thought to himself, 'If you are afraid of a blow you will never get the house.'

When the appointed time had come the three brothers met once more, and they sat down and discussed the best opportunity of showing off their skill. Just then a hare came running across the field towards them. 'Look!' said the barber, 'here comes something in the nick of time!' He seized basin and soap, made a lather whilst the hare was approaching, and then, as it ran full tilt, shaved its moustaches, without cutting it or injuring a single hair on its body.

'I like that very much indeed,' said the father. 'Unless the others exert themselves to the utmost, the house will be yours.'

Soon after they saw a man driving a carriage furiously towards them. 'Now, father, you shall see what I can do!' said the blacksmith, and he sprang after the carriage, tore off the four shoes of the horse as it was going at the top of its speed, and shod it with four new ones without checking its pace.

'You are a clever fellow!' said the father, 'and know your trade as well as your brother. I really don't know to which of you I shall give the house.'

Then the third son said, 'Father, let me also show you something;' and, as it was beginning to rain, he drew his sword and swung it in cross cuts above his head, so that not a drop fell on him, and the rain fell heavier and heavier, till at last it was coming down like a waterspout, but he swung his sword faster and faster, and kept as dry as if he were under cover.

When the father saw this he was astonished, and said, 'You have produced the greatest masterpiece: the house is yours.'

Both the other brothers were quite satisfied, and praised him too, and as they were so fond of each other they all three remained at home and plied their trades; and as they were so experienced and skilful they earned a great deal of money. So they lived happily together till they were quite old, and when one was taken ill and died the two others were so deeply grieved that they also fell ill and died too. And so, because they had all been so clever, and so fond of each other, they were all laid in one grave.

The Three Dogs

THERE WAS once upon a time a shepherd who had two children, a son and a daughter. When he was on his death-bed he turned to them and said, 'I have nothing to leave you but three sheep and a small house; divide them between you, as you like, but don't quarrel over them whatever you do.'

When the shepherd was dead, the brother asked his sister which she would like best, the sheep or the little house; and when she had chosen the house he said, 'Then I'll take the sheep and go out to seek my fortune in the wide world. I don't see why I shouldn't be as lucky as many another who has set out on the same search, and it wasn't for nothing that I was born on a Sunday.'

And so he started on his travels, driving his three sheep in front of him, and for a long time it seemed as if fortune didn't mean to favour him at all. One day he was sitting disconsolately at a cross-road, when a man suddenly appeared before him with three black dogs, each one bigger than the other.

'Hullo, my fine fellow,' said the man, 'I see you have three fat sheep. I'll tell you what, if you'll give them to me, I'll give you my three dogs.'

In spite of his sadness, the youth smiled and replied, 'What would I do with your dogs? My sheep at least feed themselves, but I should have to find food for the dogs.'

'My dogs are not like other dogs,' said the stranger; 'they will feed you instead of you them, and will make your fortune. The smallest one is called "Salt", and will bring you food whenever you wish; the second is called "Pepper", and will tear anyone to pieces who offers to hurt you; and the great one is called "Mustard", and is so powerful that it can break iron or steel with its teeth.'

The shepherd at last let himself be persuaded, and gave the stranger his sheep. In order to test the truth of his statement about the dogs, he said at once, 'Salt, I am hungry,' and before the words were out of his mouth the dog had disappeared, and returned in a

few minutes with a large basket of the most delicious food. Then the youth congratulated himself on the bargain he had made, and continued his journey in the best of spirits.

One day he met a carriage and pair, all draped in black; even the horses were covered with black trappings, and the coachman was clothed in crape from top to toe. Inside the carriage sat a beautiful girl in a black dress crying bitterly. The horses advanced slowly and mournfully, with their heads bent to the ground.

'Coachman, what's the meaning of all this grief?' asked the shepherd.

At first the coachman wouldn't say anything, but when the youth pressed him he told him that a huge dragon dwelt in the neighbourhood, and required yearly the sacrifice of a beautiful maiden. This year the lot had fallen on the King's daughter, and the whole country was filled with woe and lamentation in consequence.

The shepherd felt very sorry for the lovely maiden, and determined to follow the carriage. In a little it halted at the foot of a high mountain. The girl got out, and walked slowly and sadly to meet her terrible fate. The coachman perceived that the shepherd wished to follow her, and warned him not to do so if he valued his life; but the shepherd wouldn't listen to his advice. When they had climbed about half-way up the hill they saw a terrible-looking monster with the body of a snake, and with huge wings and claws, coming towards them, breathing forth flames of fire, and preparing to seize its victim. Then the shepherd called, 'Pepper, come to the rescue,' and the second dog set upon the dragon, and after a fierce struggle bit it so sharply in the neck that the monster rolled over, and in a few moments breathed its last. Then the dog ate up the body, all except its two front teeth, which the shepherd picked up and put in his pocket.

The Princess was quite overcome with terror and joy, and fell fainting at the feet of her deliverer. When she recovered her consciousness she begged the shepherd to return with her to her father, who would reward him richly. But the youth answered that he wanted to see something of the world, and that he would return again in three years, and nothing would make him change this resolve. The Princess seated herself once more in her carriage, and, bidding each other farewell, she and the shepherd separated, she to return home, and he to see the world.

But while the Princess was driving over a bridge the carriage suddenly stood still, and the coachman turned round to her and said, 'Your deliverer has gone, and doesn't thank you for your gratitude. It would be nice of you to make a poor fellow happy; therefore you may tell your father that it was I who slew the dragon, and if you refuse to, I will throw you into the river, and no one will be any the wiser, for they will think the dragon has devoured you.'

The maiden was in a dreadful state when she heard these words; but there was nothing for her to do but to swear that she would give out the coachman as her deliverer, and not divulge the secret to anyone. So they returned to the capital, and everyone was delighted when they saw the Princess had returned unharmed; the black flags were taken down from all the palace towers, and gay-coloured ones put up in their place, and the King embraced his daughter and her supposed rescuer with tears of joy, and, turning to the coachman, he said, 'You have not only saved the life of my child, but you have also freed the country from a terrible scourge; therefore, it is only fitting that you should be richly rewarded. Take, therefore, my daughter for your wife; but as she is still so young, do not let the marriage be celebrated for another year.'

The coachman thanked the King for his graciousness, and was then led away to be richly dressed and instructed in all the arts and graces that befitted his new position. But the poor Princess wept bitterly, though she did not dare to confide her grief to anyone. When the year was over, she begged so hard for another year's respite that it was granted to her. But this year passed also, and she threw herself at her father's feet, and begged so piteously for one more year that the King's heart was melted, and he yielded to her request, much to the Princess's joy, for she knew that her real deliverer would appear at the end of the third year. And so the year passed away like the other two, and the wedding-day was fixed, and all the people were prepared to feast and make merry.

But on the wedding-day it happened that a stranger came to the town with three black dogs. He asked what the meaning of all the feasting and fuss was, and they told him that the King's daughter was just going to be married to the man who had slain the terrible dragon. The stranger at once denounced the coachman as a liar; but no one would listen to him, and he was seized and thrown into a cell with iron doors.

While he was lying on his straw pallet, pondering mournfully on his fate, he thought he heard the low whining of his dogs outside; then an idea dawned on him, and he called out as loudly as he could, 'Mustard, come to my help,' and in a second he saw the paws of his biggest dog at the window of his cell, and before he could count two the creature had bitten through the iron bars and stood beside him. Then they both let themselves out of the prison by the window, and the poor youth was free once more, though he felt very sad when he thought that another was to enjoy the reward that rightfully belonged to him. He felt hungry too, so he called his dog Salt, and asked him to bring home some food. The faithful creature trotted off, and soon returned with a table-napkin full of the most delicious food, and the napkin itself was embroidered with a kingly crown.

The King had just seated himself at the wedding-feast with all his Court, when the dog appeared and licked the Princess's hand in an appealing manner. With a joyful start she recognised the beast, and bound her own table-napkin round his neck. Then she plucked up her courage and told her father the whole story. The King at once sent a servant to follow the dog, and in a short time the stranger was led into the King's presence. The former coachman grew as white as a sheet when he saw the shepherd, and, falling on his knees, begged for mercy and pardon. The Princess recognised her deliverer at once, and did not need the proof of the two dragon's teeth which he drew from his pocket. The coachman was thrown into a dark dungeon, and the shepherd took his place at the Princess's side, and this time, you may be sure, she did not beg for the wedding to be put off

The young couple lived for some time in great peace and happiness, when suddenly one day the former shepherd bethought himself of his poor sister and expressed a wish to see her again, and to let her share in his good fortune. So they sent a carriage to fetch her, and soon she arrived at the Court, and found herself once more in her brother's arms. Then one of the dogs spoke and said, 'Our task is done; you have no more need of us. We only waited to see that you did not forget your sister in your prosperity.' And with these words the three dogs became birds and flew away into the heavens.

The Three Dwarfs

THERE WAS once upon a time a man who lost his wife, and a woman who lost her husband; and the man had a daughter and so had the woman. The two girls were great friends and used often to play together. One day the woman turned to the man's daughter and said:

'Go and tell your father that I will marry him, and then you shall wash in milk and drink wine, but my own daughter shall wash in water and drink it too.'

The girl went straight home and told her father what the woman had said.

'What am I to do?' he answered. 'Marriage is either a success or it is a failure.'

At last, being of an undecided character and not being able to make up his mind, he took off his boot, and handing it to his daughter, said:

'Take this boot which has a hole in the sole, hang it up on a nail in the hayloft, and pour water into it. If it holds water I will marry again, but if doesn't I won't.' The girl did as she was bid, but the water drew the hole together and the boot filled up to the very top. So she went and told her father the result. He got up and went to see for himself, and when he saw that it was true and no mistake, he accepted his fate, proposed to the widow, and they were married at once.

On the morning after the wedding, when the two girls awoke, milk was standing for the man's daughter to wash in and wine for her to drink; but for the woman's daughter, only water to wash in and only water to drink. On the second morning, water to wash in and water to drink was standing for the man's daughter as well. And on the third morning, water to wash in and water to drink was standing for the man's daughter, and milk to wash in and wine to drink for the woman's daughter; and so it continued ever after. The woman hated her stepdaughter from the bottom of her heart, and did all she could to make her life miserable. She was as jealous as she could possibly be, because the girl was so beautiful and charming, while her own daughter was both ugly and repulsive.

One winter's day when there was a hard frost, and mountain and valley were covered with snow, the woman made a dress of paper, and calling the girl to her said, 'There, put on this dress and go out into the wood and fetch me a basket of strawberries!'

'Now Heaven help us,' replied her stepdaughter; 'strawberries don't grow in winter; the earth is all frozen and the snow has covered up everything; and why send me in a paper dress? It is so cold outside that one's very breath freezes; and the wind will whistle through my dress, and the brambles tear it from my body.'

'How dare you contradict me!' said her stepmother; 'be off with you at once, and don't show your face again till you have filled the basket with strawberries.'

Then she gave her a hard crust of bread, saying, 'That will be enough for you today,' and she thought to herself, 'The girl will certainly perish of hunger and cold outside, and I shan't be bothered with her any more.'

The girl was so obedient that she put on the paper dress and set out with her little basket. There was nothing but snow far and near, and not a green blade of grass to be seen anywhere. When she came to the wood she saw a little house, and out of it peeped three little dwarfs. She wished them good-day, and knocked modestly at the door. They called out to her to enter, so she stepped in and sat down on a seat by the fire, wishing to warm herself and eat her breakfast. The dwarfs said at once, 'Give us some of your food!'

'Gladly,' she said, and breaking her crust in two, she gave them the half.

Then they asked her what she was doing in the depths of winter in her thin dress.

'Oh,' she answered, 'I have been sent to get a basketful of strawberries, and I daren't show my face again at home till I bring them with me.'

When she had finished her bread they gave her a broom and told her to sweep away the snow from the back door. As soon as she left the room to do so, the three little men consulted what they should give her as a reward for being so sweet and good, and for sharing her last crust with them.

The first said, 'Every day she shall grow prettier.'

The second, 'Every time she opens her mouth a piece of gold shall fall out.'

And the third, 'A king shall come and marry her.'

The girl in the meantime was doing as the dwarfs had bidden her, and was sweeping the snow away from the back door, and what do you think she found there? Heaps of fine ripe strawberries that showed out dark red against the white snow. She joyfully picked enough to fill her basket, thanked the little men for their kindness, shook hands with them, and ran home to bring her stepmother what she had asked for. When she walked in and said, 'Good-evening,' a piece of gold fell out of her mouth. Then she told what had happened to her in the wood, and at every word pieces of gold dropped from her mouth, so that the room was soon covered with them.

'She's surely more money than wit to throw gold about like that,' said her stepsister, but in her secret heart she was very jealous, and determined that she too would go to the wood and look for strawberries. But her mother refused to let her go, saying, 'My dear child, it is far too cold; you might freeze to death.'

The girl, however, left her no peace, so the woman was forced at last to give in, but she insisted that her daughter put on a beautiful fur cloak, and she gave her bread and butter and cakes to eat on the way.

The girl went straight to the little house in the wood, and as before the three little men were looking out of the window. She took no notice of them, and without as much as 'By your leave,' or 'With your leave,' she flounced into the room, sat herself down at the fire, and began to eat her bread and butter and cakes.

'Give us some,' cried the dwarfs.

But she answered, 'No, I won't, it's hardly enough for myself; so catch me giving you any.'

When she had finished eating they said, 'There's a broom for you, go and clear up our back door.'

'I'll see myself farther,' she answered rudely. 'Do it yourselves; I'm not your servant.'

When she saw that they did not mean to give her anything, she left the house in no amiable frame of mind. Then the three little men consulted what they should do to her, because she was so rude and had as well such an evil, covetous heart, that she grudged everybody their good fortune.

The first said, 'She shall grow uglier every day.'

The second, 'Every time she speaks a toad shall jump out of her mouth.'

And the third, 'She shall die a most miserable death.'

The girl searched for strawberries, but she found none, and returned home in a very bad temper. When she opened her mouth to tell her mother what had befallen her in the wood, a toad jumped out, so that everyone was quite disgusted with her.

Then her stepmother was more furious than ever, and did nothing but plot mischief against the man's daughter, who was daily growing more and more beautiful. At last, one day the wicked woman took a large pot, put it on the fire and boiled some yarn in it. When it was well scalded she hung it round the poor girl's shoulder, and giving her an axe, she bade her break a hole in the frozen river, and rinse the yarn in it. Her stepdaughter obeyed as usual, and went and broke a hole in the ice. When she was in the act of wringing out the yarn a magnificent carriage drove by, and it was the King who sat inside. The carriage stood still, and the King asked her:

'My child, who are you, and what in the wide world are you doing here?'

'I am only a poor girl,' she answered, 'and am rinsing out my yarn in the river.' Then the King was sorry for her, and when he saw how beautiful she was he said, 'Will you come away with me?'

'Most gladly,' she replied, for she knew how willingly she would leave her stepmother and stepsister, and how glad they would be to be rid of her.

So she stepped into the carriage and drove away with the King, and when they reached his palace the wedding was celebrated with much splendour. So all turned out just as the three little dwarfs had said.

After a year the Queen gave birth to a little son. When her stepmother heard of her good fortune she came to the palace with her daughter by way of paying a call, and took up her abode there. Now one day, when the King was out and nobody else near, the bad woman took the Queen by her head, and the daughter took her by her heels, and they dragged her from her bed, and flung her out of the window into the stream which flowed beneath it. Then the step-mother laid her ugly daughter in the Queen's place, and covered her up with the bed-clothes, so that nothing of her was seen. When the King came home and wished to speak to his wife the woman called out:

'Quietly, quietly! this will never do; your wife is very ill, you must let her rest all today.' The King suspected no evil, and didn't come again till next morning. When he spoke to his wife and she answered him, instead of the usual piece of gold a toad jumped out of her mouth. Then he asked what it meant, and the old woman told him it was nothing but weakness, and that she would soon be all right again.

But that same evening the scullion noticed a duck swimming up the gutter, saying as it passed:

> 'What does the King, I pray you tell,
> Is he awake or sleeps he well?'

and receiving no reply, it continued:

> 'And all my guests, are they asleep?'

and the scullion answered:

> 'Yes, one and all they slumber deep.'

Then the duck went on:

> 'And what about my baby dear?'

and he answered:

> 'Oh, it sleeps soundly, never fear.'

Then the duck assumed the Queen's shape, went up to the child's room, tucked him up comfortably in his cradle, and then swam back down the gutter again, in the likeness of a duck. This was repeated for two nights, and on the third night the duck said to the scullion:

'Go and tell the King to swing his sword three times over me on the threshold.'

The scullion did as the creature bade him, and the King came with his sword and swung it three times over the bird, and lo and behold! his wife stood before him once more, alive, and as blooming as ever. The King rejoiced greatly, but he kept the Queen in hiding till the Sunday on which the child was to be christened. After the christening he said:

'What punishment does that person deserve who drags another out of bed, and throws him or her, as the case may be, into the water?'

Then the wicked old stepmother answered:

'No better fate than to be put into a barrel lined with sharp nails, and to be rolled in it down the hill into the water.'

'You have pronounced your own doom,' said the King; and he ordered a barrel to be made lined with sharp nails, and in it he put the bad old woman and her daughter. Then it was fastened down securely, and the barrel was rolled down the hill till it fell into the river.

The Three Little Pigs

THERE WAS once upon a time a pig who lived with her three children in a large, comfortable, old-fashioned farmyard. The eldest of the little pigs was called Browny, the second Whitey, and the youngest and best-looking Blacky. Now Browny was a very dirty little pig, and I am sorry to say spent most of his time rolling and wallowing about in the mud. He was never so happy as on a wet day, when the mud in the farmyard got soft, and thick, and slab. Then he would steal away from his mother's side, and finding the muddiest place in the yard, would roll about in it and thoroughly enjoy himself. His mother often found fault with him for this, and would shake her head sadly and say, 'Ah, Browny! some day you will be sorry that you did not obey your old mother.' But no words of advice or warning could cure Browny of his bad habits.

Whitey was quite a clever little pig, but she was greedy. She was always thinking of her food, and looking forward to her dinner; and when the farm girl was seen carrying the pails across the yard, she would rise up on her hind legs and dance and caper with excitement. As soon as the food was poured into the trough she jostled Blacky and Browny out of the way in her eagerness to get the best and biggest bits for herself. Her mother often scolded her for her selfishness, and told her that some day she would suffer for being so greedy and grabbing.

Blacky was a good, nice little pig, neither dirty nor greedy. He had nice dainty ways (for a pig), and his skin was always as smooth and shining as black satin. He was much cleverer than Browny and Whitey, and his mother's heart used to swell with pride when she heard the farmer's friends say to each other that some day the little black fellow would be a prize pig.

Now the time came when the mother pig felt old and feeble and near her end. One day she called the three little pigs round her and said:

'My children, I feel that I am growing old and weak, and that I

185

shall not live long. Before I die I should like to build a house for each of you, as this dear old sty in which we have lived so happily will be given to a new family of pigs, and you will have to turn out. Now, Browny, what sort of a house would you like to have?'

'A house of mud,' replied Browny, looking longingly at a wet puddle in the corner of the yard.

'And you, Whitey?' said the mother pig in rather a sad voice, for she was disappointed that Browny had made so foolish a choice.

'A house of cabbage,' answered Whitey, with her mouth full, and scarcely raising her snout out of the trough in which she was grubbing for some potato-parings.

'Foolish, foolish child!' said the mother pig, looking quite distressed. 'And you, Blacky?' turning to her youngest son, 'what sort of a house shall I order for you?'

'A house of brick, please mother, as it will be warm in winter, and cool in summer, and safe all the year round.'

'That is a sensible little pig,' replied his mother, looking fondly at him. 'I will see that the three houses are got ready at once. And now one last piece of advice.

'You have heard me talk of our old enemy the fox. When he hears that I am dead, he is sure to try and get hold of you, to carry you off to his den. He is very sly and will no doubt disguise himself, and pretend to be a friend, but you must promise me not to let him enter your houses on any pretext whatever.'

And the little pigs readily promised, for they had always had a great fear of the fox, of whom they had heard many terrible tales. A short time afterwards the old pig died, and the little pigs went to live in their own houses.

Browny was quite delighted with his soft mud walls and with the clay floor, which soon looked like nothing but a big mud pie. But that was what Browny enjoyed, and he was as happy as possible, rolling about all day and making himself in such a mess. One day, as he was lying half asleep in the mud, he heard a soft knock at his door, and a gentle voice said:

'May I come in, Master Browny? I want to see your beautiful new house.'

'Who are you?' said Browny, starting up in great fright, for though the voice sounded gentle, he felt sure it was a feigned voice, and he feared it was the fox.

'I am a friend come to call on you,' answered the voice.

'No, no,' replied Browny, 'I don't believe you are a friend. You are the wicked fox, against whom our mother warned us. I won't let you in.'

'Oho! Is that the way you answer me?' said the fox, speaking very roughly in his natural voice. 'We shall soon see who is master here,' and with his paws he set to work and scraped a large hole in the soft mud walls. A moment later he had jumped through it, and catching Browny by the neck, flung him on his shoulders and trotted off with him to his den.

The next day, as Whitey was munching a few leaves of cabbage out of the corner of her house, the fox stole up to her door, determined to carry her off to join her brother in his den. He began speaking to her in the same feigned gentle voice in which he had spoken to Browny; but it frightened her very much when he said:

'I am a friend come to visit you, and to have some of your good cabbage for my dinner.'

'Please don't touch it,' cried Whitey in great distress. 'The cabbages are the walls of my house, and if you eat them you will make a hole, and the wind and rain will come in and give me a cold. Do go away; I am sure you are not a friend, but our wicked enemy the fox.' And poor Whitey began to whine and to whimper, and to wish that she had not been such a greedy little pig, and had chosen a more solid material than cabbages for her house. But it was too late now, and in another minute the fox had eaten his way through the cabbage walls, and had caught the trembling, shivering Whitey, and carried her off to his den.

The next day the fox started off for Blacky's house, because he had made up his mind that he would get the three little pigs together in his den, and then kill them, and invite all his friends to a feast. But when he reached the brick house, he found that the door was bolted and barred, so in his sly manner he began, 'Do let me in, dear Blacky. I have brought you a present of some eggs that I picked up in a farm-yard on my way here.'

'No, no, Mister Fox,' replied Blacky, 'I am not going to open my door to you. I know your cunning ways. You have carried off Browny and Whitey, but you are not going to get me.'

At this the fox was so angry that he dashed with all his force against the wall, and tried to knock it down. But it was too strong and well-built; and though the fox scraped and tore at the bricks with his paws he only hurt himself, and at last he had to give it up, and limp away with his fore-paws all bleeding and sore.

'Never mind!' he cried angrily as he went off, 'I'll catch you another day, see if I don't, and won't I grind your bones to powder when I have got you in my den!' and he snarled fiercely and showed his teeth.

Next day Blacky had to go into the neighbouring town to do some marketing and to buy a big kettle. As he was walking home with it slung over his shoulder, he heard a sound of steps stealthily creeping after him. For a moment his heart stood still with fear, and then a happy thought came to him. He had just reached the top of a hill, and could see his own little house nestling at the foot of it among the trees. In a moment he had snatched the lid off the kettle and had jumped in himself. Coiling himself round he lay quite snug in the bottom of the kettle, while with his fore-leg he managed to put the lid on, so that he was entirely hidden. With a little kick from the inside he started the kettle off, and down the hill it rolled full tilt; and when the fox came up, all that he saw was a large black kettle spinning over the ground at a great pace. Very much disappointed, he was just going to turn away, when he saw the kettle stop close to the little brick house, and a moment later Blacky jumped out of it and escaped with the kettle into the house, when he barred and bolted the door, and put the shutter up over the window.

'Oho!' exclaimed the fox to himself, 'you think you will escape me that way, do you? We shall soon see about that, my friend,' and very quietly and stealthily he prowled round the house looking for some way to climb on to the roof.

In the meantime Blacky had filled the kettle with water, and having put it on the fire, sat down quietly waiting for it to boil. Just as the kettle was beginning to sing, and steam to come out of the spout, he heard a sound like a soft, muffled step, patter, patter, patter overhead, and the next moment the fox's head and fore-paws were seen coming down the chimney. But Blacky very wisely had not put the lid on the kettle, and, with a yelp of pain, the fox fell into the boiling water, and before he could escape, Blacky had popped the lid on, and the fox was scalded to death.

As soon as he was sure that their wicked enemy was really dead, and could do them no further harm, Blacky started off to rescue Browny and Whitey. As he approached the den he heard piteous grunts and squeals from his poor little brother and sister who lived in constant terror of the fox killing and eating them. But when they saw Blacky appear at the entrance to the den their joy knew no bounds. He quickly found a sharp stone and cut the cords by which they were tied to a stake in the ground, and then all three started off together for Blacky's house, where they lived happily ever after; and Browny quite gave up rolling in the mud, and Whitey ceased to be greedy, for they never forgot how nearly these faults had brought them to an untimely end.

The Three Princesses of Whiteland

THERE WAS once upon a time a fisherman, who lived hard by a palace and fished for the King's table. One day he was out fishing, but caught nothing at all. Let him do what he might with rod and line, there was never even so much as a sprat on his hook; but when day was well nigh over, a head rose up out of the water, and said, 'If you will give me what your wife shows you when you go home, you shall catch fish enough.'

So the man said 'Yes' in a moment, and then he caught fish in plenty; but when he got home at night, and his wife showed him the baby which had just been born, and fell a-weeping and wailing when he told her of the promise which he had given, he was very unhappy.

All this was soon told to the King up at the palace, and when he heard what sorrow the woman was in, and the reason of it, he said that he himself would take the child and see if he could not save it. The baby was a boy, and the King took him at once and brought him up as his own son until the lad grew up. Then one day the lad begged to have leave to go out with his father to fish; he had a strong desire to do this, he said. The King was very unwilling to permit it, but at last the lad got leave. He stayed with his father, and all went prosperously and well with them the whole day, until they came back to land in the evening. Then the lad found that he had lost his pocket-handkerchief, and would go out in the boat after it; but no sooner had he got into the boat than it began to move off with him so quickly that the water foamed all round about, and all that the lad did to try to keep the boat back with the oars was done to no purpose, for it went on and on the whole night through, and at last he came to a white strand that lay far, far away. There he landed, and when he had walked on for some distance he met an old man with a long white beard.

'What is the name of this country?' said the youth.

'Whiteland,' answered the man, and then he begged the youth to tell him whence he came and what he was doing, and the youth did so.

'Well, then,' said the man, 'if you walk on farther along the sea-shore here, you will come to three Princesses who are standing in the earth so that their heads alone are out of it. Then the first of them will call you – she is the eldest – and will beg you very prettily to come to her and help her, and the second will do the same, but you must not go near either of them. Hurry past, as if you neither saw nor heard them; but you shall go to the third and do what she bids you; it will bring you good fortune.'

When the youth came to the first Princess, she called to him and begged him to come to her very prettily, but he walked on as if he did not even see her, and he passed by the second in the same way, but he went up to the third.

'If thou wilt do what I tell thee, thou shalt choose among us three,' said the Princess.

So the lad said that he was most willing, and she told him that three trolls had planted them all three there in the earth, but that formerly they had dwelt in the castle which he could see at some distance in the wood.

'Now,' she said, 'thou shalt go into the castle, and let the trolls beat thee one night for each of us, and if thou canst but endure that, thou wilt set us free.'

'Yes,' answered the lad, 'I will certainly try to do so.'

'When thou goest in,' continued the Princess, 'two lions will stand by the doorway, but if thou only goest straight between them they will do thee no harm; go straight forward into a small dark chamber; there thou shalt lie down. Then the troll will come and beat thee, but thou shalt take the flask which is hanging on the wall, and anoint thyself wheresoever he has wounded thee, after which thou shalt be as well as before. Then lay hold of the sword which is hanging by the side of the flask, and smite the troll dead!'

So he did what the Princess had told him. He walked straight in between the lions just as if he did not see them, and then into the small chamber, and lay down on the bed.

The first night a troll came with three heads and three rods, and beat the lad most unmercifully; but he held out until the troll was done with him, and then he took the flask and rubbed himself. Having done this, he grasped the sword and smote the troll dead.

In the morning when he went to the sea-shore the Princesses were out of the earth as far as their waists.

The next night everything happened in the same way, but the troll who came then had six heads and six rods, and he beat him much more severely than the first had done, but when the lad went out of doors next morning, the Princesses were out of the earth as far as their knees.

On the third night a troll came who had nine heads and nine rods, and he struck the lad and flogged him so long, that at last he swooned away; so the troll took him up and flung him against the wall, and this made the flask of ointment fall down, and it splashed all over him, and he became as well as ever again, and filled with strength.

Then, without loss of time, he grasped the sword and struck the troll dead, and in the morning when he went out of the castle the Princesses were standing there entirely out of the earth. So he took the youngest for his Queen, and lived with her very happily for a long time.

At last, however, he took a fancy to go home for a short time to see his parents. His Queen did not like this, but when his longing grew so great that he told her he must and would go, she said to him:

'One thing shalt thou promise me, and that is, to do what thy father bids thee, but not what thy mother bids thee,' and this he promised.

So she gave him a ring, which enabled him who wore it to obtain two wishes.

He wished himself at home, and instantly found himself there; but his parents were so amazed at the splendour of his apparel that their wonder never ceased.

When he had been at home for some days his mother wanted him to go up to the palace, to show the King what a great man he had become.

The father said, 'No; he must not do that, for if he does we shall have no more delight in him this time;' but he spoke in vain, for the mother begged and prayed until at last the son went as his mother bade him.

When he arrived there he was more splendid, both in raiment and in all else, than the King, who did not like it, and said:

'Well, you can see what kind of Queen mine is, but I can't see yours. I do not believe you have such a pretty Queen as I have.'

'Would to heaven she were standing here, and then you would be able to see!' said the young King, and in an instant she was standing there.

But she was very sorrowful, and said to him, 'Why didst thou not remember my words, and listen only to what thy father said? Now must I go home again at once, and thou hast wasted both thy wishes.'

Then she tied a ring in his hair, which had her name upon it, and wished herself at home again.

And now the young King was deeply afflicted, and day out and day in went about thinking of naught else but how to get back again to his Queen. 'I will try to see if there is any place where I can learn how to find Whiteland,' he thought, and journeyed forth out into the world.

When he had gone some distance he came to a mountain, where he met a man who was lord over all the beasts in the forest – for they all came to him when he blew upon a horn. So the King asked where Whiteland was.

'I do not know that,' he answered, 'but I will ask my beasts.' Then he blew his horn and inquired whether any of them knew where Whiteland lay, but there was not one who knew that.

So the man gave him a pair of snow shoes. 'When you have these on,' he said, 'you will come to my brother, who lives hundreds of miles from here; he is lord over all the birds in the air – ask him. When you have got there, just turn the shoes so that the toes point this way, and then they will come home again of their own accord.'

When the King arrived there he turned the shoes as the lord of the beasts had bidden him, and they went back.

And now he once more asked after Whiteland, and the man summoned all the birds together, and inquired if any of them knew where Whiteland lay. No, none knew this. Long after the others there came an old eagle. He had been absent ten whole years, but he too knew no more than the rest.

'Well, well,' said the man, 'then you shall have the loan of a pair of snow shoes of mine. When you wear them you will get to my brother, who lives hundreds of miles from here. He is lord of all the fish in the sea – you can ask him. But do not forget to turn the shoes round.'

The King thanked him, put on the shoes, and when he had got to him who was lord of all the fish in the sea, he turned the snow shoes round, and back they went just as the others had gone, and he asked once more where Whiteland was.

The man called the fish together with his horn, but none of them knew anything about it. At last came an old, old pike, which he had great difficulty in calling home, it was such a great way off.

When he asked the pike, it said, 'Yes, Whiteland is well known to me, for I have been cook there these ten years. Tomorrow morning I have to go back there, for now the Queen, whose King is staying away, is to marry someone else.'

'If that be the case I will give you a piece of advice,' said the man. 'Not far from here on a moor stand three brothers, who have stood there a hundred years fighting for a hat, a cloak, and a pair of boots. If anyone has these three things he can make himself invisible, and if he desires to go to any place, he has but to wish and he is there. You can tell them you wish first to try these things, and that then you will be able to decide who is to have them.'

So the King thanked him and went, and did what he had said.

'What is this that you are standing fighting about for ever and ever?' said he to the brothers; 'let me make a trial of these things, and then I will judge between you.'

They willingly consented to this; but when he had got the hat, the cloak, and the boots, he said, 'Next time we meet you shall have my decision,' and hereupon he wished himself away.

While he was going quickly through the air he came up with the North Wind.

'And where may you be going?' said the North Wind.

'To Whiteland,' said the King, and then he related what had happened to him.

'Well,' said the North Wind, 'you can easily go faster than I can, for I have to puff and blow into every corner; but when you get there, place yourself on the stairs by the side of the door, and then I will come blustering in as if I wanted to blow down the whole castle, and when the Prince who is to have your Queen comes out to see what is

astir, just take him by the throat and fling him out, and then I will
see if I can carry him away from Court.'

As the North Wind had said, so did the King. He stood on the
stairs, and when the North Wind came howling and roaring, and
battered the roof and walls of the castle till they shook again, the
Prince went out to see what was the matter; but as soon as he came
the King took him by the neck and flung him out, and then the North
Wind laid hold of him and carried him off. And when he was rid of
him the King went into the castle. At first the Queen did not know
him, because he had grown so thin and pale from having travelled so
long and so sorrowfully; but when she saw her ring she was heartily
glad, and then the rightful wedding feast was held in such a way that
it was talked about far and wide.

The Three Robes

LONG, LONG ago, a King and Queen reigned over a large and powerful country. What their names were nobody knows, but their son was called Sigurd, and their daughter Lineik, and these young people were famed throughout the whole kingdom for their wisdom and beauty.

There was only a year between them, and they loved each other so much that they could do nothing apart. When they began to grow up the King gave them a house of their own to live in, with servants and carriages, and everything they could possibly want.

For many years they all lived happily together, and then the Queen fell ill, and knew that she would never get better.

'Promise me two things,' she said one day to the King; 'one, that if you marry again, as indeed you must, you will not choose as your wife a woman from some small state or distant island, who knows nothing of the world, and will be taken up with thoughts of her grandeur. But rather seek out a Princess of some great kingdom, who has been used to Courts all her life, and holds them at their true worth. The other thing I have to ask is, that you will never cease to watch over our children, who will soon become your greatest joy.'

These were the Queen's last words, and a few hours later she was dead. The King was so bowed down with sorrow that he would not attend even to the business of the kingdom, and at last his Prime Minister had to tell him that the people were complaining that they had nobody to right their wrongs. 'You must rouse yourself, sir,' went on the minister, 'and put aside your own sorrows for the sake of your country.'

'You do not spare me,' answered the King; 'but what you say is just, and your counsel is good. I have heard that men say, likewise, that it will be for the good of my kingdom for me to marry again, though my heart will never cease to be with my lost wife. But it was her wish also; therefore, to you I entrust the duty of finding a lady fitted to share my throne; only, see that she comes neither from a small town nor a remote island.'

So an embassy was prepared, with the minister at its head, to visit the greatest courts in the world, and to choose out a suitable Princess. But the vessel which carried them had not been gone many days when a thick fog came on, and the captain could see neither to the right nor to the left. For a whole month the ship drifted about in darkness, till at length the fog lifted and they beheld a cliff jutting out just in front. On one side of the cliff lay a sheltered bay, in which the vessel was soon anchored, and though they did not know where they were, at any rate they felt sure of fresh fruit and water.

The minister left the rest of his followers on board the ship, and taking a small boat rowed himself to land, in order to look about him and to find out if the island was really as deserted as it seemed.

He had not gone far, when he heard the sound of music, and, turning in its direction, he saw a woman of marvellous beauty sitting on a low stool playing on a harp, while a girl beside her sang. The minister stopped and greeted the lady politely, and she replied with friendliness, asking him why he had come to such an out-of-the-way place. In answer he told her the object of his journey.

'I am in the same state as your master,' replied the lady; 'I was married to a mighty King who ruled over this land, till Vikings (sea-robbers) came and slew him and put all the people to death. But I managed to escape, and hid myself here with my daughter.'

And the daughter listened, and said softly to her mother, 'Are you speaking the truth now?'

'Remember your promise,' answered the mother angrily, giving her a pinch which was unseen by the minister.

'What is your name, madam?' asked he, much touched by this sad story.

'Blauvor,' she replied, 'and my daughter is called Laufer;' and then she inquired the name of the minister, and of the King his master. After this they talked of many things, and the lady showed herself learned in all that a woman should know, and even in much that men only were commonly taught. 'What a wife she would make for the King,' thought the minister to himself, and before long he had begged the honour of her hand for his master. She declared at first that she was too unworthy to accept the position offered her, and that the minister would soon repent his choice; but this only made him the more eager, and in the end he gained her consent, and prevailed on her to return with him at once to his own country.

The minister then conducted the mother and daughter back to the ship; the anchor was raised, the sails spread, and a fair wind was behind them.

Now that the fog had lifted they could see as they looked back that, except just along the shore, the island was bare and deserted and not fit for men to live in; but about that nobody cared. They had a quick voyage, and in six days they reached the land, and at once set out for the capital, a messenger being sent on first by the minister to inform the King of what had happened.

When his Majesty's eyes fell on the two beautiful women, clad in dresses of gold and silver, he forgot his sorrows and ordered preparations for the wedding to be made without delay. In his joy he never remembered to inquire in what kind of country the future Queen had been found. In fact his head was so turned by the beauty of the two ladies that when the invitations were sent by his orders to all the great people in the kingdom, he did not even recollect his two children, who remained shut up in their own house!

After the marriage the King ceased to have any will of his own and did nothing without consulting his wife. She was present at all his councils, and her opinion was asked before making peace or war. But when a few months had passed the King began to have doubts as to whether the minister's choice had really been a wise one, and he noticed that his children lived more and more in their palace and never came near their stepmother.

It always happens that if a person's eyes are once opened they see a great deal more than they ever expected; and soon it struck the King that the members of his Court had a way of disappearing one after the other without any reason. At first he had not paid much attention to the vacant place. As, however, man after man vanished without leaving any trace, he began to grow uncomfortable and to wonder if the Queen could have anything to do with it.

Things were in this state when, one day, his wife said to him that it was time for him to make a progress through his kingdom and see that his governors were not cheating him of the money that was his due. 'And you need not be anxious about going,' she added, 'for I will rule the country while you are away as carefully as you could yourself.'

The King had no great desire to undertake this journey, but the Queen's will was stronger than his, and he was too lazy to make a fight for it. So he said nothing and set about his preparations, ordering his finest ship to be ready to carry him round the coast. Still his heart was heavy, and he felt uneasy, though he could not have told why; and the night before he was to start he went to the children's palace to take leave of his son and daughter.

He had not seen them for some time, and they gave him a warm welcome, for they loved him dearly and he had always been kind to them. They had much to tell him, but after a while he checked their merry talk and said:

'If I should never come back from this journey I fear that it may not be safe for you to stay here; so directly there is no more hope of my return leave instantly and take the road eastwards till you reach a high mountain, which you must cross. Once over the mountain keep along by the side of a little bay till you come to two trees, one green and the other red, standing in a thicket, and so far back from the road that without looking for them you would never see them. Hide each in the trunk of one of the trees and there you will be safe from all your enemies.'

With these words the King bade them farewell and entered sadly into his ship. For a few days the wind was fair, and everything seemed going smoothly; then suddenly, a gale sprang up, and a fearful storm of thunder and lightning, such as had never happened within the memory of man. In spite of the efforts of the frightened sailors the vessel was driven on the rocks, and not a man on board was saved.

That very night Prince Sigurd had a dream, in which he thought his father appeared to him in dripping clothes, and, taking the crown from his head, laid it at his son's feet, leaving the room as silently as he had entered it.

Hastily the Prince awoke his sister Lineik, and they agreed that their father must be dead, and that they must lose no time in obeying his orders and putting themselves in safety. So they collected their

jewels and a few clothes and left the house without being observed by anyone.

They hurried on till they arrived at the mountain without once looking back. Then Sigurd glanced round and saw that their stepmother was following them, with an expression on her face which made her uglier than the ugliest old witch. Between her and them lay a thick wood, and Sigurd stopped for a moment to set it on fire; then he and his sister hastened on more swiftly than before, till they reached the grove with the red and green trees, into which they jumped, and felt that at last they were safe.

Now, at that time there reigned over Greece a King who was very rich and powerful, although his name has somehow been forgotten. He had two children, a son and a daughter, who were more beautiful and accomplished than any Greeks had been before, and they were the pride of their father's heart.

The Prince had no sooner grown out of boyhood than he prevailed on his father to make war during the summer months on a neighbouring nation, so as to give him a chance of making himself famous. In winter, however, when it was difficult to get food and horses in that wild country, the army was dispersed, and the Prince returned home.

During one of these wars he had heard reports of the Princess Lineik's beauty, and he resolved to seek her out, and to ask for her hand in marriage. All this Blauvor, the Queen, found out by means of her black arts, and when the Prince drew near the capital she put a splendid dress on her own daughter and then went to meet her guest.

She bade him welcome to her palace, and when they had finished supper she told him of the loss of her husband, and how there was no one left to govern the kingdom but herself.

'But where is the Princess Lineik?' asked the Prince when she had ended her tale.

'Here,' answered the Queen, bringing forward the girl, whom she had hitherto kept in the background.

The Prince looked at her and was rather disappointed. The maiden was pretty enough, but not much out of the common.

'Oh, you must not wonder at her pale face and heavy eyes,' said the Queen hastily, for she saw what was passing in his mind. 'She has never got over the loss of both father and mother.'

'That shows a good heart,' thought the Prince; 'and when she is happy her beauty will soon come back.' And without any further delay he begged the Queen to consent to their betrothal, for the marriage must take place in his own country.

The Queen was enchanted. She had hardly expected to succeed so soon, and she at once set about her preparations. Indeed she wished to travel with the young couple, to make sure that nothing should go wrong; but here the Prince was firm, that he would take no one with him but Laufer, whom he thought was Lineik.

They soon took leave of the Queen, and set sail in a splendid ship; but in a short time a dense fog came on, and in the dark the captain steered out of course, and they found themselves in a bay which was quite strange to all the crew. The Prince ordered a boat to be lowered, and went on shore to look about him, and it was not long before he noticed the two beautiful trees, quite different from any that grew in Greece. Calling one of the sailors, he bade him cut them down, and carry them on board the ship. This was done, and as the sky was now clear they put out to sea, and arrived in Greece without any more adventures.

The news that the Prince had brought home a bride had gone before them, and they were greeted with flowery arches and crowns of coloured lights. The King and Queen met them on the steps of the palace, and conducted the girl to the women's house, where she would have to remain until her marriage. The Prince then went to his own rooms and ordered that the trees should be brought in to him.

The next morning the Prince bade his attendants bring his future bride to his own apartments, and when she came he gave her silk which she was to weave into three robes – one red, one green, and one blue – and these must all be ready before the wedding. The blue one was to be done first and the green last, and this was to be the most splendid of all, 'for I will wear it at our marriage,' said he.

Left alone, Laufer sat and stared at the heap of shining silk before her. She did not know how to weave, and burst into tears as she thought that everything would be discovered, for Lineik's skill in weaving was as famous as her beauty. As she sat with her face hidden and her body shaken by sobs, Sigurd in his tree heard her and was moved to pity. 'Lineik, my sister,' he called, softly. 'Laufer is weeping; help her, I pray you.'

'Have you forgotten the wrongs her mother did to us?' answered Lineik, 'and that it is owing to her that we are banished from home?'

But she was not really unforgiving, and very soon she slid quietly out of her hiding-place, and taking the silk from Laufer's hands began to weave it. So quick and clever was she that the blue dress was not only woven but embroidered, and Lineik was safe back in her tree before the Prince returned.

'It is the most beautiful work I have ever seen,' said he, taking up a bit. 'And I am sure that the red one will be still better, because the stuff is richer,' and with a low bow he left the room.

Laufer had hoped secretly that when the Prince had seen the blue dress finished he would have let her off the other two; but when she found she was expected to fulfil the whole task, her heart sank and she began to cry loudly. Again Sigurd heard her, and begged Lineik to come to her help, and Lineik, feeling sorry for her distress, wove and embroidered the second dress as she had done the first, mixing gold thread and precious stones till you could hardly see the red of the stuff. When it was done she glided into her tree just as the Prince came in.

'You are as quick as you are clever,' said he, admiringly. 'This looks as if it had been embroidered by the fairies! But as the green robe must outshine the other two I will give you three days in which to finish it. After it is ready we will be married at once.'

Now, as he spoke, there rose up in Laufer's mind all the unkind things that she and her mother had done to Lineik. Could she hope that they would be forgotten, and that Lineik would come to her rescue for the third time? And perhaps Lineik, who had not forgotten the past either, might have left her alone, to get on as best she could, had not Sigurd, her brother, implored her to help just once more. So Lineik again slid out of her tree, and to Laufer's great relief, set herself to work. When the shining green silk was ready she caught the sun's rays and the moon's beams on the point of her needle and wove them into a pattern such as no man had ever seen. But it took a long time, and on the third morning, just as she was putting the last stitches into the last flower the Prince came in.

Lineik jumped up quickly, and tried to get past him back to her tree; but the folds of the silk were wrapped round her, and she would have fallen had not the Prince caught her.

'I have thought for some time that all was not quite straight here,' said he. 'Tell me who you are, and where you come from?'

Lineik then told her name and her story. When she had ended the

Prince turned angrily to Laufer, and declared that, as a punishment for her wicked lies, she deserved to die a shameful death.

But Laufer fell at his feet and begged for mercy. It was her mother's fault, she said, 'It was she, and not I, who passed me off as the Princess Lineik. The only lie I have ever told you was about the robes, and I do not deserve death for that.'

She was still on her knees when Prince Sigurd entered the room. He prayed the Prince of Greece to forgive Laufer, which he did, on condition that Lineik would consent to marry him. 'Not till my stepmother is dead,' answered she, 'for she has brought misery to all that came near her.' Then Laufer told them that Blauvor was not the wife of a King, but an ogress who had stolen her from a neighbouring palace and had brought her up as her daughter. And besides being an ogress she was also a witch, and by her black arts had sunk the ship in which the father of Sigurd and Lineik had set sail. It was she who had caused the disappearance of the courtiers, for which no one could account, by eating them during the night, and she hoped to get rid of all the people in the country, and then to fill the land with ogres and ogresses like herself.

So Prince Sigurd and the Prince of Greece collected an army swiftly, and marched upon the town where Blauvor had her palace. They came so suddenly that no one knew of it, and if they had, Blauvor had eaten most of the strong men; and others, fearful of something they could not tell what, had secretly left the place. Therefore she was easily captured, and the next day was beheaded in the market-place. Afterwards the two Princes marched back to Greece.

Lineik had no longer any reason for putting off her wedding, and married the Prince of Greece at the same time that Sigurd married the Princess. And Laufer remained with Lineik as her friend and sister, till they found a husband for her in a great nobleman; and all three couples lived happily until they died.

Tritill, Litill and the Birds

ONCE UPON a time there lived a Princess who was so beautiful and so good that everybody loved her. Her father could hardly bear her out of his sight, and he almost died of grief when, one day, she disappeared, and though the whole kingdom was searched through and through, she could not be found in any corner of it. In despair, the King ordered a proclamation to be made that whoever could bring her back to the palace should have her for his wife. This made the young men start afresh on the search, but they were no more successful than before, and returned sorrowfully to their homes.

Now there dwelt, not far from the palace, an old man who had three sons. The two eldest were allowed by their parents to do just as they liked, but the youngest was always obliged to give way to his brothers. When they were all grown up, the eldest told his father that he was tired of leading such a quiet life, and that he meant to go away and see the world.

The old people were very unhappy at the thought that they must part with him, but they said nothing, and began to collect all that he would want for his travels, and were careful to add a pair of new boots. When everything was ready, he bade farewell, and started merrily on his way.

For some miles his road lay through a wood, and when he left it he suddenly came out on a bare hillside. Here he sat down to rest, and pulling out his wallet prepared to eat his dinner.

He had only eaten a few mouthfuls when an old man, badly dressed, passed by, and seeing the food, asked if the young man could not spare him a little.

'Not I, indeed!' answered he; 'why, I have scarcely enough for myself. If you want food you must earn it.' So the beggar went on his way.

After the young man had finished his dinner he rose and walked on for several hours, till he reached a second hill, where he threw himself down on the grass, and took food from his wallet. While he was eating an old man came by, yet more wretched than the first, and begged for a few mouthfuls. But instead of food he only got hard words, and limped sadly away.

Towards evening the young man reached an open space in the wood, and by this time he thought he would like some supper. The birds saw the food, and flew round his head in numbers hoping for some crumbs, but he threw stones at them, and frightened them off. Then he began to wonder where he should sleep. Not in the open space he was in, for that was bare and cold, and though he had walked a long way that day, and was tired, he dragged himself up, and went on seeking for shelter.

At length he saw a deep sort of hole or cave under a great rock, and as it seemed quite empty, he went in, and lay down in a corner. About midnight he was awakened by a noise, and peeping out he beheld a terrible ogress approaching. He implored her not to hurt him, but to let him stay there for the rest of the night, to which she consented, on condition that he should spend the next day in doing any task which she might choose to set him. To this the young man willingly agreed, and turned over and went to sleep again. In the morning, the ogress bade him sweep the dust out of the cave, and to have it clean before her return in the evening, otherwise it would be the worse for him. Then she left the cave.

The young man took spade and broom, and began to clean the floor of the cave, but try as he would to move it the dirt still stuck to its place. He soon gave up the task, and sat sulkily in the corner, wondering what punishment the ogress would find for him, and why she had set him to do such an impossible thing.

He had not long to wait, after the ogress came home, before he knew what his punishment was to be! She just gave one look at the floor of the cave, then dealt him a blow on the head which cracked his skull, and there was an end of him.

Meanwhile his next brother grew tired of staying at home, and let his parents have no rest till they had consented that he also should be given some food and some new boots, and go out to see the world. On his road, he also met the two old beggars, who prayed for a little of his food and wine, but this young man had never been taught to help other people, and had made it a rule through his life to keep all he had to himself. So he turned a deaf ear and finished his dinner.

By and by he, too, came to the cave, and was bidden by the ogress to clean the floor, but he was no more successful than his brother, and his fate was the same.

Anyone would have thought that, when the old people had only one son left, at least they would have been kind to him, even if they did not love him. But for some reason they could hardly bear the sight of him, though he worked much harder for their comfort than his brothers had ever done. So when he asked their leave to go out into the world they gave it at once, and seemed quite glad to be rid of him. They felt it was quite generous of them to provide him with a pair of new boots and some bread and milk for his journey.

Besides the pleasure of seeing the world, the youth was very anxious to discover what had become of his brothers, and he determined to trace, as far as he could, the way that they must have gone. He followed the road that led from his father's cottage to the hill, where he sat down to rest, saying to himself, 'I am sure my brothers must have stopped here, and I will do the same.'

He was hungry as well as tired, and took out some of the food his parents had given him. He was just going to begin to eat when the old man appeared, and asked if he could not spare him a little. The young man at once broke off some of the bread, begging the old man to sit down beside him, and treating him as if he was an old friend. At last the stranger rose, and said to him, 'If ever you are in trouble call me, and I will help you. My name is Tritill.' Then he vanished, and the young man could not tell where he had gone.

However, he felt he had now rested long enough, and that he had better be going on his way. At the next hill he met with the second old man, and to him also he gave food and drink. And when this old man had finished he said, like the first, 'If you ever want help in the smallest thing call to me. My name is Litill.'

The young man walked on till he reached the open space in the wood, where he stopped for dinner. In a moment all the birds in the world seemed to be flying round his head, and he crumbled some of his bread for them and watched them as they darted down to pick it up. When they had cleared off every crumb the largest bird with the gayest plumage said to him, 'If you are in trouble and need help say,

"My birds, come to me!" and we will come.' Then they flew away.

Towards evening the young man reached the cave where his brothers had met their deaths, and, like them, he thought it would be a good place to sleep in. Looking round, he saw dead men's bones and some pieces of clothing. The sight made him shiver, but he resolved to await the return of the ogress, for such he knew she must be.

Very soon she came striding in, and he asked politely if she would give him a night's lodging. She answered as before, that he might stay on condition that he should do any work that she might set him to next morning. So, the bargain being concluded, the young man curled himself up in a corner and went to sleep.

The dirt lay thicker than ever on the floor of the cave when the young man took the spade and broom and began his work. He could not clear it any more than his brothers had done, and at last the spade itself stuck in the earth so that he could not pull it out. The youth stared at it in despair. Then the old beggar's words flashed into his mind, and he cried, 'Tritill, Tritill, come and help me!'

And Tritill stood beside him and asked what he wanted. The youth told him all his story, and when he had finished, the old man said, 'Spade and broom, do your duty,' and they danced about the cave till, in a short time, there was not a speck of dust left on the floor. As soon as it was quite clean Tritill went his way.

With a light heart the young man awaited the return of the ogress. When she came in she looked carefully round, and then said to him, 'You did not do that quite alone. However, as the floor is clean I will leave your head on.'

The following morning the ogress told the young man that he must take all the feathers out of her pillows and spread them to dry in the sun. But if one feather was missing when she came back at night his head should pay for it.

The young man fetched the pillows, and shook out all the feathers, and oh! what quantities of them there were! He was thinking to himself, as he spread them out carefully, how lucky it was that the sun was so bright and that there was no wind, when suddenly a breeze sprang up, and in a moment the feathers were dancing high in the air. At first the youth tried to collect them again, but he soon found that it was no use, and he cried in despair, 'Tritill, Litill, and all my birds, come and help me!'

He had hardly said the words when there they all were; and when the birds had brought all the feathers back again, he, helped by Tritill and Litill, put them away in the pillows, as the ogress had bidden him. But one little feather they kept out, and told the young man that if the ogress missed it he was to thrust it up her nose. Then they all vanished, Tritill, Litill, and the birds.

Directly the ogress returned home she flung herself with all her weight on the bed, and the whole cave quivered under her. The pillows were soft and full instead of being empty, which surprised her, but that did not content her. She got up, shook out the pillow-cases one by one, and began to count the feathers that were in each. 'If one is missing I will have your head,' said she, and at that the young man drew the feather from his pocket and thrust it up her nose, crying, 'If you want your feather, here it is.'

'You did not sort those feathers alone,' answered the ogress calmly; 'however, this time I will let that pass.'

That night the young man slept soundly in his corner, and in the morning the ogress told him that his work that day would be to slay one of her great oxen, to cook its heart, and to make drinking cups of its horns, before she returned home. 'There are fifty oxen,' added she, 'and you must guess which of the herd I want killed. If you guess right, tomorrow you shall be free to go where you will, and you shall choose besides three things as a reward for your service. But if you slay the wrong ox your head shall pay for it.'

Left alone, the young man stood thinking for a little. Then he called, 'Tritill, Litill, come to my help!'

In a moment he saw them, far away, driving the biggest ox the youth had ever seen. When they drew near, Tritill killed it, Litill took out its heart for the young man to cook, and both began quickly to turn the horns into drinking cups. The work went merrily on, and they talked gaily, and the young man told his friends of the payment promised him by the ogress if he had done her bidding. The old men warned him that he must ask her for the chest which stood at the foot of her bed, for whatever lay on the top of the bed, and for what lay under the side of the cave. The young man thanked them for their counsel, and Tritill and Litill then took leave of him, saying that for the present he would need them no more.

Scarcely had they disappeared when the ogress came back, and found everything ready just as she had ordered. Before she sat down to eat the bullock's heart she turned to the young man, and said, 'You did not do that all alone, my friend; but, nevertheless, I will keep my word, and tomorrow you shall go your way.' So they went to bed and slept till dawn.

When the sun rose the ogress awoke the young man, and called to him to choose any three things out of her house.

'I choose,' answered he, 'the chest which stands at the foot of your bed; whatever lies on the top of the bed, and whatever is under the side of the cave.'

'You did not choose those things by yourself, my friend,' said the ogress; 'but what I have promised, that will I do.'

And then she gave him his reward.

'The thing which lay on the top of the bed' turned out to be the lost Princess. 'The chest which stood at the foot of the bed' proved full of gold and precious stones; and 'what was under the side of the cave' he found to be a great ship, with oars and sails that went of itself as well on land as in the water. 'You are the luckiest man that ever was born,' said the ogress as she went out of the cave as usual.

With much difficulty the youth put the heavy chest on his shoulders and carried it on board the ship, the Princess walking by his side. Then he took the helm and steered the vessel back to her father's kingdom. The King's joy at receiving back his lost daughter was so great that he almost fainted, but when he recovered himself he made the young man tell him how everything had really happened. 'You have found her, and you shall marry her,' said the King; and so it was done. And this is the end of the story.

The Twelve Dancing Princesses

ONCE UPON a time there lived in the village of Montignies-sur-Roc a young herdsman, without either father or mother. His real name was Michael, but he was always called the Star Gazer, because when he drove his cows over the commons to seek for pasture, he went along with his head in the air, gazing straight before him.

As he had a white skin, blue eyes, and hair that curled all over his head, the village girls pursued him and used to cry after him, 'Well, Star Gazer, what are you doing?' and Michael would answer, 'Oh, nothing,' and go on his way without even turning to look at them.

The fact was he thought them very ugly, with their sunburnt necks, their great red hands, their coarse petticoats and their wooden shoes. He had heard that somewhere in the world there were girls whose necks were white and whose hands were small, who were always dressed in the finest silks and laces, and were called Princesses, and while his companions round the fire saw nothing in the flames but common everyday fancies, he dreamed that he had the happiness to marry a Princess.

One morning about the middle of August, just at mid-day when the sun was hottest, Michael ate his dinner of a piece of dry bread, and went to sleep under an oak. And while he slept he dreamt that there appeared before him a beautiful lady, dressed in a robe of cloth of gold, who said to him, 'Go to the castle of Belœil, and there you shall marry a Princess.'

That evening the herd-boy, who had been thinking a great deal about the advice of the lady in the golden dress, told his dream to the farm people. But, as was natural, they only laughed at the Star Gazer.

The next day at the same hour he went to sleep again under the same tree. The lady appeared to him a second time, and said, 'Go to the castle of Belœil, and you shall marry a Princess.'

In the evening Michael told his friends that he had dreamt the same dream again, but they only laughed at him more than before.

'Never mind,' he thought to himself; 'if the lady appears to me a third time, I will do as she tells me.'

The following day, to the great astonishment of all the village, about two o'clock in the afternoon a voice was heard singing:

> 'Raleo, raleo,
> How the cattle go!'

It was the herd-boy driving his cows back to the byre.

The farmer began to scold him furiously, but he answered quietly, 'I am going away,' made his clothes into a bundle, said good-bye to all his friends, and boldly set out to seek his fortune.

There was great excitement through all the village, and on the top of the hill the people stood holding their sides with laughing, as they watched the Star Gazer trudging bravely along the valley with his bundle at the end of his stick.

It was enough to make anyone laugh, certainly.

Now it was well known, for full twenty miles round, that there lived in the castle of Belœil twelve Princesses of wonderful beauty, and as proud as they were beautiful, and who were besides so very sensitive and of such truly royal blood, that they would have felt at once the presence of a pea in their beds, even if the mattresses had been laid over it.

It was whispered about that they led exactly the lives that Princesses ought to lead, sleeping far into the morning, and never getting up till mid-day. They had twelve beds all in the same room, but what was very extraordinary was the fact that though they were locked in by triple bolts, every morning their satin shoes were found worn into holes.

When they were asked what they had been doing all night, they always answered that they had been asleep; and, indeed, no noise was ever heard in the room, yet the shoes could not wear themselves out alone!

At last the Duke of Belœil had ordered that the trumpet be sounded, and a proclamation made that whoever could discover how his daughters wore out their shoes should choose one of them for his wife.

On hearing the proclamation a number of Princes arrived at the castle to try their luck. They watched all night behind the open door

of the Princesses' room, but each time, when the morning came, they had all disappeared, and no one could tell what had become of them.

When he reached the castle, Michael went straight to the gardener and offered his services. Now it happened that the garden boy had just been sent away, and though the lad did not look very sturdy, the gardener agreed to take him, as he thought that his pretty face and golden curls would please the Princesses. And so the Star Gazer became garden boy at the castle.

The first thing he was told was that when the Princesses got up he was to present each one with a bouquet, and Michael thought that if he had nothing more unpleasant to do than that he should get on very well.

Accordingly he placed himself behind the door of the Princesses' room, with twelve bouquets in a basket. He gave one to each of the sisters, and they took them without even deigning to look at the lad, except Lina the youngest, who fixed her large black eyes as soft as velvet on him, and exclaimed, 'Oh, how pretty he is – our new flower boy!' The rest all burst out laughing, and the eldest pointed out that a Princess ought never to lower herself by looking at a garden boy.

Now Michael knew all about the disappearance of the other suitors, but notwithstanding, the beautiful eyes of the Princess Lina inspired him with a violent longing to try his fate. Unhappily he did not dare to come forward, being afraid that he should only be jeered at, or even turned away from the castle on account of his impudence.

Nevertheless, the Star Gazer had another dream. The lady in the golden dress appeared to him once more, holding in one hand two young laurel trees, a cherry laurel and a rose laurel, and in the other hand a little golden rake, a little golden bucket, and a silken towel. She thus addressed him:

'Plant these two laurels in two large pots, rake them over with the rake, water them with the bucket, and wipe them with the towel. When they have grown as tall as a girl of fifteen, say to each of them, "My beautiful laurel, with the golden rake I have raked you, with the golden bucket I have watered you, with the silken towel I have wiped you." Then after that ask anything you choose, and the laurels will give it to you.'

Michael thanked the lady in the golden dress, and when he woke he found the two laurel bushes beside him. So he carefully obeyed the orders he had been given by the lady.

The trees grew very fast, and when they were as tall as a girl of fifteen he said to the cherry laurel, 'My lovely cherry laurel, with the golden rake I have raked thee, with the golden bucket I have watered thee, with the silken towel I have wiped thee. Teach me how to become invisible.' Then there instantly appeared on the laurel a pretty white flower, which Michael gathered and stuck into his button-hole.

That evening, when the Princesses went upstairs to bed, he followed them barefoot, so that he might make no noise, and hid himself under one of the twelve beds, so as not to take up much room.

The Princesses began at once to open their wardrobes and boxes. They took out of them the most magnificent dresses, which they put on before their mirrors, and when they had finished, turned themselves all round to admire their appearances.

Michael could see nothing from his hiding-place, but he could hear everything, and he listened to the Princesses laughing and jumping with pleasure. At last the eldest said, 'Be quick, my sisters, our partners will be impatient.' At the end of an hour when the Star Gazer heard no more noise, he peeped out and saw the twelve sisters in splendid garments, with their satin shoes on their feet, and in their hands the bouquets he had brought them.

'Are you ready?' asked the eldest.

'Yes,' replied the other eleven in chorus, and they took their places one by one behind her.

Then the eldest Princess clapped her hands three times and a trap door opened. All the Princesses disappeared down a secret staircase, and Michael hastily followed them.

As he was following on the steps of the Princess Lina, he carelessly trod on her dress.

'There is somebody behind me,' cried the Princess; 'they are holding my dress.'

'You foolish thing,' said her eldest sister, 'you are always afraid of something. It is only a nail which caught you.'

They went down, down, down, till at last they came to a passage with a door at one end, which was only fastened with a latch. The eldest Princess opened it, and immediately they were in a lovely little wood, where the leaves of the trees were spangled with drops of silver which shone in the brilliant light of the moon.

They next crossed another wood where the leaves were sprinkled with gold, and after that another still, where the leaves glittered with diamonds.

At last the garden boy perceived a large lake, and on the shores of the lake twelve little boats with awnings, in which were seated twelve Princes, who, grasping their oars, awaited the Princesses.

Each Princess entered one of the boats, and Michael slipped into that which held the youngest. The boats glided along rapidly, but Lina's, from being heavier, was always behind the rest. 'We never went so slowly before,' said the Princess; 'what can be the reason?'

'I don't know,' answered the Prince. 'I assure you I am rowing as hard as I can.'

On the other side of the lake the garden boy saw a beautiful castle splendidly illuminated, whence came the lively music of fiddles, kettle-drums, and trumpets.

In a moment they touched land, and the company jumped out of the boats; and the Princes, after having securely fastened their barques, gave their arms to the Princesses and conducted them to the castle.

Michael followed, and entered the ballroom in their train. Everywhere were mirrors, lights, flowers, and damask hangings. He was quite bewildered at the magnificence of the sight.

He placed himself out of the way in a corner, admiring the grace and beauty of the Princesses. Their loveliness was of every kind. Some were fair and some were dark; some had chestnut hair, or curls darker still, and some had golden locks. Never were so many beautiful Princesses seen together at one time, but the one whom Michael thought the most beautiful and the most fascinating was the little Princess with the velvet eyes.

With what eagerness she danced! Leaning on her partner's shoulder she swept by like a whirlwind. Her cheeks were flushed, her eyes sparkled, and it was plain that she loved dancing better than anything else.

The poor boy envied those handsome young men with whom she danced so gracefully, but he did not know how little reason he had to be jealous of them. The young men were really the Princes who, to the number of fifty at least, had tried to discover the Princesses' secret. The Princesses had made them drink a philtre, which froze the heart and left nothing in it but the love of dancing.

They all danced on till the shoes of the Princesses were worn into holes. When the cock crowed the third time the fiddles stopped, and a delicious supper was served by Negro boys, consisting of sugared orange flowers, crystallised rose leaves, powdered violets, cracknels, wafers, and other dishes, which are, as everyone knows, the favourite food of Princesses.

After supper, the dancers all went back to their boats, and this time Michael entered that of the eldest Princess. They crossed again the wood with the diamond-spangled leaves, the wood with gold-sprinkled leaves, and the wood where the leaves glittered with drops of silver, and as a proof of what he had seen, the boy broke a small branch from a tree in the last wood. Lina turned as she heard the noise made by the breaking of the branch.

'What was that noise?' she said.

'It was nothing,' replied her eldest sister. 'It was only the screech of the barn-owl that roosts in one of the turrets of the castle.'

While she was speaking Michael managed to slip in front, and running up the staircase, he reached the Princesses' room first. He flung open the window, and sliding down the vine which climbed up the wall, found himself in the garden just as the sun was beginning to rise, and it was time for him to set about his work.

Later that morning, when he made up the bouquets, Michael hid the branch with the silver drops in the nosegay intended for the youngest Princess. When Lina discovered it she was much surprised. However, she said nothing to her sisters, but as she met the garden boy by accident while she was walking under the shade of the elms, she suddenly stopped as if to speak to him; then, altering her mind, went on her way.

The same evening the twelve sisters went again to the ball, and Michael again followed them and crossed the lake in Lina's boat. This time it was the Prince who complained that the boat seemed very heavy.

'It is the heat,' replied the Princess. 'I, too, have been feeling very warm.'

During the ball she looked everywhere for the garden boy, but she never saw him.

As they came back, Michael gathered a branch in the wood with the gold-spangled leaves, and now it was the eldest Princess who heard the noise that it made in breaking.

'It is nothing,' said Lina; 'only the cry of the owl which roosts in one of the turrets of the castle.'

In the morning Lina found the branch in her bouquet. When the sisters went down she stayed a little behind and said to the garden boy, 'Where does this branch come from?'

'Your Royal Highness knows well enough,' answered Michael.

'So you have followed us?'

'Yes, Princess.'

'How did you manage it? We never saw you.'

'I hid myself,' replied Michael quietly.

The Princess was silent a moment, and then said:

'You know our secret! – keep it. Here is the reward of your discretion.' And she flung him a purse of gold.

'I do not sell my silence,' answered Michael, and he went away without picking up the purse.

For three nights Lina neither saw nor heard anything unusual; on the fourth she heard a rustling among the diamond-spangled leaves of the wood. That day there was a branch from those trees in her bouquet.

She took the garden boy aside, and said to him in a harsh voice, 'You know what price my father has promised to pay for our secret?'

'I know, Princess,' answered Michael.

'Don't you mean to tell him?'

'That is not my intention.'

'Are you afraid?'

'No, Princess.'

'What makes you so discreet, then?'

But Michael was silent.

Lina's sisters had seen her talking to the garden boy, and jeered at her for it.

'What prevents your marrying him?' asked the eldest. 'You would become a gardener too; it is a charming profession. You could live in a cottage at the end of the park, and help your husband to draw up water from the well, and when we get up you could bring us our bouquets.'

The Princess Lina was very angry, and when the boy presented her bouquet, she received it in a disdainful manner. Michael behaved most respectfully. He never raised his eyes to her, but nearly all day she felt him at her side without ever seeing him.

One day she made up her mind to tell everything to her eldest sister.

'What!' said she, 'this rogue knows our secret, and you never told me! I must lose no time in getting rid of him.'

'But how?'

'Why, by having him taken to the tower with the dungeons, of course.'

For this was the way that in old times beautiful Princesses got rid of people who knew too much.

But the astonishing part of it was that the youngest sister did not seem at all to relish this method of stopping the mouth of the garden boy, who, after all, had said nothing to their father.

It was agreed that the question should be submitted to the other ten sisters. All were on the side of the eldest. Then the youngest sister declared that if they laid a finger on the garden boy, she would herself go and tell their father the secret of the holes in their shoes.

At last it was decided that Michael should be put to the test; that they would take him to the ball, and at the end of supper would give him the philtre which was to enchant him like the rest.

They sent for the Star Gazer, and asked him how he had contrived to learn their secret; but still he remained silent.

Then, in commanding tones, the eldest sister gave him the order they had agreed upon.

He only answered, 'I will obey.'

He had really been present, invisible, at the council of princesses, and had heard all; but he had made up his mind to drink of the philtre, and sacrifice himself to the happiness of her he loved. Not wishing, however, to cut a poor figure at the ball by the side of the other dancers, he went at once to the laurels, and said:

'My lovely rose laurel, with the golden rake I have raked thee, with the golden bucket I have watered thee, with a silken towel I have dried thee. Dress me like a Prince.'

A beautiful pink flower appeared. Michael gathered it, and found himself in a moment clothed in velvet, which was as black as the eyes of the little Princess, with a cap to match, a diamond aigrette, and a blossom of the rose laurel in his button-hole.

Thus dressed, he presented himself that evening before the Duke of Belœil, and obtained leave to try and discover his daughters' secret. He looked so distinguished that hardly anyone would have known who he was.

The twelve Princesses went upstairs to bed. Michael followed them, and waited behind the open door till they gave the signal for departure.

This time he did not cross in Lina's boat. He gave his arm to the eldest sister, danced with each in turn, and was so graceful that everyone was delighted with him. At last the time came for him to dance with the little Princess. She found him the best partner in the world, but he did not dare to speak a single word to her.

When he was taking her back to her place she said to him in a mocking voice:

'Here you are at the summit of your wishes: you are being treated like a Prince.'

'Don't be afraid,' he replied gently. 'You shall never be a gardener's wife.'

The little Princess stared at him with frightened eyes, and he left her without waiting for an answer.

When the satin slippers were worn through the fiddles stopped, and the Negro boys set the table. Michael was placed next to the eldest sister, and opposite to the youngest.

They gave him the most exquisite dishes to eat, and the most delicate wines to drink; and in order to turn his head more completely, compliments and flattery were heaped on him from every side. But he took care not to be intoxicated, either by the wine or the compliments.

At last the eldest sister made a sign, and one of the black pages brought in a large golden cup.

'The enchanted castle has no more secrets for you,' she said to Michael. 'Let us drink to your triumph.'

He cast a lingering glance at the little Princess, and without hesitation lifted the cup.

'Don't drink!' suddenly cried out the little Princess. 'I would rather marry a gardener.'

And she burst into tears.

Michael flung the contents of the cup behind him, sprang over the table and cast himself at Lina's feet. The rest of the Princes fell likewise at the knees of the Princesses, each of whom chose a husband and raised him to her side. The charm was broken.

The twelve couples embarked in the boats, which crossed back many times in order to carry over the other Princes. Then they all went through the three woods, and when they had passed the door of the underground passage a great noise was heard, as if the enchanted castle was crumbling to the earth.

They went straight to the room of the Duke of Belœil, who had just awakened. Michael held in his hand the golden cup, and he revealed the secret of the holes in the shoes.

'Choose, then,' said the Duke, 'whichever you prefer.'

'My choice is already made,' replied the boy, and he offered his hand to the youngest Princess, who blushed and lowered her eyes.

The Princess Lina did not become a gardener's wife; on the contrary, it was the Star Gazer who became a Prince: but before the marriage ceremony the Princess insisted that her lover should tell her how he came to discover the secret.

So he showed her the two laurels which had helped him, and she, like a prudent girl, thinking they gave him too much advantage over his wife, cut them off at the root and threw them in the fire.

And this is why the country girls go about singing:

> '*Nous n'irons plus au bois,*
> *Les lauriers sont coupés,*'

as they dance in summer by the light of the moon.

The Two Frogs

ONCE UPON a time in the country of Japan there lived two frogs, one of whom made his home in a ditch near the town of Osaka, on the sea coast, while the other dwelt in a clear little stream which ran through the city of Kioto. At such a great distance apart, they had never even heard of each other; but, funnily enough, the idea came into both their heads at once that they should like to see a little of the world, and the frog who lived at Kioto wanted to visit Osaka, and the frog who lived at Osaka wished to go to Kioto, where the great Mikado had his palace.

So one fine morning in the Spring they both set out along the road that led from Kioto to Osaka, one from one end and the other from the other. The journey was more tiring than they expected, for they did not know much about travelling, and half-way between the two towns there arose a mountain which had to be climbed. It took them a long time and a great many hops to reach the top, but there they were at last, and what was the surprise of each to see another frog before him! They looked at each other for a moment without speaking, and then fell into conversation, explaining the cause of their meeting so far from their homes. It was delightful to find that they both felt the same wish – to learn a little more of their native country – and as there was no sort of hurry they stretched themselves out in a

223

cool, damp place, and agreed that they would have a good rest before they parted to go on their ways.

'What a pity we are not bigger,' said the Osaka frog; 'for then we could see both towns from here, and tell if it is worth our while going on.'

'Oh, that is easily managed,' returned the Kioto frog. 'We have only got to stand up on our hind legs, and hold on to each other, and then we can each look at the town he is travelling to.'

This idea pleased the Osaka frog so much that he at once jumped up and put his front paws on the shoulders of his friend, who had risen also. There they both stood, stretching themselves as high as they could and holding each other tightly, so that they might not fall down. The Kioto frog turned his nose towards Osaka, and the Osaka frog turned his nose towards Kioto; but the foolish things forgot that when they stood up their great eyes lay in the backs of their heads, and that though their noses might point to the places to which they wanted to go their eyes beheld the places from which they had come.

'Dear me!' cried the Osaka frog, 'Kioto is exactly like Osaka. It is certainly not worth such a long journey. I shall go home!'

'If I had had any idea that Osaka was only a copy of Kioto I should never have travelled all this way,' exclaimed the frog from Kioto, and as he spoke he took his hands from his friend's shoulders, and they both fell down on the grass. Then they took a polite farewell of each other, and set off for home again, and to the end of their lives they believed that Osaka and Kioto, which are as different to look at as two towns can be, were as like as two peas.

Two in a Sack

WHAT A life that poor man led with his wife, to be sure! Not a day passed without her scolding him and calling him names, and indeed sometimes she would take the broom from behind the stove and beat him with it. He had no peace or comfort at all, and really hardly knew how to bear it.

One day, when his wife had been particularly unkind and had beaten him black and blue, he strolled slowly into the fields, and as he could not endure to be idle he spread out his nets.

What kind of bird do you think he caught in his net? He caught a crane, and the crane said, 'Let me go free, and I'll show myself grateful.'

The man answered, 'No, my dear fellow. I shall take you home, and then perhaps my wife won't scold me so much.'

But the crane said, 'You had better come with me to my house,' and so they went to the crane's house.

When they got there, what do you think the crane took from the wall? He took down a sack, and he said:

'Two out of a sack!'

Instantly two pretty lads sprang out of the sack. They brought in oak tables, which they spread with silken covers, and placed all sorts of delicious dishes and refreshing drinks on them. The man had never seen anything so beautiful in his life, and he was delighted.

Then the crane said to him, 'Now take this sack to your wife.'

The man thanked him warmly, took the sack, and set out.

His home was a good long way off, and as it was growing dark, and he was feeling tired, he stopped to rest at his cousin's house by the way.

The cousin had three daughters, who laid out a tempting supper, but the man would eat nothing, and said to his cousin, 'Your supper is poor.'

'Oh, make the best of it,' said she, but the man only said, 'Clear away!' and taking out his sack he cried, as the crane had taught him:

'Two out of the sack!'

And out came the two pretty boys, who quickly brought in the oak tables, spread the silken covers, and laid out all sorts of delicious dishes and refreshing drinks.

Never in their lives had the cousin and her daughters seen such a supper, and they were delighted and astonished at it. But the cousin quietly made up her mind to steal the sack, so she called to her daughters, 'Go quickly and heat the bathroom: I am sure our dear guest would like to have a bath before he goes to bed.'

When the man was safe in the bathroom she told her daughters to make a sack exactly like his, as quickly as possible. Then she changed the two sacks, and hid the man's sack away.

The man enjoyed his bath, slept soundly, and set off early next morning, taking what he believed to be the sack the crane had given him.

All the way home he felt in such good spirits that he sang and whistled as he walked through the wood, and never noticed how the birds were twittering and laughing at him.

As soon as he saw his house he began to shout from a distance, 'Hallo! Old woman! Come out and meet me!'

His wife screamed back, 'You come here, and I'll give you a good thrashing with the poker!'

The man walked into the house, hung his sack on a nail, and said, as the crane had taught him:

'Two out of the sack!'

But not a soul came out of the sack.

Then he said again, exactly as the crane had taught him:

'Two out of the sack!'

His wife, hearing him chattering goodness knows what, took up her wet broom and swept the ground all about him.

The man took flight and rushed off into the field, and there he found the crane marching proudly about, and to him he told his tale.

'Come back to my house,' said the crane, and so they went to the crane's house, and as soon as they got there, what did the crane take down from the wall? Why, he took down a sack, and he said:

'Two out of the sack!'

And instantly two pretty lads sprang out of the sack, brought in oak tables, on which they laid silken covers, and spread all sorts of delicious dishes and refreshing drinks on them.

'Take this sack,' said the crane.

The man thanked him heartily, took the sack, and went. He had a long way to walk, and as he presently got hungry, he said to the sack, as the crane had taught him:

'Two out of the sack!'

And instantly two rough men with thick sticks crept out of the bag and began to beat him, crying as they did so:

> 'Don't boast to your cousins of what you have got,
>   One – two – one – two –
> Or you'll find you will catch it uncommonly hot,
>   One – two – one – two – '

And they beat on till the man panted out:
'Two into the sack!'
The words were hardly out of his mouth, when the two crept back into the sack.

Then the man shouldered the sack, and went off straight to his cousin's house. He hung the sack up on a nail, and said, 'Please have the bathroom heated, cousin.'

The cousin heated the bathroom, and the man went into it, but he neither washed nor rubbed himself, he just sat there and waited.

Meantime his cousin felt hungry, so she called her daughters, and all four sat down to table. Then the mother said:
'Two out of the sack!'
Instantly the two rough men crept out of the sack, and began to whack the woman soundly as they cried:

> 'Greedy pack! Thievish pack!
>   One – two – one – two –
> Give your cousin back his sack!
>   One – two – one – two – '

And they went on beating. The woman cried to her eldest daughter, 'Go and fetch your cousin from the bathroom. Tell him those two ruffians are beating me black and blue.'

'I've not finished rubbing myself yet,' said the peasant.
And the two ruffians kept on beating as they sang:

> 'Greedy pack! Thievish pack!
>   One – two – one – two –
> Give your cousin back his sack!
>   One – two – one – two – '

Then the woman said to her second daughter, 'Quick, quick, get him to come to me.'

'I'm just washing my head,' said the man.

Then she sent the youngest girl, and he said, 'I've not done drying myself.'

At last the woman could hold out no longer, and sent him the sack she had stolen.

Now he had quite finished his bath, and as he left the bathroom he cried,

'Two into the sack!'

And the two crept back at once into the sack.

Then the man took both sacks, the good and the bad one, and went away home.

When he was near the house he shouted, 'Hallo! Old woman! Come out and meet me!'

His wife only screamed out, 'You broomstick, come here! Your back shall pay for this.'

The man went into the cottage, hung his sack on a nail, and said, as the crane had taught him:

'Two out of the sack!'

Instantly two pretty lads sprang out of the sack, brought in oak tables, laid silken covers on them, and spread them with all sorts of delicious food and refreshing drinks.

The woman ate and drank, and praised her husband.

'Well, now, old man, I won't beat you any more,' said she.

When they had done eating, the man carried off the good sack, and put it away in his store-room, but hung the other sack up on the nail. Then he went out and strolled up and down in the yard.

Meantime his wife became thirsty. She looked with longing eyes at the sack, and at last she said, as her husband had done:

'Two out of the sack!'

And at once the two rogues with their big sticks crept out of the sack, and began to belabour her as they sang:

'Would you beat your husband true?
Don't cry so!
Now we'll beat you black and blue!
Oh! Oh!

The woman screamed out, 'Old man, old man! Come here, quick! Here are two ruffians pommelling me fit to break my bones.'

Her husband only laughed and said, 'Yes, they'll beat you well, old lady.'

And the two thumped away and sang again:

> 'Blows will hurt, remember, crone,
> We mean you well, we mean you well;
> In future leave the stick alone,
> For how it hurts, you now can tell,
> Whack, whack, whack!'

At last her husband took pity on her, and cried:
'Two into the sack!'

He had hardly said the words before they were back in the sack again.

From this time the man and his wife lived so happily together that it was a pleasure to see them, and so this story comes to an end.

The White Dove

A KING had two sons. They were a pair of reckless fellows, who were always up to some foolishness. One day they rowed out alone on the sea in a little boat. It was beautiful weather when they set out, but as soon as they had got some distance from the shore there arose a terrific storm. The oars went overboard at once, and the little boat was tossed about on the rolling billows like a nut-shell. The Princes had to hold fast by the seats to keep from being thrown out of the boat.

At the height of the storm they saw a dough-trough, in which there sat an old woman. She called to them, and said that they could still get to shore alive if they would promise her the son that was next to come to their mother the Queen.

'We can't do that,' shouted the Princes; 'he doesn't belong to us, so we can't give him away.'

'Then you can rot at the bottom of the sea, both of you,' said the old woman; 'and perhaps it may be the case that your mother would rather keep the two sons she has than the one she hasn't got yet.'

Then she rowed away in her dough-trough, while the storm howled still louder than before, and the water dashed over their boat until it was almost sinking. Then the Princes thought that there was something in what the old woman had said about their mother, and being, of course, eager to save their lives, they shouted to her, and promised that she should have their brother if she would deliver them from this danger. As soon as they had done so the storm ceased and the waves fell. The boat drove ashore below their father's castle, and both Princes were received with open arms by their father and mother, who had suffered great anxiety for them.

The two brothers said nothing about what they had promised, neither at that time nor later on when the Queen's third son came, a beautiful boy, whom she loved more than anything else in the world. He was brought up and educated in his father's house until he was full grown, and still his brothers had never seen or heard anything

about the witch to whom they had promised him before he was born.

It happened one evening that there arose a raging storm, with mist and darkness. It howled and roared around the King's palace, and in the midst of it there came a loud knock on the door of the hall where the youngest Prince was. He went to the door and found there an old woman with a dough-trough on her back, who said to him that he must go with her at once; his brothers had promised him to her if she would save their lives.

'Yes,' said he; 'if you saved my brothers' lives, and they promised me to you, then I will go with you.'

They therefore went down to the beach together, where he had to take his seat in the trough, along with the witch, who sailed away with him, over the sea, home to her dwelling.

The Prince was now in the witch's power, and in her service. The first thing she set him to was to pick feathers. 'The heap of feathers that you see here,' said she, 'you must get finished before I come home in the evening, otherwise you shall be set to harder work.' He started to the feathers, and picked and picked until there was only a single feather left that had not passed through his hands. But then there came a whirlwind and sent all the feathers flying, and swept them along the floor into a heap, where they lay as if they were trampled together. He had now to begin all his work over again, but this time it only wanted an hour of evening, when the witch was to be expected home, and he easily saw that it was impossible for him to be finished by that time.

Then he heard something tapping at the window pane, and a thin voice said, 'Let me in, and I will help you.' It was a white dove, which sat outside the window, and was pecking at it with its beak. He opened the window, and the dove came in and set to work at once, and picked all the feathers out of the heap with its beak. Before the hour was past the feathers were all nicely arranged: the dove flew out at the window, and at the same moment the witch came in at the door.

'Well, well,' said she, 'it was more than I would have expected of you – to get all the feathers put in order so nicely. However, such a Prince might be expected to have neat fingers.'

Next morning the witch said to the Prince, 'Today you shall have some easy work to do. Outside the door I have some firewood lying; you must split that for me into little bits that I can kindle the fire with. That will soon be done, but you must be finished before I come home.'

The Prince got a little axe and set to work at once. He split and clove away, and thought that he was getting on fast; but the day wore on until it was long past mid-day, and he was still very far from having finished. He thought, in fact, that the pile of wood rather grew bigger than smaller, in spite of what he took off it; so he let his hands fall by his side, and dried the sweat from his forehead, and was ill at ease, for he knew that it would be bad for him if he was not finished with the work before the witch came home.

Then the white dove came flying and settled down on the pile of wood, and cooed and said, 'Shall I help you?'

'Yes,' said the Prince, 'many thanks for your help yesterday, and for what you offer today.' Thereupon the little dove seized one piece of wood after another and split it with its beak. The Prince could not take away the wood as quickly as the dove could split it, and in a short time it was all cleft into little sticks.

The dove then flew upon his shoulder and sat there; and the Prince thanked it, and stroked and caressed its white feathers, and kissed its little red beak. With that it was a dove no longer, but a beautiful young maiden, who stood by his side. She told him then that she was a Princess whom the witch had stolen, and had changed to this shape, but with his kiss she had got her human form again; and if he would be faithful to her, and take her to wife, she could free them both from the witch's power.

The Prince was quite captivated by the beautiful Princess, and was quite willing to do anything whatsoever to get her for himself.

She then said to him, 'When the witch comes home you must ask her to grant you a wish, when you have accomplished so well all that she has demanded of you. When she agrees to this you must ask her straight out for the Princess that she has flying about as a white dove. But just now you must take a red silk thread and tie it round my little finger, so that you may be able to recognise me again, into whatever shape she turns me.'

The Prince made haste to get the silk thread tied round her little white finger; at the same moment the Princess became a dove again and flew away, and immediately after that the old witch came home with her dough-trough on her back.

'Well,' said she, 'I must say that you are clever at your work, and it is something too, that such princely hands are not accustomed to.'

'Since you are so well pleased with my work,' said the Prince, 'you will, no doubt, be willing to give me a little pleasure too, and give me something that I have taken a fancy to.'

'Oh, yes, indeed,' said the old woman; 'what is it that you want?'

'I want the Princess here who is in the shape of a white dove,' said the Prince.

'What nonsense!' said the witch. 'Why should you imagine that there are Princesses here flying about in the shape of white doves? But if you *will* have a Princess, you can get one such as we have them.' She then came to him, dragging a shaggy little grey ass with long ears. 'Will you have this?' said she; 'you can't get any other Princess!'

The Prince used his eyes and saw the red silk thread on one of the ass's hoofs, so he said, 'Yes, just let me have it.'

'What will you do with it?' asked the witch.

'I will ride on it,' said the Prince; but with that the witch dragged it away again, and came back with an old wrinkled, toothless hag, whose hands trembled with age. 'You can have no other Princess,' said she. 'Will you have *her*?'

'Yes, I will,' said the Prince, for he saw the red silk thread on the old woman's finger.

At this the witch became so furious that she danced about and knocked everything to pieces that she could lay her hands upon, so that the splinters flew about the ears of the Prince and the Princess, who now stood there in her own beautiful shape.

Then their marriage had to be celebrated, for the witch had to stick to what she had promised, and he must get the Princess whatever might happen afterwards.

The Princess now said to him, 'At the marriage feast you may eat what you please, but you must not drink anything whatever, for if you do that you will forget me.'

This, however, the Prince forgot on the wedding day, and stretched out his hand and took a cup of wine; but the Princess was keeping watch over him, and gave him a push with her elbow, so that the wine ran over the tablecloth.

Then the witch got up and laid about her among the plates and dishes, so that the pieces flew about their ears, just as she had done when she was cheated the first time.

They were then taken to the bridal chamber, and the door was shut. Then the Princess said, 'Now the witch has kept her promise, but she will do no more if she can help it, so we must fly immediately. I shall lay two pieces of wood in the bed to answer for us when the witch speaks to us. You can take the flower-pot and the glass of water that stands in the window, and we must slip out by that and get away.'

No sooner said than done. They hurried off out into the dark night, the Princess leading, because she knew the way, having spied it out while she flew about as a dove.

At midnight the witch came to the door of the room and called in to them, and the two pieces of wood answered her, so that she believed they were there, and went away again. Before daybreak she was at the door again and called to them, and again the pieces of wood answered for them. She thus thought that she had them, and when the sun rose the bridal night was past; she had then kept her promise, and could vent her anger and revenge on both of them. With the first sunbeam she broke into the room, but there she found no Prince and no Princess – nothing but the two pieces of firewood, which lay in the bed, and stared, and spoke not a word. These she threw on the floor, so that they were splintered into a thousand pieces, and off she hastened after the fugitives.

With the first sunbeam the Princess said to the Prince, 'Look round; do you see anything behind us?'

'Yes, I see a dark cloud, far away,' said he.

'Then throw the flower-pot over your head,' said she.

When this was done there was a large thick forest behind them.

When the witch came to the forest she could not get through it until she went home and brought her axe to cut a path.

A little after this the Princess said again to the Prince, 'Look round; do you see anything behind us?'

'Yes,' said the Prince, 'the big black cloud is there again.'

'Then throw the glass of water over your head,' said she.

When he had done this there was a great lake behind them, and this the witch could not cross until she ran home again and brought her dough-trough.

Meanwhile the fugitives had reached the castle which was the Prince's home. They climbed over the garden wall, ran across the garden, and crept in at an open window. By this time the witch was just at their heels, but the Princess stood in the window and blew upon the witch; hundreds of white doves flew out of her mouth, fluttered and flapped around the witch's head until she grew so angry that she turned into flint, and there she stands to this day, in the shape of a large flint stone, outside the window.

Within the castle there was great rejoicing over the Prince and his bride. His two elder brothers came and knelt before him and confessed what they had done, and said that he alone should inherit the kingdom, and they would always be his faithful subjects.

The White Wolf

ONCE UPON a time there was a King who had three daughters; they were all beautiful, but the youngest was the fairest of the three. Now it happened that one day their father had to set out for a tour in a distant part of his kingdom. Before he left, his youngest daughter made him promise to bring her back a wreath of wild flowers. When the King was ready to return to his palace, he bethought himself that he would like to take home presents to each of his three daughters; so he went into a jeweller's shop and bought a beautiful necklace for the eldest Princess; then he went to a rich merchant's and bought a dress embroidered in gold and silver thread for the second Princess, but in none of the flower shops nor in the market could he find the wreath of wild flowers that his youngest daughter had set her heart on. So he had to set out on his homeward way without it. Now his journey led him through a thick forest. While he was still about four miles distant from his palace, he noticed a white wolf squatting on the roadside, and, behold! on the head of the wolf, there was a wreath of wild flowers.

Then the King called to the coachman, and ordered him to get down from his seat and fetch him the wreath from the wolf's head. But the wolf heard the order and said, 'My Lord and King, I will let you have the wreath, but I must have something in return.'

'What do you want?' answered the King. 'I will gladly give you rich treasure in exchange for it.'

'I do not want rich treasure,' replied the wolf. 'Only promise to give me the first thing that meets you on your way to your castle. In three days I shall come and fetch it.'

And the King thought to himself, 'I am still a good long way from home; I am sure to meet a wild animal or a bird on the road; it will be quite safe to promise.' So he consented, and carried the wreath away with him. But all along the road he met no living creature till he turned into the palace gates, where his youngest daughter was waiting to welcome him home.

238

That evening the King was very sad, remembering his promise; and when he told the Queen what had happened, she too shed bitter tears. And the youngest Princess asked them why they both looked so sad, and why they wept. Then her father told her what a price he would have to pay for the wreath of wild flowers he had brought home to her, for in three days a white wolf would come and claim her and carry her away, and they would never see her again. But the Queen thought and thought and at last she hit upon a plan.

There was in the palace a servant-maid the same age and the same height as the Princess, and the Queen dressed her up in a beautiful dress belonging to her daughter, and determined to give her to the white wolf, who would never know the difference.

On the third day the wolf strode into the palace yard and up the great stairs, to the room where the King and the Queen were seated. 'I have come to claim your promise,' he said. 'Give me your youngest daughter.'

Then they led the servant-maid up to him, and he said to her, 'You must mount on my back and I will take you to my castle.' And with these words he swung her on to his back and left the palace.

When they reached the place where he had met the King and given him the wreath of wild flowers, he stopped, and told her to dismount that they might rest a little.

So they sat down by the roadside.

'I wonder,' said the wolf, 'what your father would do if this forest belonged to him?'

And the girl answered, 'My father is a poor man, so he would cut down the trees, and saw them into planks, and he would sell the planks, and we should never be poor again, but would always have enough to eat.'

Then the wolf knew that he had not got the real Princess, and he swung the servant-maid on to his back and carried her to the castle. And he strode angrily into the King's chamber, and spoke.

'Give me the real Princess at once. If you deceive me again I will cause such a storm to burst over your palace that the walls will fall in, and you will all be buried in the ruins.'

Then the King and the Queen wept, but they saw there was no escape. So they sent for their youngest daughter, and the King said to her, 'Dearest child, you must go with the white wolf, for I promised you to him, and I must keep my word.'

So the Princess got ready to leave her home; but first she went to her room to fetch her wreath of wild flowers, which she took with her. Then the white wolf swung her on his back and bore her away. But when they came to the place where he had rested with the servant-maid, he told her to dismount that they might rest for a little at the roadside. Then he turned to her and said, 'I wonder what your father would do if this forest belonged to him?'

And the Princess answered, 'My father would cut down the trees and turn it into a beautiful park and gardens, and he and his courtiers would come and wander among the glades in the summer time.'

'This is the real Princess,' said the wolf to himself. But aloud he said, 'Mount once more on my back, and I will bear you to my castle.'

And when she was seated on his back he set out through the woods, and he ran, and ran, till at last he stopped in front of a stately court-yard, with massive gates.

'This is a beautiful castle,' said the Princess, as the gates swung back and she stepped inside. 'If only I were not so far away from my father and my mother!'

But the wolf answered, 'At the end of a year we will pay a visit to your father and mother.'

And at these words the white furry skin slipped from his back, and the Princess saw that he was not a wolf at all, but a beautiful youth, tall and stately; and he gave her his hand, and led her up the castle stairs.

One day, at the end of half a year, he came into her room and said, 'My dear one, you must get ready for a wedding. Your eldest sister is going to be married, and I will take you to your father's palace. When the wedding is over, I shall come and fetch you home. I will whistle outside the gate, and when you hear me, pay no heed to what your father or mother say, leave your dancing and feasting, and come to me at once; for if I have to leave without you, you will never find your way back alone through the forests.'

When the Princess was ready to start, she found that he had put on his white fur skin, and was changed back into the wolf; and he swung her on to his back, and set out with her to her father's palace, where he left her, while he himself returned home alone. But, in the evening, he went back to fetch her, and, standing outside the palace gate, he gave a long, loud whistle. In the midst of her dancing the Princess heard the sound, and at once she went to him, and he swung her on his back and bore her away to his castle.

Again, at the end of half a year, the Prince came into her room, as the white wolf, and said, 'Dear heart, you must prepare for the wedding of your second sister. I will take you to your father's palace today, and we will remain there together till tomorrow morning.'

So they went together to the wedding. In the evening, when the two were alone together, he dropped his fur skin, and, ceasing to be a wolf, became a Prince again. Now they did not know that the Princess's mother was hidden in the room. When she saw the white skin lying on the floor, she crept out of the room, and sent a servant to fetch the skin and to burn it in the kitchen fire. The moment the flames touched the skin there was a fearful clap of thunder heard, and the Prince disappeared out of the palace gate in a whirlwind, and returned to his palace alone.

But the Princess was heartbroken, and spent the night weeping bitterly. Next morning she set out to find her way back to the castle, but she wandered through the woods and forests, and she could find no path or track to guide her. For fourteen days she roamed in the forest, sleeping under the trees, and living upon wild berries and roots, and at last she reached a little house. She opened the door and went in, and found the wind seated in the room all by himself, and she spoke to the wind and said, 'Wind, have you seen the white wolf?'

And the wind answered, 'All day and all night I have been blowing round the world, and I have only just come home; but I have not seen him.'

But he gave her a pair of shoes, in which, he told her, she would be able to walk a hundred miles with every step. Then she walked through the air till she reached a star, and she said, 'Tell me, star, have you seen the white wolf?'

And the star answered, 'I have been shining all night, and I have not seen him.'

But the star gave her a pair of shoes, and told her that if she put them on she would be able to walk two hundred miles at a stride. So she drew them on, and she walked to the moon, and she said, 'Dear moon, have you not seen the white wolf?'

But the moon answered, 'All night long I have been sailing through the heavens, and I have only just come home; but I did not see him.'

But he gave her a pair of shoes, in which she would be able to cover four hundred miles with every stride. So she went to the sun, and said, 'Dear sun, have you seen the white wolf?'

And the sun answered, 'Yes, I have seen him, and he has chosen another bride, for he thought you had left him, and would never return, and he is preparing for the wedding. But I will help you. Here are a pair of shoes. If you put these on you will be able to walk on glass or ice, and to climb the steepest places. And here is a spinning-wheel, with which you will be able to spin moss into silk. When you leave me you will reach a glass mountain. Put on the shoes that I have given you and with them you will be able to climb it quite easily. At the summit you will find the palace of the white wolf.'

Then the Princess set out, and before long she reached the glass mountain, and at the summit she found the white wolf's palace, as the sun had said.

But no one recognised her, as she had disguised herself as an old woman, and had wound a shawl round her head. Great preparations were going on in the palace for the wedding, which was to take place the next day. Then the Princess, still disguised as an old woman, took out her spinning-wheel, and began to spin moss into silk. And as she spun the new bride passed by, and seeing the moss turned into silk, she said to the old woman, 'Little mother, I wish you would give me that spinning-wheel.'

And the Princess answered, 'I will give it to you if you will allow me to sleep tonight on the mat outside the Prince's door.'

And the bride replied, 'Yes, you may sleep on the mat outside the door.'

So the Princess gave her the spinning-wheel. And that night, winding the shawl all round her, so that no one could recognise her, she lay down on the mat outside the Prince's door. And when everyone in the palace was asleep she began to tell the whole of her story. She told how she had been one of three sisters, and that she had been

the youngest and the fairest of the three, and that her father had
betrothed her to a white wolf. And she told how she had gone first to
the wedding of one sister, and then with her husband to the wedding
of the other sister, and how her mother had ordered the servant to
throw the white fur skin into the kitchen fire. And then she told of her
wanderings through the forest; and of how she had sought the Prince
weeping; and how the wind and star and moon and sun had be-
friended her, and had helped her to reach his palace. And when the
Prince heard all the story, he knew that it was his first wife, who had
sought him, and had found him, after such great dangers and difficulties.

But he said nothing, for he waited till the next day, when many
guests – Kings and Princes from far countries – were assembled in the
banqueting hall. He spoke to them and said, 'Hearken to me, ye
Kings and Princes, for I have something to tell you. I had lost the
key of my treasure casket, so I ordered a new one to be made; but I
have since found the old one. Now, which of these keys is the better?'

Then all the Kings and royal guests answered, 'Certainly the old
key is better than the new one.'

'Then,' said the Prince, 'if that is so, my former bride is better than my new one.'

And he sent for the new bride, and he gave her in marriage to one of the Princes who was present, and then he turned to his guests, and said, 'and here is my former bride' – and the beautiful Princess was led into the room and seated beside him on his throne. 'I thought she had forgotten me, and that she would never return. But she has sought me everywhere, and now we are together once more we shall never part again.'

THE END

Epilogue

Looking back from his late forties, Andrew Lang wrote nostalgically in his 'Ballade of the Bookworm':

> Far in the past I peer, and see
> A child upon the nursery floor,
> A child with books upon his knee,
> Who asks, like Oliver, for more!

> . . .

> One gift the Fairies gave me: (three
> They commonly bestowed of yore)
> The love of books, the golden key
> That opens the enchanted door;
> Behind it BLUEBEARD lurks, and o'er –
> And o'er doth JACK his giants kill,
> And there is all ALADDIN'S store, –
> The books I loved, I love them still!

When I look back from much the same time of life memory conjures up a surprisingly similar picture. But instead of the little chapbooks which the boy at Selkirk read more than a century ago, I see myself turning the pages of the Colour Fairy Books edited by Andrew Lang –

> Books Yellow, Red, and Green and Blue,
> All true, or just as good as true,
> And here's the Yellow Book for *you*!

So began the dedicatory poem in the one which I loved best – and in a sense I took it to myself, and stored away a name I found on the title-page of each of these magic volumes which seemed to be the talisman that raised them above our other volumes of fairy tales, even above the big volume of Grimm with its uninteresting pictures. Perhaps their only rivals were the Andersen and *The Arabian Nights* with their strangely haunting illustrations by Helen Stratton, though the pictures in the Fairy Books made a far more vivid and lasting impression: Lancelot Speed in the *Red* and that genius H. J. Ford in the others – Ford who has never, in my opinion, been equalled as the artist of Fairyland.

How clearly one's favourite fairy stories remain in the mind, with even an echo of the thrill, the last whisp of the glamour that fell upon us at that first reading! 'Soria Moria Castle', 'The Twelve Dancing Princesses', 'Jack and the Beanstalk', 'The Golden Goose', 'The Fortunes of Moti' – the enchanted pageant stretches out into the distance, and the very names ring in my ears like echoes of a spell that was once so potent and even now has not lost its magic:

> Old songs that sung themselves to me
> Sweet through a boy's day-dream.

The name on the title pages, in the days before one thought of authors, remained also like a word of power. And some years later it cropped up again when my mother read out loud the lovely old French song-story of *Aucassin and Nicolete*, and I found the magic name 'Andrew Lang' on the title-page as its translator. At much that same time my favourite author was Rider Haggard, and the something more than sheer excitement, the mythopoeic quality which makes him alone of the storytellers an author whom one continues to read in later life, was beginning to dawn on me and take me in thrall. But of all his books *The World's Desire* spoke most compellingly, while the songs in it woke suddenly a love for poetry that had been only an interest before – and in that one book Haggard was writing 'in collaboration with Andrew Lang'.

Now I was beginning to follow up the writings of any author whose books had impressed me particularly, and *The Poetical Works of Andrew Lang*, 4 vols, was still obtainable and made a perfect Christmas present from my parents.

The World's Desire, many of the shorter poems and verse translations from the Greek, and the narrative poem 'Helen of Troy' now linked themselves with another early love, that for Greek myth and legend which had hitherto been fed only by Kingsley and Amy Cruse and A. J. Church's simple re-tellings of Homer and Virgil. Lang wrote in his superb sonnets on the *Iliad* and the *Odyssey* of 'where that Æaean isle forgets the main', and of 'dark Cassandra lying low in rich Mycenae', and these and others sang themselves to me on my first visit to Greece – the islands in 'the wine-dark sea', Delphi, the loveliest spot on earth, and Mycenae, still a haunted place for all its beauty ('The curse is still here!' exclaimed C. S. Lewis in a hushed voice as we walked through the Lion Gate some thirty years later).

On my return from Greece I began at once on my first readings of Homer. And here again Lang was waiting to be my guide with his prose translations of both the epics, and with essays and books on Homer which I was soon to find. For that Hellenic cruise gave me also the friendship of the Georgian poet and dramatist Gordon Bottomley who speedily became my 'literary godfather' and first of all lent me many volumes of Lang's literary essays, and even gave me duplicates from his own library.

About this time also I remember buying for sixpence in the market at Bath a first edition of Lang's little volume on book-collecting, *The Library*. This, and the copy of his *Books and Bookmen* which Gordon Bottomley lent me until I could find it for myself, made me determine to be a bibliophile – if not a bibliomaniac. Obviously I could not collect Shakespeare quartos, or even the early editions of Perrault; but Lang's advice to those of slender means was to choose one's favourite minor author, one who was not yet sought by the great collectors – for thus a large collection, or at least a unique one, might be built over the years with perhaps even more enjoyment than if one were a Grolier or a Folger.

Of course the choice of a special author to collect admitted of little doubt: Andrew Lang himself was the obvious answer. His books were still plentiful in the second-hand bookshops; my weekly pocket money, or the omission of my Saturday lunch on the way home from Liverpool College, would often secure me another first edition – and, until I got to Oxford and could consult the Bodleian catalogue, there was always the chance of discovering some book by him of which I had never even heard.

Oxford held for me another and delightfully unexpected link with Lang. My parents had already decided that, if I passed the necessary exams, I should go to Merton College. What coincidence could be more surprising and delightful than, on picking up a copy of one of his more learned works, *Custom and Myth*, to read on the title-page: 'By Andrew Lang, Late Fellow of Merton College, Oxford'.

And, just before going up to Merton, there was a meeting in Edinburgh with a very old lady, Mrs MacCunn, who was Lang's favourite cousin Florence Sellar. She gave me a copy of his first book, *Ballads and Lyrics of Old France* (1872), which he had inscribed for her; and she wrote me several letters about him during my first year at Merton – 'It is as if I touched his hand' – for she said that here she was addressing letters to Merton in big, shaky writing (owing to extreme age), while the last time she had done so was also in big, shaky writing (owing to extreme youth) – but then they were to Andrew Lang.

At Merton I had the rooms under those in which Lang lived seventy years earlier – the 'White Rose on the gay garden wall' was still blooming outside my windows: 'Once more I hear the sister towers Each unto each reply' and could indeed feel:

> There is no change this happy day
> Within the College gardens gray!

Up in the college library the old volume of the Fellows' Library List showed his signature opposite the books on folklore and the Classics which he had taken out; the Senior Fellow remembered several stories about him, and met him when he dined in hall as an Honorary Fellow at the College Gaudy in 1911; and each Sunday on my way out of Chapel I would pause a moment below the plaque on the wall dedicated 'In Memory of Andrew Lang, M.A., Hon. D.Litt, Sometime Fellow and afterwards Honorary Fellow . . . '

And finally, when the time came for me to choose a subject for research for the degree of Bachelor of Letters, and I had to suggest several alternatives, there came the moment which probably decided my literary future when my beloved Professor, David Nichol Smith, exclaimed: 'But of course you must write about Andrew Lang!' and carried his conviction through the English faculty, some of whose members thought Thomas Parnell or Francis Gentleman more suitable for the 'academic exercise in research' – as the B.Litt. thesis was described at that time.

Two years of research for the thesis under Nichol Smith's supervision, and an additional term of revision with the inspiring criticism of J. R. R. Tolkien, my other examiner, who had 'referred back' the thesis – 'because I want to know more about Lang and fairy tales' – made me master of the basic material out of which grew my first major work: *Andrew Lang: A Critical Biography* (1946) – the only full-scale book on Lang that has yet appeared.

This did not end my interest in Lang; indeed I have been reading him ever since, taking holidays in the British Museum and the Bodleian to follow him further still through the files of old newspapers and magazines, and writing about him whenever I got the chance – as, for example, in the Bodley Head Monograph of 1962 and the special Andrew Lang number of the *Indiana Bookman* in 1965. And collecting him too, until my Lang library has become one of the four biggest in existence – with several items (both printed and in manuscript) which none of the three rival collections possess.

For the magic of Andrew Lang is a deep and abiding influence. George Saintsbury once estimated that his works, collected and uncollected, would fill two hundred volumes of a library edition – and I am probably nearer to having read everything that he wrote than almost anybody since Lang himself. I have been asked why I read and sometimes re-read his more obsolete and erudite books on Australian Totemism and the obscurer corners of Scottish history when neither subject is of any particular interest to me: I can only answer that there is something which comes through all that he wrote – not merely an attractive and arresting style, but something that I can only assume to be the personal charm of the man himself.

The individuality of his writing and the delight which so many of his contemporaries took in it has been described by many of them, and two of the longest survivors, Bernard Shaw and Gilbert Murray, both confirmed these recollections of its potency, telling me how eagerly they turned each day in the eighties and nineties to see if there were a literary leader by Lang in the *Daily News* – unsigned, but instantly to be recognised as his. And two of his closest friends, Florence Sellar and A. E. W. Mason, were as unanimous in their confirmation of what Rider Haggard had written in his autobiography: 'of the friend I know not what to say, save that I reckon it as one of the privileges of my life to be able to call him by that much-misused name; the tenderest, the purest and the highest-minded of human creatures, one from whom true goodness and nobility of soul radiate in every common word and act, though often half-hidden in a jest, the most perfect of gentlemen – such is Andrew Lang.'

Something of this magic, even though much of it may be at second hand, comes through in the Fairy Books. The tales may have been translated or adapted in the main by Mrs Lang and her assistants, who ranged from W. A. Craigie, the Icelandic scholar, and Major Campbell, who collected most of the Indian tales orally, to May Kendall, the poetess, and many friends, cousins and nieces of Lang and his wife: but Lang is the presiding genius, leaning over their shoulders to advise and inspire.

'My part has been that of Adam, according to Mark Twain, in the Garden of Eden,' wrote Lang in the last of the Fairy Books, the *Lilac*, in 1910. 'Eve worked, Adam superintended. I also superintend. I find out where the stories are, and advise, and, in short, superintend ... Nobody really *wrote* most of the stories. People told them in all parts of the world long before Egyptian hieroglyphics or Cretan signs or Cyprian syllabaries, or alphabets were invented. They are older than reading and writing, and arose like wild flowers before men had any education to quarrel over.'

We owe it to Lang that the world's fairy tales, the wild flowers of literature, were collected with such loving care and presented for the delight of young readers (and for those of mature age who are still sufficiently young in heart). That love began when Lang was a boy at Selkirk on the

Scottish Border and would listen eagerly to tales told by an old shepherd who regaled him and his friends in the barn on Saturday nights; probably he heard 'The Black Bull of Norroway' in the actual words given in this selection of stories. His love grew through the years as he read and compared the folk-tales of the ancient world preserved in the literatures of Greece and Rome, of Egypt and Babylon, in the chronicles of the conquistadores of Mexico and Peru, in the reports of missionaries and finally in the carefully compiled narratives of field anthropologists.

From the original twelve volumes of the Fairy Books, Kathleen Lines culled her *Fifty Favourite Fairy Tales* in 1963, and found her basket of literary wild flowers so popular that she has been sent questing back to Fairyland for *More Favourite Fairy Tales from Andrew Lang*, collected in the present volume – tales drawn from all nations ancient and modern, from Armenia and Iceland, from Scotland and the Punjab, China, Japan, Russia and many more. And, as in the earlier selection, it is still Lang's text, though amended where necessary to yield either a more exact translation or smoother telling. The pressed flowers of Lang's many imitators have mostly turned to dust, but his, as the present volume shows, are still blooming as freshly as ever beside the road which leads to Fairyland:

> And you once more may voyage through
> The forests that of old we knew,
> The fairy forests deep in dew.

ROGER LANCELYN GREEN